About

CU00407991

Joel Hames lives in rural Lancashire with his wife and two daughters, where he works hard at looking serious and pretending to be a proper novelist. Joel writes what he wants, when he wants to (which by coincidence is when the rest of the family choose to let him). His first novel, *Bankers Town*, was published in 2014.

If you want to know what Joel has planned for the future, what he thinks right now, or just stalk him a little, you can find him on Facebook at facebook.com/joelhamesauthor or Twitter at @joel_hames.

Also by Joel Hames

Bankers Town

THE ART OF STAYING DEAD

Joel Hames

First published in 2015
Copyright © 2015 by Joel Hames

All rights reserved. This book or any portion
thereof may not be reproduced or used in any
manner whatsoever without the express
written permission of the publisher except for
the use of brief quotations in a book review.

This is a work of fiction. Names, characters,
businesses, places, events and incidents are
either the products of the author's
imagination or used in a fictitious manner.
Any resemblance to actual persons, living or
dead, or actual events is purely coincidental.
If by chance I have stumbled upon a genuine
conspiracy, I promise I know nothing about
it.

Cover art by John Bowen

For My Daughters, Eve and Rose

Contents

PART 1: In the Metal Box

1: Going Dark

Sure, it was small and dark, and a little boring, and it didn't smell great, but that wasn't so bad. If you'd told me people would be dying in a few minutes' time I'd have rolled my eyes and laughed.

It was tight. Twelve of us, plus a couple of guards, plus some official whose name I hadn't caught, in a security office designed for three or four. No space to sit down. We were all standing there holding pads and pens, they'd taken everyone's tablets and phones when we arrived. Most of us had those little notebooks you can fit in your pocket, but the guy to my left was writing furiously on a hard plastic clipboard that kept jabbing into my arm. I grunted each time it happened, and he apologised, but went on writing and jabbing anyway.

The CCTV screens were small and silent, black and white, a bit blurry. If I concentrated on one at a time I could just about make out what was going on, but then a movement in one of the others would catch my attention and I'd lose focus and have to start all over again. It didn't matter. We'd be in there ourselves soon enough. I gave up and looked at the clipboard guy instead.

He was big. And by big, I mean fat. Which didn't help, with the clipboard and everyone else in the small dark room. He looked vaguely familiar, and I thought I might have seen him before, in the papers maybe, or in court, but then everyone in the Delegation looked vaguely familiar from the papers or from court, partly because I expected them to and partly because I'd never bothered keeping track of all those thousands of faces over thirteen years. Mid-forties, I guessed, with a lump of curly black hair that belonged on someone twenty years younger perched on top of his fat, open face, and a sleek black beard that belonged on someone from the sixties. Che Guevara. That was it. It wasn't the papers or court, it was Che Guevara, if halfway round that bike tour of Argentina Che Guevara had discovered steak and red wine and decided the revolution could take care of itself. He was still writing, and I couldn't think what the hell he was writing about because the screens were about as useful as a microwave in a powercut and it wasn't like anything was happening anywhere else, either. It had been four hours since they'd picked us up in three minibuses outside the Royal Courts of Justice like a bunch of legal groupies, and the only thing I'd written in my own notebook was the name of the girl standing the other side of Che.

I tried to look at her, past the beard, but that would have meant moving forward and making it obvious I wasn't interested in the images on the screens. I'd been pleased with myself, earlier, comfortably spread across a double seat on the minibus. It was early, I was hungover, I didn't really want to spend more time than I had to talking to strangers, and there was always the possibility David Brooks-Powell would show up, which would be as welcome as a brain tumour. And then I'd seen her, in front of me, sitting down next to the German guy who kept nodding at everyone like he was pretending he understood what was going on. She'd introduced herself – to him, not to me – said her name was Claire, and she was a journalist, and I'd realised straight away what an idiot I'd been, because the whole point of doing this was to raise my profile, get my name out there, and here was the perfect opportunity, plus she was almost good-looking enough to be out of my league. And yet instead of patting the empty seat beside me in invitation when I realised there wasn't enough room for everyone to have a whole row to themselves, I'd shoved my bag on it and turned to look out of the window at a bunch of barristers in the rain.

The German guy was standing the other side of me now. Hans, I think he'd said. He was still nodding, this time at the screens, like they were telling him something only he could hear. Che had finished writing, thank Christ, and leaned back, which meant his arms were touching mine and I was glad I'd chosen to wear a long-sleeved top. Even so, I couldn't help a quiet sigh. I could see Claire now. Che's other arm was in front of her, not far off crushing her against the metal wall behind us, and she was sighing, too. She looked up, saw me, and winked, and I thought *sod this*, and before Che could start writing again I leaned forward, across him, and said "Hi, I'm Sam."

"Claire," she said, "Daily Sentinel," and I raised an eyebrow in interest like I didn't already know.

"I'm just another lawyer," I replied. She laughed. Che looked from one of us to the other and frowned, and I found myself grinning back at her. It was just possible this thing might not turn out to be a complete waste of time.

Really, it shouldn't have been a waste of time at all. I needed this badly, and if I played it right it could be the perfect opportunity to build things back up. Because I might not be the most scrupulous lawyer, or the best, but I was sharp enough to know something needed rebuilding. Not so many years ago I'd been moaning about the quality of the clients I was getting. I'd have sniffed at another Maloney. These days I was delighted to get any client at all. Thirteen years in human rights, and I was lucky if I got to fight speeding fines for bearded junkies with trust funds and more Ferraris than brain cells. It would have been OK, maybe, if the bearded junkies were famous, if I was dealing with the worthless brats of one-shot celebrities and getting my own name out there and maybe, one day, getting someone walking in with a real case to deal with. But my clients, when they turned up at all, weren't famous. They were just rich, and boring, and stupid, and more often than not they weren't there at all. I'd have paid good money for a Maloney right now.

It was Paul's idea, this tour, sorry, "Delegation", with a capital "D". I guessed Paul felt sorry for me, no, I was sure of it, because back when we started I was the guy with a future in front of him, I was the guy doing him favours, putting work his way, and now he was a hotshot barrister with the kind of clients I'd have killed for, and I was nobody at all. The place I'd taken should have been his, and when he'd realised he had to be in court that day he should have thrown it to someone else in his Chambers, or at least to a solicitor that was more use to him than I was, which meant most of the names on the Roll, but instead he'd called me and I hadn't even had the grace or sense, at first, to realise what a great opportunity he was giving me.

So that's where I was, and it was a big opportunity for a nobody like me, part of a "Delegation of Interested Parties" put together by one of those human rights NGOs with an overdeveloped sense of their own importance, to visit what was without doubt one of the nastiest places in the country.

Dovesham. Odds are you've never heard of the place. It's not famous like Pentonville or Belmarsh, or packed to the rafters with celebrity lunatics like Broadmoor. But if they get caught, and convicted, and manage to stay alive long enough, the worst people in Britain tend to end up in Dovesham.

It's a prison with an international flavour. Most of the inmates are only here because the Home Office can't deport them and isn't quite useless enough to just let them all out. Violent psychopaths from all over the world are catered for, rapists and serial killers from North America, sadistic cartel lieutenants from Mexico and Guatemala, zealots from Syria and Egypt, terrorists and diamond smugglers from West Africa, wannabe warlords from Somalia, anyone with an exotic tang but enough of a local connection to get themselves locked up in Blighty eventually finds their way to Dovesham. It's not like there's anything secret about the place or the prisoners; every trial gets reported, every conviction and sentence properly noted down. If you were that way inclined, you could get your hands on the names and crimes of every inmate there. But the press just aren't that interested. No poor British victims, no young naked British bodies dug up in the snow. The British press like their crimes local. Distance dulls the appetite.

Not for Human Rights International, though. Prisoners from all over the world, crimes that could, if you ran round in circles and squinted hard enough, be seen as political, little access to the outside world, the appeal process, the media: no wonder HRI wanted in. They'd been pushing for a visit for years, and the Home Secretary wanted some decent press for a change. I guess HRI were surprised how easy it was, because they'd got everything agreed and ready to go before they realised they didn't have anyone to stuff into their Delegation. A bunch of self-important pricks with their own little kingdoms of expertise, they decided. Politics, prisons, drugs, psychiatry. And for the rest, journalists and lawyers. Which is how they ended up with me.

Something was happening on one of the screens. I still couldn't see what it was, but Hans clearly could because his head was jerking up and down even faster than it had been before. Che was back to the clipboard. I looked around. Everyone seemed to be writing or frowning in concentration, even Claire. I followed the collective gaze to a screen in the bottom right where the blurs bore a vague resemblance to someone shouting at someone else. I couldn't see why. I couldn't even figure out who it was doing the shouting, but after a moment the scribbling slowed and the tension seemed to drain from the room, so whatever it was that had happened or promised to happen had either finished or never really kicked off in the first place. I glanced at Che's clipboard, you could hardly miss the thing, and read the most recent line he'd written. "*Prisoner appears somewhat bruised*", it said, in a clear, slanting, almost ladylike script. If he'd got that from the blurs I'd been looking at then he had better eyesight than I did, or a better imagination.

I yawned and took another look around the room. Still staring at the screens, all of them, but looking as bored as I was now the excitement was over. Even Che had relaxed, and Hans had stopped nodding altogether. I picked a screen and stared at it, and after a minute I could see it. A room. A table. There were four people, one guard, standing, a prisoner sitting at one side of the table, and a couple of the delegates from Group A on the other. It looked like everyone was smiling. Not much for Che to write about there. I picked another screen, and tried the same method. Ignore everything else and wait for the shapes to resolve. A cell. Same formation, one guard, one prisoner, two delegates. Another screen. Canteen. Multiply everything by three: three guards, three prisoners, six delegates. Nothing happening. And even if it did, it would take us so long to notice it would probably be over by the time we did.

We'd been sorted into our three groups in advance, instructed to assemble at Point A, B or C outside the

Royal Courts according to the designation at the top of the letters we'd been sent. I was in Group B, the second minibus, the second group in.

In theory, it was an excellent idea. Check, double-check, triple-check. Each group gets to spend a little time with the inmates. Guards present, but no questions out of bounds. We couldn't make the prisoners talk to us, but the assumption was they'd want to, most of them. The delegates in there at the moment were from Group A. While one group was talking, another group would be watching their progress upstairs in the CCTV operations room. That way we might spot things the prison staff didn't want us seeing. Guards applying pressure. Items being moved. Great idea, only it didn't take into account the size or quality of the screens. Unless the guards started executing prisoners in front of us, there wasn't much we were going to spot from out here.

While all this was going on, the third group would be wandering around the other bits of the prison, a couple of senior officials in tow. I couldn't figure out what great truths they were supposed to uncover – I suppose, in theory (again), expert eyes might spot ill-concealed lapses, breaches, hints of mistreatment and the rest. In reality it sounded more like we were getting taken for a nice little walk while the rest of the Delegation got to do their business.

The minibuses had stopped for a few minutes at the prison entrance and then driven straight in. I couldn't believe they hadn't searched the vehicle. There was a brief chance to mingle when we were herded out into a central courtyard, patchy grass and tar overlooked by barred windows on all four sides, but I blew that one too, angling for a chat with Claire but finding my way blocked immediately by Hans and a pair of older women with that sweet, encouraging look I'd seen a thousand times on the faces of barristers as sweet as a barrel of acid. I didn't have a chance in hell of getting past them. Instead I drifted over to Group A and managed a couple of minutes desultory conversation with a tall, middle-aged man with a carefully-sculpted sweep of hair that had me thinking of the guy who played Face in the A-Team. He was "from the military", he said, and I couldn't think what he was doing there, but it wasn't like I was expecting to contribute a great deal myself. There was also a young, serious-looking woman wearing the kind of rimless glasses I couldn't help associating with the Gestapo. I'd thought she looked familiar, and I was right, because she turned out to be Jayati Mehta, yet another lawyer, a far better and more successful one than me. I knew her by reputation, I told her, which was true. I even reeled off a couple of her recent cases, which must have made me sound more like a star-struck teenager than a colleague and peer. She smiled and thanked me, and didn't bother trying to reciprocate. She'd have been a confident liar to claim she knew who I was.

A couple of minutes was all we got before being sorted back into our groups and individually searched – not as thoroughly as I'd expected, but no doubt there were scanners all over the place primed for the scent of a weapon. And then some stairs, a corridor or two, and the Black Hole of Dovesham.

So, OK, I'd figured out how to look at the screens, but it wasn't like there was much for me to look at. Like everyone else, I was there for the inmates. Ask some questions, hope they weren't the same questions someone else had already asked, get the kind of answer I could turn into a campaign or a scandal or a statement in the House of Commons or anything that would get me a bit of press. I looked round the bulk to my left, at Claire. She was staring at the screens, like everyone else, but I could tell from the way her eyes kept flicking from one to another that she wasn't taking in what she was seeing any more than I was.

I looked back at the screens myself, I was gazing at them when it happened, so if someone had seen it, what started it, how it started, then it could just as easily have been me as anyone else. But I didn't see a thing.

It started with a loud crash. I couldn't tell where it had come from. We all looked up, looked around. The guards shrugged and the prison official smiled, so after a moment we all went back to the screens. There was another crash, something metallic and heavy, by the sound of it, and the prison official smiled again, but the smile didn't look as confident as it had done a moment ago. Then another noise, further off, duller, not metallic this time, and the part of my brain I was already trying to ignore told me that was what an explosion sounded like, but then everything went quiet again, and the screens were still there in front of us, still as difficult to read as they had been before, and nothing obvious staring out at us. *Piss off*, I told the part of my brain that was telling me something bad was about to happen. *Piss off and leave me alone.*

And then everything went dark.

2: Heat

For a moment, there was silence. Just a moment; then all hell broke loose. More crashes, more of those dull sounds, only closer this time, less dull, and I couldn't pretend they didn't sound like explosions any more. Sharper noises, which that same part of my brain told me were gunfire and the rest of my brain didn't argue with. Inside the cramped little room, shouts and questions fast and loud and all at the same time. No one screaming. Yet. There was another noise, faint, fast, familiar, and it took a few seconds before I realised it was my own pulse, the blood in my head, the sound I always heard when I didn't want to be awake or where I was.

During those first few seconds my eyes were adjusting to the darkness and already I could see there were gaps. Amazingly, the screens were still on, still functioning, but whatever had taken out the lights in here had taken them out down there, too, so there was even less to see than there had been before. Flashes, every now and then. I didn't like to think what that might be. The shouting inside had stopped, I couldn't think why, until I heard one voice, louder than the rest, slower and less panicked.

"Everyone stay calm. There are emergency generators and the door to this room's so thick no one's getting in unless we open it. OK?"

I couldn't see who had spoken but I was guessing it was the official, not the guards. Now I wanted to picture him, I couldn't even remember what the guy looked like. Stupid selective bloody memory. I thought about the door and the walls. Nice and thick. A thick metal box. I liked that. It reminded me of me. Solid, thick, impermeable.

Keeping bad things out of Sam Williams since 2004.

Silence, now, inside and out, and then faintly, shouts from beyond the door, downstairs, outside, which had me wondering quite how thick that door and those walls really were. I tried to decipher the shouts, to work out whether it was pain or anger or desperation I could hear, but they were so distant they might as well have been Happy Bloody Birthday. We waited. I kept expecting the lights to come back on, we'd just been told there were emergency generators, but then I realised the power wasn't the problem. The screens were still on. Whatever had happened, it had happened to the lighting circuits, all of them, simultaneously, not the power supply, and a generator wasn't going to fix it.

I was starting to get nervous. Bullshit. I was already nervous. Now I was starting to get scared. Everyone was quiet, even the breathing muted, a collective breath held against the promise of some other sound underneath. I could feel Che's arm against my top and it felt damp but I didn't care. This was ridiculous. It was daytime. Still light outside, and we were trapped in a tiny locked room in the dark. We needed to get out. I looked around for help, for someone to agree with me, but I couldn't see more than solid black and slightly less black on top of it.

The crashes, explosions, gunshots, they were all still going on, but less frequently and further away. The shouts had stopped altogether. I seized on that. Whatever was happening out there I could feel it moving away from us, I could almost see it, like a giant dog or a fox or a wolf or something, hunting us out, failing to find the scent, moving on and leaving us behind. I stopped myself before the idea went further. A fox. I'm in a prison and there's people getting shot and blown up and I'm thinking about a giant fucking fox. Fear and the dark can do strange things.

A more familiar noise, suddenly, and close by, an engine starting up. I thought about it. No windows here, why should there be windows, why not leave us all in the dark to die, but I thought the courtyard was close by and it sounded like it could be one of the minibuses. It got louder. Whatever it was, it was moving. The sharper sounds – the gunshots – started up again too, closer, and suddenly the engine died. I could feel eyes in the darkness, eyes seeking out faces, something or someone to look at, but there was nothing to see. If I'd been next to Claire I'd have reached out a hand, as much for my sake as for hers, but I wasn't holding hands with Che or Hans. Not even if they might be the last hands I'd hold. Especially if they might be the last hands I'd hold.

The engine started up again. *Come on*, I thought, *whoever the hell you are*. It wasn't that I was hoping someone else would make it out, or not just that. I had the idea that if they could, I could too. More shots. A crash, this time definitely a crash, metal on stone, hard, grinding, painful. The engine died again. For a moment there was complete silence, and I could feel it again, everyone desperate to see everyone else and unable to see anything at all.

The silence was broken by a hiss and crackle. *The screens*, I thought, stupidly, as if they'd suddenly sprouted speakers. It wasn't the screens, it was a radio, the official, or one of the guards.

"Monitoring Group B, Monitoring Group B, do you read?"

A rustling, scrambling, the owner of the radio trying to get to it and hit the right buttons in the dark.

"Yes. Yes, we're here. What the hell's going on out there?"

I was surprised by the voice. Surprised how calm it was. Christ knows what would have come out if I'd opened my mouth to speak, but sure as dead birds drop it wouldn't have been as steady and clear as those eleven words.

"There's a major situation."

Well I could have told you that.

"So what should we do?"

"Wait."

Nice.

"You coming?"

"Yes. Keep it quiet in there, if you can. Not sure anyone knows you're there, yet. Best you keep it that way."

I could see the logic in that.

"You coming any time soon?"

"As soon as we can. Need to clear some lines of fire first. Out."

Clear some lines of fire. I had no idea what that meant and I didn't think I liked the sound of it. Ten, maybe twenty seconds silence, and again I was sure I knew, in the darkness, what everyone was thinking. *How long?* And *what the hell are lines of fire?*

"The courtyard. The windows, look onto it. Lots of windows. Men must be there, with guns, clear sight onto the courtyard. So we cannot go out there until these men have been dealt with. Those are the lines of fire."

I was so surprised by the voice from my right it took me a moment to be amazed he'd read my mind. And then I realised if an idiot like me knew what we were all thinking then chances were everyone else in the room did too. He spoke quietly, Hans, hardly a trace of an accent, just an occasional out-of-place pause. Better English than half my English clients. The sound of my blood in my ears had faded, and in the silence that followed I suddenly realised how loud the slightest noises had become, the tapping of a finger against a thigh, the tiny adjustments of arms and feet as cramp, or the fear of cramp, wrapped tendrils round limbs. And the breathing. Fifteen people and I thought I could hear every single one taking in their share of the hot still air and handing back sweet foul breath. Che most of all. The shooting and explosions had stopped or got so far away we couldn't hear them any more, and ridiculously, irrationally, I found myself hating the silence so much I'd have welcomed the sounds of violence again.

I don't know how much more I could have stood or what I would have done when it got too much. It felt like I had seconds until I broke. Maybe everyone else was thinking the same, because the small movements got bigger and more frequent. Someone cleared their throat, someone else sniffed. Three people coughed. Hans spoke, again, "We have only to wait. They will tell us when it is safe."

If he meant to be reassuring, he'd missed by a mile. But a moment after he fell silent the noises outside started up again and I was left wondering whether the silence wasn't better after all. No explosions this time, but crashes, still, and those hard, sharp sounds I couldn't pretend weren't clearly gunshots. The little staccato cracks got closer, and for fifteen, twenty seconds it seemed like they were right on top of us, then they receded into the background and it was like things were almost normal.

Another stupid thought, that. *Normal.* As if to prove just how stupid it was there was light, suddenly. Not a lot, not enough to see anything in the room by, but light on the screens, which meant that someone somewhere had reconnected at least part of the lighting circuit and the cells and the canteen weren't dark any more.

No movement in any of them. The flashes had stopped a while ago, whether that was minutes or seconds I couldn't say, and from the stillness in front of us it looked like no one had waited around for the lights to come back on. I looked from one screen to another, taking my time, waiting for the shapes to resolve into things I could understand. A table. A door.

There was a noise to my left. A sob. Claire, I thought, and then she spoke and I was irrationally satisfied I'd got it right.

"There. Bottom right."

Fourteen pairs of eyes pointed where she'd said. A moment's silence, then fourteen gasps. The screen showed the interior of a cell. A table. A door. And, this time, a body, and sure, I couldn't see blood or a wound but it was still and lying on the floor with the face pointing up and just to the side of the camera, and it wasn't like anyone was going to be taking a nap right now. I recognised that face. Jayati Mehta. A solicitor. A human rights lawyer. Someone like me, female, clever, successful, but otherwise just like me.

Dead.

I could feel my forehead crease and my jaw tense and I realised that I was thinking, thinking hard and entirely involuntarily. My brain had decided to do the work for me, which was probably a good thing because even in the state I was in I could tell I wasn't capable of a decent conscious decision. My brain was telling me it didn't really matter, because I didn't have any decisions to make. The guards, the prison official, Hans. There were at least four people in the room who'd do a better job at keeping me alive than I could, and probably closer to a dozen.

There was movement to my left, a jerk I couldn't quite interpret, and then a voice, surprisingly high-pitched for someone so large.

"We need to get the fuck out of here."

So Che wasn't one of the dozen.

"Come on. Isn't anyone going to say anything? Isn't

anyone going to fucking well do anything?"

The voice had got even higher and the movements more pronounced, like he was flinging his arms around, trying to emphasise his point in the darkness. And then, suddenly, there was more noise, movement in the room, and I could sense an emptiness in the space he'd just been occupying.

"Get out of the fucking way."

People were talking back, now, telling him to calm down, to stop it, to think for a moment, but nothing seemed to be getting through and the disturbance was moving further away from me and closer to the door. There was a thud of flesh against metal, a scratching, a shuffling, and then Che, again.

"Unlock this door."

"No."

It was the guard who'd been on the radio, the calm, sensible guard. I liked him, I decided. If he was saying *no* I was happy to agree with him.

"Unlock this fucking door or I'll fucking kill you."

It sounded ridiculous, in that voice, but then I pictured the man, the bulk of him, and thought maybe he could, if he felt he had to.

"Wait."

This time it was Hans. Hans knew about lines of fire, so as far as I was concerned Hans was up there with the sensible guard. There was movement to my right, I felt myself pushed back, firmly but gently, and then a whole new series of sounds, faster, more purposeful, as Hans worked his way to the other end of the room.

"If he wants to go, let him go."

"Really?" said the guard.

"Yes. He loses his head in here, he is a danger to everybody. Out there, just to him. And maybe he is right. But he goes first. It is his risk."

There was a short pause while we all took in what he was saying, before he went on.

"You may die, you know." Hans had turned now, his voice suddenly louder as he spoke directly to Che. "You do not know if anybody is out there and if they are, you do not know who they are. It would be more wise to wait here."

"Wait here for someone to turn up and do that to me?" Che shouted the words into the darkness, and I turned back to the screen. I could feel the others turning too. We'd been facing the door, as if there was anything there to see, but we all knew what Che meant. Jayati Mehta.

More sounds at the door.

"You really want to do this?" asked the guard.

"Yeah. I'm not ready to die." But Che's voice had dropped, the pitch was down a bit, the volume too. Maybe he was having second thoughts.

"You don't have to do this, you know."

"Yes I do."

A creak, then light, suddenly, a vertical bar of faint light and the grey of the opposite wall of the corridor, but it felt like sunrise. I could see the inside of the room, now, just, and faint outlines of faces. Che followed the door out, hunched, slow, looking one way, then another, as if he was expecting something to send him scurrying back. There was nothing. Che stood a little straighter, pushed the door wide open, stepped out into the corridor.

The shot, when it came, was so loud I thought it must have come from inside the room. Che screamed. I'd turned to stare at the screens, stupidly, but now I looked up and saw Hans pulling at him, scrambling wildly to get lean German arms around that gigantic frame, tugging him back and into the room as one of the guards pulled the door shut behind him and the other slammed the locks into place. Che was still screaming. Outside I thought I could hear voices too, shouting. Hans was speaking quietly, telling Che he was OK, it was just a scratch, just his arm, he'd be OK. I hadn't had much time to look at Che in the moment between the gunshot and the door shutting and leaving us all in the dark again, but I convinced myself I'd seen blood, lots of blood. An artery, maybe. Or just a flesh wound. Che had plenty of flesh to get wounded.

He was whimpering, now, Hans still speaking softly, and the shouting clearer outside, someone demanding *what the fuck did you do that for?* and someone else swearing in reply. They reverberated, the voices. Everything was metal round here, metals walls on the corridor and the room we were in. No wonder the shot had been loud.

Strangely, I found myself able to think again, clearly, consciously, perversely, because the horror had got closer and it was obvious we were worse off now than we had been a minute ago, back in the dark with a wounded man and at least one person outside who wanted to kill us. Someone would come for us, I thought. There would be more guards, police, maybe even the army. The metal door looked solid enough to keep us safe, for a while at least. Che might not have a while. He might be fine. I had no way of knowing.

The crackle, again, and a voice.

"What's going on in there? We heard shots."

The scrambling took a little longer this time. The radio must have fallen to the floor at some point during Che's failed suicide mission, and from the grunts and bumps I thought maybe half a dozen people had bent down to find it at the same time.

"You there? Group B? You there?"

"We're here. We've got a wounded man. How long will you be?"

"We're close. Sit tight. A couple of minutes."

"OK. Come quick."

Silence. Even the whimpering had stopped. I reckoned my heart was doing about one twenty a minute, so if they weren't with us in a few hundred beats I could start to panic. Again.

Footsteps, loud, in the corridor. Then banging, even louder, on the door. Movement inside and the voice of Hans: "Wait. The radio."

Static, then the guard.

"Is that you?"

"Yes. We're at the door. It's safe to come out."

It's safe to come out. I thought I'd engrave those words on something precious, something more expensive than I could really afford, and look at them every day. More scrambling, then Hans again.

"Wait."

"What is it now?"

The guard didn't sound any happier than I felt. Hans clearly knew what he was doing, and I appreciated his caution, but by now I just wanted to get out.

"Do you have a codeword?"

"What?"

"A call signal, identity code, something only your colleagues would know?"

"Oh for Christ's sake, man. Look, they're outside now, waiting for us. Ask them yourself. Just get the hell out of the way and let me open the door."

"Please."

The scrambling stopped. Che had started moaning again, quietly. I didn't know how much more of this I could stand.

"Hello?"

"Hi guys. Are you going to open the door or what?"

"Just do me a favour, right?"

"Whatever you want. Come on out we'll sort you out, no problem."

"What's your call-sign?"

"Eh?"

"Your call-sign."

Silence.

"Hello?"

"Yeah, sorry. What was it you wanted?"

"Your call-sign. You're gamma section, right?"

"Eh, yeah, sure."

Silence, for a moment. The static had died, the guard must have switched off the radio. Then the other guard spoke.

"There isn't a gamma section."

Nobody spoke. Nobody had to. Fifteen breaths held, silent, in the darkness, in the sudden knowledge that outside the door was nothing but swift and violent death.

"Stay calm. Everybody quiet, they will come. We just have to wait."

Hans was still managing to keep himself calm, or at least to sound like it, even though things had somehow just got even worse.

More static. The radio must have come back on.

"You coming out?"

"No. No, I think we'll sit tight."

A laugh, and even through the static it sounded like the laugh of the kind of man I wouldn't pick as a friend.

"You sure about that?"

"Yeah."

"OK. But I wouldn't wait too long. It's a jungle out there, you know. Come with us, you might live."

Hostages, I suddenly realised. If they were trying to get out of prison, the one thing they'd want was hostages, and here we were, civilians, lawyers, journalists, all vaguely public figures. We'd be perfect. Shooting at Che made no sense, but if you can't expect a little irrationality from a high-security prisoner with a gun you can't expect it from anyone. And the others out there hadn't seemed too pleased when it happened.

"Oh," from the radio again, "by the way, I hope you like it hot."

I don't know why, but while he was still speaking I'd already turned back to the screens, seen something that caught my attention, focused until I could be sure I knew what I was looking at, and digested the implications. So it was me that spoke next, first time I'd opened my mouth since introducing myself to Claire, back in another life.

"There. Middle row, left hand side."

I didn't need to say anything more. We could all see what we could see. A cell. A table. A chair. A mattress, burning. Everything around us was metal, and one thing I knew about metal was that if one end of it gets hot, the rest won't stay cool for long. It didn't matter if they couldn't get smoke or fire into our little room. All they needed to do was heat the place up until we started to fry. Heat the box. Singe the skin. I hadn't thought of that. I could already feel my feet getting warmer, even though I knew that was just the tension and my mind ganging up on me.

At least, I hoped it was.

3: Five Minutes, Thirty Seconds

Silence, again, bar the occasional gasp from Che. It wasn't like there was anything helpful to be said. The silence grew. The heat grew with it.

More shots, close by. More running outside, more shouting, no chance of hearing what was being said. More hammering on the door, but no one was thinking of opening it this time.

Then the radio, again.

"Group B, Group B, are you still in there?"

It was a different voice this time. I was sure of it.

"Yes."

"You can come out now. You're safe."

"Call-sign?"

"Rich? It's Elliot. Bravo-Delta-Four. You know me. Afternoon, B-Wing."

This sounded promising. The radio went dead and the guard spoke.

"It all checks out. I'm opening the door."

It was a question. Only Hans could answer it.

"Yes," he said, and I allowed myself to think I might not die today after all.

The next five minutes were pure chaos. I've been over them since, with the police later that day, in my own mind in the days and weeks that followed, but I couldn't make much more sense of it afterwards than I managed at the time. There were three men and one woman in the group that had rescued us, and they weren't police or Special Forces or anything like that, they were just regular screws, prison guards, people with guns who knew their way around the place. I could settle for that. That meant six guards, plus the prison official, plus Hans, shepherding the rest of us to safety. Che was still moaning but the blood seemed to be coming slowly and he could still move, so I decided it probably wasn't an artery after all. We moved fast, too, so I only got a glimpse at the body in the corridor outside the door and what looked like another one further back. More corridors, a couple of staircases, stopping at every corner to check everything was clear and make radio contact with the people in charge of saving our lives.

There were more bodies in the courtyard. Two of the minibuses were just where we'd left them but the other one was on its side, blocking the exit. I thought I could see someone slumped in the driver's seat but I wasn't sure. The shouting had been replaced, or drowned out, by something else, a rushing noise, wind or sea, but the sea was miles away. There was room, between the stone arch which led outside and the vertical roof of the broken minibus, for us to crawl through one by one. A line had formed, I hadn't noticed when, but I crouched in my place and watched Claire enter the gap and disappear from view, then one of the guards, and Hans, a couple more from the group, another guard. Che was in front of me, unbelievable luck, still just in front of me, fat and bleeding, and I thought if this bastard got me shot I'd kill him for it, and then I realised how ridiculous that was and just waited and hoped. It was slow, but he got through, and I was there with him a few seconds later wondering if maybe it would have been better to stay inside, because now I could hear gunshots again, and they were coming from in front of us, not behind. There was a bit of scrubland, a few hundred metres square, with a road going through it and a wood beyond, and it sounded to me like the gunshots were coming from the wood. If the prison had been cleared out and the armed convicts were out there, wasn't the prison the best place to be? I looked back, over my shoulder. It was solid enough. Hundreds of years old, probably, apart from the metal bits. Then I saw smoke and remembered, and gave up trying to work out which was the least likely way to die.

The rushing noise got closer. A helicopter. Brilliant. I could see it now, not it, them, three glorious blue and red choppers heading our way and looking like nothing short of Armageddon was getting in their way. I can't see a helicopter without thinking Valkyries and there it was, in my head, the smell of victory, or survival at least, and never more appropriate. The gunshots had stopped, too. I looked back down and saw maybe a dozen people staring at me, their mouths moving as if they were shouting, which of course they were but nothing except the choppers was getting through. We'd already started moving out and I hadn't even noticed. The first of the choppers was coming down, right in the middle of the open land, and they were running, but so was I, and head-start or no head-start there was no way I was getting to that chopper behind Che.

I was past him within a few seconds and the chopper was maybe a hundred yards away and just a few feet up. I wasn't planning on slowing down. There were a few more behind me, way behind, then Che, and the rest of the group were still in front. I didn't fancy being stuck in the middle with the bleeding giant.

And that was the five minutes of chaos, because of the next thirty seconds I can remember every single one, every tenth of every one. I can remember it like it's happening now, I can see it, feel it, hear it.

It starts with two people just in front of me. A few more have already climbed onto the helicopter, I have an image of feet on the steps, there's one climbing now, one waiting, several more sprinting the last few metres. I can see Hans, too, waiting with one foot on the steps, helping people on, Hans is a genuine red-blooded action hero, half John Wayne, half John McClane, and that's great, but even as I'm running I'm wondering how many of us are getting on that first chopper and who's going to have to wait for the next one, and if it's between Hans and me, I'd rather he played *Die Hard* a little longer.

Of the two in front, the closest to the chopper is a young guy, fresh out of university by the look of his beardless face and white-boy dreads. Since I'd put him down in the "no possible use" column the moment I'd set eyes on him, all I can remember about him right now is an interest in drugs, though whether that was personal or professional I never got round to asking. The other one is Claire. They're close together, paces almost matching, and the same part of me that's hoping I get onto the helicopter before Hans decides he wants out himself has a brief but powerful urge to see the drug guy fall over or just slow down so that it's me and Claire getting out of Saigon together. But it's the opposite that happens, and in my memory I can see it's about to happen before it does, even though that can't be true, because even a selfish shit like me would have called out something like *look out* or *there's a bump* or something like that. That's all it is, really, a bump, nothing more than a bump, too small to be a hill or a mound. A bump, and Claire's looking ahead and up at the chopper when anyone with a brain knows if you're running on uneven ground you want to be looking at what's in front of your feet. She hits the ground earlier than she expects to with her right foot and that's it, she's down.

A few seconds later I'm almost on top of her and the drug guy's way ahead and already slowing down to grab

Hans' outstretched hand. Claire hasn't moved, she's on her side, looking up, one arm on the ground where it broke her fall, the other up in the air like a child trying to get a grown-up's attention. I have those few seconds to decide what to do and regardless of what happened afterwards, all the stuff that followed that I couldn't have guessed at the time, forgetting all that, I reckon I weighed things up pretty well.

On the one side you've got the fact that I want to be on that chopper, there's murderers and a burning building out there, and the sooner I'm away from all that the better. On the other side, though, I'm thinking *where are the murderers?* because I haven't heard any shots for a while, I haven't seen anyone at all except us and the helicopter pilots, the runners have probably run, the dead are dead, the fire's hundreds of metres behind me and I don't see it getting much closer. It's not like I'm safe, but it's a good bet the drama's over. There's Claire, she's young, attractive, she's a journalist, she's exactly the kind of person I want to get to know for every reason in the book, and playing the hero isn't a bad way to get to know someone.

I slow down.

As I'm bending down to grab her by that conveniently raised arm, I hear something above the thud of the blades. Something I don't want to hear. *Crack! Crack!* it goes, pauses for a moment, then starts again, *Crack! Crack! Crack!* I look up. No idea where it's coming from but if I'm picking it up this close to the chopper it can't be far. Thing is, it's too late. I've stopped, bent down, I'm committed.

I haul her to her feet, keep hold of her arm, start running. It doesn't work. I look back to see why. Claire isn't running, she's bent over, or trying to bend over only the arm I'm holding means she can't, quite. She's breathing hard, her mouth an "O", her face red. I shout at her.

"Come on!"

She looks up at me, says something and shakes her head. Whatever she's saying I can't hear it because there's three things that are louder: the chopper, rapidly filling up, the gunshots, not getting any further away, and Che, lumbering his way past like a mammoth with a spear in its side and breathing like an asthmatic donkey with a megaphone. That's how bad it's got. The wounded donkey-mammoth's going to beat me to the chopper. I look back up and realise I can't let her go, not now, because if I do let her go and she doesn't make it out it'll be like I've killed her. I have another go, pull her hard towards me and shout, again, right into her face, "Come on!"

She shakes her head again and points down, at her foot. It doesn't look right. It's not pointing the wrong way or anything obvious, just turned on its side. Twisted when she fell. This is ridiculous. No one's going to die because of a twisted ankle. The sound around us gets more intense and I look up again and see the chopper, our chopper, start to move higher over the ground. Another one's coming in, that's OK, as long as I get out I don't care if I'm first or last. Che hasn't made it yet, he's still on his way, and Hans, the idiot, has actually got off the first chopper and is now standing there waiting for him, waiting for all of us, even the guards didn't do that. I pull Claire, harder, one hand on her arm and the other round her (I can't help noticing, even now) rather shapely waist, and she stops shaking her head and starts to limp alongside me. The new chopper's come down now, it's just thirty metres away. Che's on board, at last. Hans is still waiting. Twenty metres. The *Crack!* of the gunshots, again. Claire seems to be moving a little better, putting some weight on that ankle like she's realised a little pain now isn't going to kill her but a bullet just might. Ten metres. I can feel the wind from the blades pushing at me, the noise is unbelievable, there's Claire to drag along and I need to keep an eye on the ground because if I fall now there's no one behind us to pick me up. There's a miniature ladder, just two rungs leading onto the chopper, and Hans has moved onto the lower one, hand stretched out like an Olympic relay sprinter. *Crack! Crack!* I look down and force the steps, one, two, three, four, and now I can see the ladder and that outstretched hand without looking back up. I've got my left arm up round Claire's shoulder and my right hand holding her right hand like a demented bloody waltz, and I push with my left and pull with my right. The weight disappears. Hans has got her.

A moment later I'm on the lower step and looking round. The first chopper is already out of sight. The third is coming in to land and people are jumping off it, people in black with helmets and guns who look like they've stepped off the set of a space movie. There's no one behind us, no one left running across the scrubland from the burning building.

This look takes less than a second. I'm still on the lower step.

Crack! I turn and look the other way, towards the wood, and I can see two men at its edge, in uniform, holding guns. One of them crumples to the ground, first his left leg and then the rest of him, and even from here I can see a dark patch right in the middle of that leg. The other falls behind him, more deliberately, flattens himself to the mud and dust, looking ahead. I follow his eyes.

There's a man there. He's in the wood, in amongst the darkness of the trees, but in that instant, where he's standing, from where I'm looking, there are no trees close behind him, just a channel of faint grey light, just enough for me to see him clearly.

He looks old. His face is black, but his hair is grey, almost white. He seems to be wearing prison clothes but I'm not sure. In one hand he's holding what looks like a metal disk. In the other, there's a pistol. He's staring back at the scrubland, at the fallen man and the other behind him.

I'm still on the step. I want to move, but my legs won't work. The noise gets louder, as if the chopper blades are moving even faster.

The man looks up. He sees me. He's can't be more than twenty metres away. We're looking at each other. He doesn't blink.

He looks back down at the hand with the gun, and raises it.

I still can't move.

The arm is up and straight and pointing towards me. We're still looking at one another, and I can't believe I'm about to die, and for some unaccountable reason I blame everything on Che.

Then suddenly I'm jerked upwards. At first I think Hans has grabbed me and pulled, but then I realise I'm still on the lower step and it's the chopper that's moved. We're on our way.

The last thing I see, before I climb up and inside, is the man lowering his arm, turning, and disappearing into the wood.

4: Life Goes On

No one spoke, but with the noise of the chopper and my own heart thumping like a bucketload of frightened rabbits I doubt I'd have heard if they did. Other than the pilot, it was just the four of us, me, Claire, Hans and Che. Che was slumped across three seats with his left hand clutching the top of his right arm and blood still seeping through the fingers, and Claire was lying down massaging her ankle, so it was probably a good thing we'd missed the first chopper and had all this room to ourselves. Hans sat alone at the back, staring into middle distance. He looked blank, catatonic. If he was, it was a good thing he'd decided to go there now and not earlier.

I was trying to work out how I felt. I was alive. Physically unhurt. People had been shot – Che had been shot – people hadn't made it out at all. And at the end of it all, some bastard had pointed a gun at me, and if the pilot hadn't picked that moment to fly I'd have been just another body on the ground.

I pulled myself up, rubbed my shoulders, looked around again. I'd never felt more alive. I staggered over to where Claire was lying, across a few seats, bent down, put my hand on her shoulder. She started, looked up, saw me and smiled.

"Are you OK?"

I didn't bother shouting the words. I wouldn't have been able to shout loud enough. Mouthing them was enough.

She nodded. "Thanks," she said, or that was what it looked like. I sat down next to her and, to my surprise, she reached out and took my hand. I squeezed. She squeezed back.

Couldn't have been more than twenty minutes later we were down, off the chopper, indoors. Everything was white, clean, uniforms and serious faces. We'd been helped down off the chopper by a young man with a nondescript face and a twitch who asked us our names and ticked them off a list he was holding. Three of us went one way, Che went the other, accompanied by a woman in all-white scrubs who couldn't keep the smile off her face and gave the strong and disconcerting impression that she'd gladly rip Che's clothes off him and start operating right there. As I confirmed my name I took a glance at the list and saw Che's real name was Timothy. Timothy didn't seem right. I decided to keep thinking of him as Che.

The room we were waiting in was enormous, big enough for all three groups to sit comfortably apart in separate sections, big enough to talk with the others or be by yourself, if you wanted. In amongst the civilians I spotted plenty of uniforms and serious faces, and one at each of the four doors. Four doors, no windows. I looked round our group. I was sitting next to Claire. She hadn't let go of my hand until we were down, and I was hoping she'd take it again now we were sat waiting for I didn't know what, but I wasn't going to make the first move. Everyone else was there, everyone except Che, anyway.

Group C seemed all present and correct, too, I counted twelve and recounted them just to be sure. But Group A was looking sparse. Only eight. No Jayati Mehta, obviously, but the man with the beautiful hair who'd said he was "from the military" wasn't there either, and nor were two others, I couldn't work out who. It didn't mean anything, I reminded myself. Che was only wounded, and not badly at that, and he wasn't with us. Jayati Mehta was dead, that I was sure of, but the others might have just grazed their knees for all I knew.

One of the doors opened and another serious-looking uniform walked to what I supposed must be the front of the room. She had a long, narrow nose and one of those frowns that look like they might live there permanently. She cleared her throat for silence, which didn't make the slightest difference, because no one was talking anyway.

"I'm sorry you're being kept here. Obviously, you've been through a lot and I'm sure you want to get home as soon as you can. We just need to speak to each of you individually, and once you've been seen we'll be able to take you back to London."

I hadn't been looking outside when we flew, but I'd kind of assumed we were in London already. I looked around. More than thirty of us. Could take a while. Not that I had much to rush back for.

Five minutes later another uniform appeared and called out three names, one from each group. Three people got up – ours was a nondescript woman called Marie who'd just said she "worked in human rights", whatever that meant. I work in human rights. I've known terrorists who'd have said they worked in human rights, too. Anyway, three people, three guides, and out they went. If they could do us three at a time things might be over a little faster.

Just a little, mind. Five minutes went by. Ten drew near. Still a lot of people to get through, and the one they'd started with was Marie *Berg*, I remembered, with that sinking feeling familiar to people with names like Williams. Ten minutes, and right on cue the doors opened and the guides were back. No Marie, none of the interviewees. Looked like they were on the way home the moment they'd said their bit.

The drug guy was next. Samuel Dorran. I heard Claire sigh, and turned to her.

"What comes after Claire?" I asked her.

"Tully," she said.

"You've got it lucky, Tully. Try Williams."

She smiled at me. On any normal day I'm not one to be impressed by a smile, but this wasn't a normal day, not by a long shot. She wasn't almost good-looking enough to be out of my league after all, I realised. She was playing a whole different game.

Dorran's ten minutes were up. Talya was next, a young Turkish girl (when I'd introduced myself she'd told me she was Turkish right away, before she even said her name, sharply, almost fiercely, like I'd accused her of not being Turkish instead of just saying "Hi, I'm Sam"). The room was thinning out, fewer civilians, fewer uniforms, too. A couple of the uniforms were circulating with plastic cups full of tea and something they called coffee but which I'd have called hot, watery mud. Talya was less than ten minutes, maybe she'd just sat there telling them she was Turkish until they got bored of it, and now Hans was in. After the Bruce Willis act he'd pulled earlier I was unreasonably disappointed to find he wasn't, after all, Hans Gruber, like in *Die Hard*, but Hans Fischer. He looked round the room before he left, caught my eye, smiled and walked away. He'd saved my life, all our lives, really. I'd probably never see him again.

We started talking, quietly, because no one else in the room was talking at all. Claire had opted for tea and was insistent that there was no way the coffee could have been worse. She worked at the *Sentinel*, she said, and I didn't feel the need to remind her she'd already told me that. Not been there long. General news, not the front page stuff, or not yet, anyway, and there was that smile again. I thought about what I should tell her and settled for the sanitised truth. Nothing about Mauriers. Human rights lawyer. Immigration, corruption, abuse of power. A wrongly-issued driving penalty is an abuse of power, really. It's just not a very important one.

Another two down. The room had looked big when we were all there, but now it was huge, incongruous, like we'd stepped out of Lilliput into a world of giants. The three groups had fallen out of step, so people were coming in and out every few minutes now, which broke things up a little. Every time that happened we'd fall silent, look around, think quietly to ourselves. But each time, after a bit, we'd start talking again, usually right where we'd left off. It didn't feel strange – or at least, no stranger than everything else.

She didn't live far from me, as it turned out. Four streets and a mile or so, the same patch of Hackney-cum-Islington I'd pitched up in when I landed my first job. The world was at my feet, and if I'd looked forward a decade I'd have seen myself with a townhouse in Mayfair or a sprawling mass in the commuter belt, not half a dozen pubs and a few kebab shops from where I'd started out. Bloody David Brooks-Powell. Bloody Mauriers. I caught myself frowning and had to remember how much worse it could have been. Jayati Mehta probably had a townhouse in Mayfair.

"Peters". A lean, bespectacled middle-aged man I hadn't even registered as being in our Group stood and followed the guide to the door. I looked around. It was just the two of us. The survivors from Group A were long gone, and there were four of the C's left in their section, sat where chance and the alphabet had left them as their colleagues departed, far enough apart to feel alone and look at the walls and the ceiling and write things in their little notebooks from time to time. Even if nothing came of it – and, I had to remind myself, nothing *would* come of it – I was glad I had Claire to talk to. They hadn't given us back our phones, for all I knew the whole lot of them had gone up in smoke back at Dovesham. There was nothing here to read, which I thought was particularly bad planning before I remembered that none of this had been planned at all.

"Tully."

She stood up, took my hand, again, and squeezed. I started to stand but she pulled away, turned and left. That was it.

Ten minutes. I hadn't known ten minutes could last that long. After six there was a changeover in Group C, that at least gave me something to look at, someone standing up and walking to a door. I got up myself, and wandered over to where Group A had been sat, as if I could somehow get a feel for what they'd been through just by standing where they'd stood. All I got was more bored.

"Sam."

That was a surprise. There was a uniform, nodding towards me, but there was Claire, too. She was smiling at me and saying she'd told them we lived so close to one another they might as well take us back together. I felt something someone who'd been through what I'd been through that day had no right to feel. I felt happy.

"Samuel Williams?"

"That's me. But it's just Sam. Sam's fine."

"I'm Detective Inspector Roarkes. Please take a seat."

Detective Inspector Roarkes was sat behind a battered wooden desk, every inch of which was covered in piles of paper of varying thickness. The walls were a dirty white, the carpet looked brown but it probably wasn't supposed to. After the white sterility of the giant holding pen, this place felt shabby, old, and tired. Still no windows. I sat.

"Sorry for the delay. We've gone as fast as we could, but it's not often we have to interview this many people."

I nodded. I understood, I told him. Occupational hazard of being called Williams.

"Nominative," he said. He was looking down at a single sheet of paper on the desk.

"I beg your pardon?"

"Nominative hazard. It's your name, not your occupation."

"I see. Yes."

I did see. I saw Detective Inspector Roarkes didn't like me, and I couldn't figure out why.

"And your occupation is, it says here, lawyer. Is that right?"

"Yes. I'm a human rights lawyer."

He looked up at me and nodded. Human rights lawyers and detective inspectors don't tend to see eye to eye most of the time, which probably explained why Detective Inspector Roarkes had taken against me, but wasn't particularly fair, because I didn't really think of myself as a human rights lawyer these days. At least, not when I was trying to be honest. He looked back down at his paper.

"Hope you don't feel anything's been infringed here, Mr. Williams."

It was a statement, not a question, but I answered anyway.

"Not at all, Detective Inspector. Just happy to be alive, really."

He glanced up at me again, sharply, smiled, and seemed to relax. He looked as tired as the room did, and I couldn't blame him, if he'd been sat here all afternoon asking the same questions over and over again and getting the same answers. And him a Detective Inspector, too. Grey hair, mid-fifties, I'd have guessed, thin lips and yellow teeth through which he sucked the air for a moment every time he paused.

"So what happened?"

I told him, from the beginning, the crash before the lights went out. He stopped me from time to time, prompting, asking questions, checking things against other sets of notes from everyone else he'd spoken to, holding me back for a moment while he wrote down what I'd just said.

"Claire Tully. Had you met her, before today?"

"No."

"She says you saved her life."

"She's exaggerating. She tripped when we were running for the chopper. I helped her up. That's all."

He nodded and went back to his notes.

"OK, Mr. Williams, that's all. Thank you. I'm sorry you had to go through all this, but you can go now. If we need to speak to you again, we'll be in touch."

"Can I ask you something?"

He pushed back his chair and looked up at me.

"If you've left a phone or anything like that at Dovesham, we'll let you know if we find it. There's a lot to go through there, I'm afraid."

"I'm not thinking about my phone." That was true. It was useless, anyway. "It's something else."

"Ask away. I might not be able to answer, though."

"Sure. What happened?"

He smiled, and nodded again.

"We're still not sure. It looks like it started out as a riot. But if it was a riot there was some planning behind it, because there were firearms where they really weren't supposed to be."

"Right."

"Anything else?"

I didn't know quite how to ask it, but I felt I needed to.

"How many?"

"How many what?"

"Dead, hurt, that kind of thing."

He looked hard at me, like he was weighing me up, sucking the air through his teeth again for what felt like minutes.

"I suppose I can tell you. You're not a journalist. And it's not like there's any great secret. We've got two prison officers dead and one wounded. We've got two dead from your lot, and three wounded. We've got three dead inmates, a couple wounded, and a couple more they're expecting to find when they've been through what the fire left behind."

"Anyone escape?"

"Everyone who got out got caught."

Everyone who got out got caught. I knew people were dead, people less lucky than me, and now I was away the whole thing had nothing to do with me any more, but I still wanted to hear it and I was pleased I had. He'd seen me, the man with the pistol, he'd shot a guard and turned and seen me, looked right at me, pointed his gun at my face. Nothing to do with me. But I wouldn't have been happy if he'd still been out there.

Claire was waiting in the room. Alone, bar a single uniform, who saw me and marched smartly over. Claire looked up and followed.

Five minutes later the two of us were sat in the back of a police Land Rover. Not an unusual event for me. I represent scum, which makes me the enemy as far as the police are concerned, but when you meet the same officers day after day and you decide not to act like a prick, you can't help getting along well enough with most of them. Not all, but I can't stop anyone else acting like a prick. So I've been given my fair share of lifts by people whose professional interest would have been better served leaving me by the side of a road next to the wreckage of a hundred grand sports car or outside a house flaunting the shattered-glass scars of a drunken rage or in a corridor staring into a hotel room still dotted with the remnants that never made it up my client's nose.

It was dark. I shouldn't have been surprised but I was, stuck inside without windows so long. Darkness was fine, because I didn't want to talk, right now, I didn't know quite what to talk about, and the darkness made that acceptable. After forty-five minutes we were off the motorway and into the forest of shopping centres and semis that mark the gateway to North London. Twenty minutes later we were nearly home.

"Fancy a drink?"

I looked at her and nodded. There was a pub at the end of the road we were on, a crappy run-down unfashionable place that was just the sort of pub I liked when I was alone.

"Can you let us out here?" I asked. The car pulled up and the driver got out. She was a sergeant, I now saw, which made the whole thing seem an appalling waste of a useful officer's time. Of course seniority doesn't always mean competence, with police any more than with lawyers. She looked around, suspicious, uncertain. A quiet road, fog, dark, distant shouts and what sounded like fighting.

"You're sure you're OK here?"

"We're fine. Thanks."

We weren't, as it happened. I hadn't been in the Butchers for a year and either the clientele had changed or we'd caught it on a bad night, because it was the same noisy crowd I tried to avoid in the high street bars, only nastier and much more drunk. We sat down at the only empty table, she with a gin and tonic, me with a Guinness, and the glasses were still half-full when I suggested moving on and she nodded her agreement.

Moving on. I hadn't thought where, just kind of assumed another pub would materialise out of the fog and the dark. It hadn't, and now we'd been walking five minutes and there was my street. Claire had tucked her arm into mine the moment we stepped outside, and shivered, even though she was wearing what looked like a good thick coat. She was bound to think I'd planned this – but then, it had been her idea to get a drink in the first place, hadn't it?

"My flat's just round the corner."

She looked at me, screwed up her face in a display of concentration.

"Got anything to drink?"

"Beer. Whisky. Wine."

"Wine's good," she said. "Come on, then."

One bottle down. I'd had a momentary panic as I turned the key, trying to think back to that morning, the state I'd left the place in, but it wasn't so bad, or at least not so bad that half a bottle of wine and artfully-dimmed lights couldn't make it look pretty enough. We were sitting on the big old sofa, which looked best with the lights off entirely, but artfully-dimmed would have to do, and Claire was flicking through the selection on my iPod. She'd found some eighties soul I didn't even know I had and couldn't remember liking enough to buy. Something made me look at my watch, and then something else, something stupid, made me grab the remote and turn on the TV.

There it was. Dovesham by night. Lights everywhere, blue lights flashing, torches, headlights, spot-lights dangling from ladders and platforms and the helicopters circling overhead. Claire had been lounging back but now she sat up, alert, and turned down the music.

"....were killed in the riot, alongside two guards and three prisoners, although we have been told that this tally may rise as the more seriously-burnt sections of the complex are searched."

The TV cut to an image of the minibus, on its side. An image from earlier in the day, while it was still light. Probably not long after we'd crawled past the thing. Claire reached for my hand.

"Police and prison officials have, however, confirmed that all three of the inmates known to have penetrated areas outside the main building have been apprehended. The three have been named as Dejan Stankovic, and brothers Marko and Pedrag Ilic, all of whom were convicted in two thousand and six of a number of offences related to organised crime in Serbia and Great Britain. Pedrag Ilic was injured in the operation to recapture him, and has been transferred to a secure hospital. His brother and Dejan Stankovic are back behind bars."

Images of the three men flashed onto the screen. I didn't recognise any of them.

All were white.

"Our sources have stressed that even at the height of the riot, all other inmates were kept within the main building. A number of bodies are expected to be found when the more seriously damaged parts of the building are declared safe, and officers are confident that at that point all inmates will be accounted for. We understand that the police, too, are confident that there is no longer any threat to the public and the situation is now fully under control."

I turned to Claire.

"What about that guy?"

She didn't seem to know what I meant.

"The guy in the woods. Didn't you see him?"

It wasn't until I said the words that I realised she probably hadn't. She'd got onto the helicopter ahead of me, dragged to safety by Hans. While I stood there waiting to get shot she was face down across a row of seats gripping her right ankle. Hans had been on the chopper. Che had been on the chopper. The only person who hadn't been on the chopper was me. I tried to explain.

"While I was getting on the helicopter."

"What happened?"

"There was a guy. In the woods. Black guy, had a gun, pointed it at me."

Claire took the remote from my hand and switched the TV off.

"What are you saying, Sam?"

"I'm saying there was another guy. He got outside. I saw him shoot one of the guards."

"Are you sure?"

"Yes."

I was sure. I knew what I'd seen. One man, two guards. He'd shot at them and then he'd turned and seen me. He wasn't one of the men on TV. I don't forget a face. And he wasn't white.

"Did you see the guard?"

"What?"

"The guard he shot. Did you see what he looked like?"

I couldn't see why that mattered.

"No, but that's not the point."

"It is the point, Sam. They've just shown us the three men who got out and they're all white. Your guard, do you think maybe *he* was the inmate and the guy who shot him might have been a guard?"

"No. Definitely not."

I stopped. I could see his face clear as anything. He'd been in prison clothes, I thought, but now I went back through it I wasn't so sure. He'd shot someone, and he'd pointed his gun at me, and he'd been wearing something drab and possibly greenish, though I couldn't even be sure of that. Maybe it wasn't prison uniform after all.

"He shot a guard, though. There were two of them after him, and he got one in the leg."

Claire was frowning now.

"Two of them?"

"Yes."

"Wearing officers' uniforms?"

I hesitated.

"They were definitely wearing uniforms. Can't be certain what type."

"I think you've got it the wrong way round, Sam."

I looked at her, trying to work out if there was a chance in hell she could be right.

"The brothers, probably. I bet what you saw was the brothers getting caught. One of them was injured, did you hear, they just said it, on the news. That's your guy getting shot in the leg."

"But why did he point his gun at me?"

"Did he fire?"

"No."

"Probably just instinct. Have you ever fired a gun?"

I looked at her. I'd had her down as young, probably intelligent, certainly pretty. Now she seemed – I couldn't think of the word, and then I could. She seemed streetwise.

"No."

"Nor me. But the kind of people who do, people who do it for a living, they don't know who's a friend and who's trying to kill them. Split second decisions and all that. Probably just scoping you out, making sure you weren't one of the bad guys."

I didn't say anything, just thought about it. The silence lengthened, and she spoke again.

"And I'm glad he gave himself the time to think."

I grinned. She was right. Probably right. And – I remembered – it was nothing to do with me anyway. She picked up the iPod again, and her glass of wine, and gave a long, satisfied sigh as the first notes of *Sergeant Pepper* filled the room. I waited to the end of the first chorus, gently removed the glass from her hand, and leaned in. She smiled.

She didn't leave till long past one. I'd told her she could stay, but she had to work in the morning and she didn't think she'd get much sleep if she spent the rest of the night with me. I made it as far as the front door, my eyes straining through the darkness until I was sure I could see her getting in the cab, and staggered back to bed. I lay there turning things over in my mind, everything fuzzy now, the prison and the bodies and then Claire. Given the choice, I'd have focused on Claire, but in my experience brains don't give you the choice. Instead, as I drifted out of consciousness, I could see him, his face, looking at me as I stood on that step like an enormous wingless duck with a great big cross painted on its back.

Was she right? He didn't look like a guard. They didn't look like inmates. Did it matter? My last thought, as the wine and the last eighteen intense hours finally pushed me into sleep, was that it didn't matter, not really, because it wasn't really anything to do with me.

I wish I'd been right.

5: Imagination

I didn't have a case on at the moment, which was lucky because the state I woke up in, I'd have struggled to defend a white man in Mississippi. At least, that's what I told myself. Truth was, it had been a while since I'd had a case. If this was luck, I could have done with a bit less of it

Still, at least there was something to join the Grimshaws. Ten years, it had been, ten years of Bill and Eileen Grimshaw turning and staring at me like I'd just killed their little girl all over again. Every night, for ten years, and now, suddenly, the Grimshaws had company, and that company was a man pointing a gun at my face. It wasn't what I'd call a happy dream, but at least it was a change.

I looked at the clock by my bed and tried to work out what the hell was going on in my head. It took me a moment to realise it wasn't in my head, it was outside, the phone ringing. I couldn't see the phone. I heard my own voice, a lot more serious and business-like than I was feeling, asking the caller to leave a message, and managed to push myself up and into the living room, still naked and half-asleep.

"Mr Williams, this is the security and administration office at HMP Dovesham. Please call us back when you get this message."

I still couldn't see where the damned phone was.

"It's nothing urgent."

Which was a relief, because I could tell already it would be a while before I was fit to talk sensibly to anyone at all, even the screws at Dovesham.

"But please do call back when you can."

There. There was the phone. Under the sofa. Of course.

"The number is –"

"Hello, this is Sam."

"Oh, hello Mr Williams, I didn't realise you were in."

It was a friendly sort of voice. Sensible, normal, cheery, not the kind of voice you'd expect to accompany someone who spent the working day guarding a prison full of dangerous psychopaths. Administration more than security, I thought.

"Sorry. Couldn't find the phone."

"Well it's your lucky day then, because you've just found two."

"Eh?"

It was too early in the day for cryptic. It was half past ten. Not too early. Just too early for me.

"Your phone."

"Right?"

"Old Samsung, cracked screen?"

Of course.

"Yes, have you found it?"

"I'm talking to you on it. Hope you don't mind. Best way to work out what belongs to who. Just dial Ice or Home and see who answers."

"Ice? Who's Ice?"

"In Case of Emergency. You should have a contact there yourself."

A good idea, in theory. But whose number would I put there?

"Yeah, I suppose so." Something occurred to me. "You know, if you go through all the phones ringing Home and Ice you'll end up getting through to someone whose husband or wife died yesterday."

There was a brief silence.

"I know."

She didn't sound so cheery now.

"I'm sorry. Already happened, right?"

"Five minutes ago. A Mr Mehta. His wife was shot."

"I know."

"Right there in the cell. Shot in the head."

"I know. I saw it."

"Sorry. Of course. On the screens, right?"

I nodded, which pretty much summed up how together I was, nodding at a phone. She didn't seem to need an answer, though.

"So anyway, we can send you the phone, if you want."

"I'm surprised you managed to get anything out at all. The fire, and everything."

"It wasn't as bad as everyone thought. The fire."

"That's good."

"I mean, it was out by midnight, in the end, we've had all night to go through the place and see what was left."

The cheerful voice had disappeared completely. Even in the state I was in, I thought I knew why.

"I'm sorry."

"What for?"

"Your colleagues."

There was another silence, during which I wondered whether I'd said the right thing. Then fast, shallow breathing, like she was trying to hold herself back from crying. I waited till she was ready to speak again.

"Thanks," she said. "Sorry you had to go through it all."

"Glad you got all the bastards, anyway."

"Should have shot the lot of them. No, I shouldn't have said that. Forget I said that."

"Don't worry about it. And at least you got one of them."

"What?"

"One of them got shot, didn't he? The Serbian guy. Whatever his name was."

"Ilic?"

"That's the one."

"No. Stupid idiot broke his ankle jumping off a wall."

She laughed. I didn't.

"Are you sure?"

"Couldn't be surer. It was me that found him. Lying there crying like a baby. You'd have thought his bloody leg had come off. His brother and his mate had just left him there and he was scared he was going to burn to death. I told him I had to go but I'd be back in a while, if he was lucky. Told him the fire was close. Course it wasn't, it was quarter of a mile away."

I wasn't listening, not properly. Pedrag Ilic hadn't been shot. She was sure he hadn't been shot. But I'd seen someone get shot and if that someone wasn't Pedrag Ilic, then who the hell was it?

"Lucky for him I wasn't supposed to be there. Off shift. Otherwise I might have had a gun with me, and then the fire would have been the least of his worries."

Now she was sounding more like someone who belonged to the world of Dovesham. And more like security than administration, too. If I'd been thinking straight I'd have started recording the call, stuff like this was pure gold to a human rights lawyer who wanted to get his name out there. *Prison guard regrets not shooting injured inmate*. At the very least I'd get a few lines in the *Daily Mirror*. But for once, my career was the last thing on my mind. I needed to think fast.

"Can you do me a favour?"

"Sure. Want the phone sent round?"

"Oh, yes. Please. But there's something else. When I was being questioned by the police, I'm not sure I told them everything I saw."

"Oh, right. Anything in particular you want me to pass on."

"Well, is there someone there at Dovesham who's been putting together the whole picture, everything that happened, that sort of thing?"

"Jim Connolly. He's my boss. Been talking to the police all night. If anyone knows what happened, it's him."

"Can you ask him to call me?"

There was a pause.

"Well, I can ask him, but he's been here since yesterday morning. He *was* on shift, see. Been a bit to deal with."

"I understand. But I think it might be important. I really do."

"I'll see what I can do. Goodbye, Mr Williams."

She didn't sound so friendly any more. I could see why, after everything she'd had to deal with, and her boss, and then some jumped-up prick of a lawyer starts digging around. I didn't really care. If I couldn't handle being disliked by a guard at a high security prison then I might as well chuck it all in and retrain as a florist with a line in witty insults. Everyone likes a funny florist.

I made my way slowly back to the bedroom, lay back down and closed my eyes. I didn't want to go back to sleep, and there was too much going on in my head to let me, but I needed a bit of quiet and darkness to let it all ferment.

Thirty seconds was all I got before the phone rang again. I hadn't brought it with me, but at least I knew where it was.

"Hello?"

"Hello Mr Williams." It was her again, my friend of a minute earlier. If I ever found out her name, maybe I could put her down as my In Case of Emergency.

"Hello again."

"Jim'll call you some time this morning. Some time in the next couple of hours."

"Thanks. I appreciate it."

"Sure."

She didn't even say goodbye this time. I made a mental note to be sure I never got locked up in Dovesham.

Some time in the next couple of hours. Nice and vague. I gave up on the bed. Coffee would help, I thought, but it didn't. Going back in time and drinking less might have helped. At least I'd had some sleep. I couldn't imagine how Claire must be feeling. I took a quick shower, keeping an ear out all the time for the phone. Nothing. I booted up the old laptop, which was no happier about being woken up than I'd been, and hit Google. Apart from the usual off-the-wall conspiracy crap everyone was spouting the same line on the Dovesham escapees, three got out, one got hurt, all got caught. Nothing on precisely how Ilic got hurt, but regardless of her personal issues there was no reason to believe the woman from Dovesham had been lying to me.

The phone rang, and this time I had it in my hand and was saying my name before I had a chance to think.

"Sam. So you're alive."

"Paul."

I sat back down. I hadn't even realised I'd got to my feet.

"You OK, mate? Not hurt?"

"Nah. Fine. Hungover."

"I feel your pain. I've got a bastard between the eyes myself, and the worst thing I had to handle yesterday was a VAT cockup by my clerk."

I managed a laugh.

"So you're sure you're OK?"

"Sure."

"And that's it?"

I realised I was being rude. The guy had given me his spot, after all. He'd helped me out. And yeah, I'd come as close to dying as I'd managed in the first thirty-six years of my life, but I could hardly say that was his fault.

"Sorry, Paul. Just a lot happening at the moment."

"Oh. OK."

I could sense his disappointment. Not annoyance. Nothing as obvious as that.

"Look, really, I am sorry. Listen, are you around tonight? Or tomorrow?"

"Tonight's a no-go. Tomorrow depends on work. Big case, solicitors busting my balls, you know how it is."

Anyone else, I'd have thought he was trying to wind me up. Not Paul.

"Tell the bastards they only came to you because you're good enough to wing it and still win their bloody case."

"It's Mauriers, Sam."

I see the word in my head a dozen times a day, I might say it, quietly, under my breath, the same way someone else might say "shit", but hearing it out loud still made me freeze, for a moment. Not helpful for a lawyer in the same field. Heaven help me if I ever came up against them for real.

"If I bought you a drink would you lose the thing on purpose?"

Paul laughed. He knew how I felt about Mauriers.

"Listen, Sam, I'll try to get myself clear tomorrow evening. We need to catch up. You're sure you're OK now though, right?"

"Tip top."

"Speak tomorrow then."

"See you."

I put the phone down, wondering why I'd picked that particular moment to say *tip top* for the first time in my life, and tried to remember what I'd been doing before it rang. The story was on the screen in front of me. They didn't have to spell out the details: Stankovic and the Ilic brothers had been nasty customers. The convictions were for people-trafficking and money-laundering, but it was pretty clear they'd done a little killing on the side to keep everything running smoothly. A couple of years on the run, hunted down throughout the old Yugoslavia, and when they were finally caught it turned out they'd been living the high life in London the whole time. There were rumours about people who'd known all along and been paid to forget. The police ran an investigation, suspended a couple of junior officers for "incompetence", let the whole thing die. The army ran their own investigation which ended when the sole remaining subject of their enquiries, a Major Dawes of the 2nd Battalion, The Princess of Wales's Royal Regiment, was found dead at the foot of a South Devon cliff with a note in his pocket insisting he'd never known a thing. Stankovic and the Ilic brothers got nearly sixty years between them and were forgotten about. Until now.

The phone rang. I answered and found myself holding the thing about a foot from my face. Jim Connolly wasn't one of your quiet types.

"You Sam Williams? This is Jim Connolly, HMP Dovesham. Hear you've got some questions."

Loud and fast, too. Regimental Sergeant Major sort. And already I was on the back foot, starting to apologise for wasting his time, before I remembered that I might, just possibly, be helping him.

I explained what I'd seen. And what I'd since been told, about the broken ankle. It didn't tally. He gave a grunt, which I interpreted as his version of thoughtful. If I was right, the thinking didn't go on long.

"I'm sorry, Mr Williams. You must have got it wrong. No one shot in the leg. One of our boys got it in the head, but that was inside. No one shot outside at all. And none of the cons."

One of our boys got it in the head. And on with the show. That was it. Jim Connolly wasn't the sentimental type.

"I wouldn't forget something like that."

"I'm sure you wouldn't, Mr Williams. Which means you must have imagined it. All that time locked in the room, then a sprint through the building, crawling past the bus, hearing the choppers, fire behind you, gunshots inside, running across the field? It's no surprise you thought you saw something that wasn't there. Quite frankly, I'm surprised none of your lot saw the Loch Ness Monster."

"So what I saw, you're saying it couldn't have happened."

"Not at Dovesham, sir. You say the man you think you saw was black with grey hair?"

"That's right."

"We have twenty-three black prisoners and seven black officers, and every one of them is under the age of forty, Mr Williams."

He said it like it was final. The whole thing was impossible. I thanked him and apologised for wasting his time.

Was he right?

I'd seen something and interpreted it one way. Claire had been sure that interpretation was wrong – which was feasible, at the time. But now – had I imagined it all? Was it possible that the fear and the sensations, all that darkness followed by sudden light, the sounds, the shock of seeing the dead, could all of that have come together into something no one else could see because it was never really there in the first place?

Roarkes had given me his card, and as luck would have it he was sitting at his desk eating his lunch when I called. I apologised. I seemed to be doing a lot of apologising lately.

"No need. Cress."

"Huh?"

There was a short pause in which I could almost see him wiping the back of his hand across his mouth.

"Cress sandwich. Wife says I've got to eat healthy. Won't even let me put egg in it."

"Nasty. You're going to have to start making your own sandwiches."

"I do. I put the damned egg in there. Sneaky cow must have taken it all out while I was getting dressed."

I couldn't help laughing.

"Bad enough that she hides my fags."

"Sorry. That's not a laughing matter."

"So what can I do for you, Mr Williams?"

I explained. What I'd seen, which he already knew about from the debrief. What I'd since found out, from the news and Jim Connolly. How it didn't add up. Roarkes chewed for a moment before he spoke.

"Any chance you've just, well, misremembered the whole thing?"

"Nope."

"That's it? Nope?"

I thought about it. I didn't want to come across as an arsehole. I'd done that too often in the last thirteen years.

"Look, I don't forget things. Especially things like that. But I guess it's possible I just imagined the whole thing."

"That's the same thing."

No it wasn't. There's a world of difference between remembering something wrong and imagining it in the first place. I didn't say anything.

"Look, Sam – mind if I call you Sam?"

"Go ahead."

"I don't know what you want from me, Sam. I've been over the briefings, been over everything Dovesham sent over, and from what I've seen Connolly's spot on. The only person who saw what you think you saw is you. If it makes you happy, feel free to keep asking the same people the same questions. But if you want my advice, I'd forget about it. It's nothing to do with you any more."

I thanked him and hung up, and then without thinking too much about it I reached for a scrap of paper on the coffee table by the sofa and dialled the number on it.

"Claire Tully, Sentinel."

"Hi Claire, it's Sam."

"Oh."

Oh. Difficult to interpret. I couldn't tell if she was pleased to hear from me or not.

"Listen, are you around tonight?"

"Aren't you supposed to give it a few days?"

She was teasing me. Which was good, because it meant she probably was pleased to hear from me.

"Why waste a few days?"

"I'll take that as a compliment."

"You should. But listen, there's something I need to talk to you about."

And for what felt like the hundredth time that day, I explained how the official line didn't tally with what I thought I'd seen, or with the refracted version she'd come up with herself.

"Hmmm," she said.

"Hmmm?" I replied.

"Will you be offended if I tell you what I think might have happened?"

"Only if you insult me at the end of it."

"I think Roarkes and Connolly are probably right. You've got images in your head, people getting shot – we saw someone hit in the arm, we saw a body on the screen, there were others in the corridor. You see something like that, it's not just going to get filed away like a train journey or an episode of EastEnders. It's going to come back. I think what you saw came back, a few minutes later."

"You're saying I hallucinated it?"

"You can call it that if you want to. I'm saying you had a flashback."

"I've always associated flashbacks with more enjoyable activities than getting shot at."

She laughed, and I could see that smile again.

"OK then. I'm saying you were confused."

"Confused. Sounds less insane than a flashback. I'll take that."

"You wanted my opinion, Sam."

"Fair enough. I'm still not sure I buy it, mind. Sure you don't want to write a story on it?"

"What, this guy I hooked up with imagined someone shooting at him?"

"Could win you the Pulitzer."

"Not really *Sentinel* stuff is it, Sam?"

"I'm serious, Claire. Look, you're probably right, all of you. I'll give you that. But only because I can't think of anything else that makes sense. Anyway, how about tonight?"

Nothing, for a moment, just the gentle buzz of the phone.

"OK. Do you know the new Turkish place on Upper Street?"

"The one with all the big pipes hanging on the wall?"

I'd walked past it a couple of times, but I hadn't been in. It looked expensive.

"That's the one. Eight OK for you?"

"Perfect."

I was smiling as I put the phone down, but the smile

didn't last long. Claire thought I was confused. Connolly thought I'd imagined the whole thing. Roarkes thought it was nothing to do with me. Even I thought it was nothing to do with me.

So why did I have a strong and unsettling feeling that I hadn't heard the last of it?

6: Your Everyday Kind of Grey

I was hungry and there was nothing viable in the fridge, which meant a two minute walk to the kebab and burger bar at the corner of the road. As I strolled back, trying to shield my eyes from the glare of the sun and keep the steady drip of chilli sauce away from my shoes, I noticed someone standing outside the door of my building.

The building was a Victorian terraced house split into three single-storey apartments, and I'd been there seven years, which was about six years longer than I'd meant to stay. The ground floor had the garden, which was a tiny paved square that caught the sun for about fifteen minutes each summer. I had the roof terrace, which you could only reach by crawling up a ladder through a trapdoor which never properly closed and meant the whole place was freezing from October through to March. First floor had no outside space at all, but the current occupant had got himself a piano by way of revenge. The piano would have been more use than the roof terrace. First floor and ground floor came and went so fast it felt like I'd only just found out their names by the time they were gone and the next lot in. They seemed to be getting younger, too.

Anyway, there was a grey Volkswagen parked on the double yellows by the flat, and a man standing outside the door wearing one of those bright yellow tabards that make people think they've got some kind of authority over everyone else. I'd toyed with the idea of wearing one to court one day, see if it helped, but the magistrates and judges I came across weren't exactly known for their easy-going sense of humour.

"Can I help you?" I asked. He turned around and stared at me, a white guy, bodybuilder, by the look of him, tattoos all over his face.

"I'm looking for Sam Williams." The voice was surprisingly gentle.

"That's me."

"Can you sign for this, please?"

I put the kebab down carefully on the ground and took the small brown package he was holding. "*HMP Dovesham*" was printed down one side. I signed and watched him walk to a motorbike parked on the other side of the street.

The phone didn't look any more battered than it had done before yesterday. I checked my messages. Paul had called three times before he finally reached me at home. No one else knew where I'd been, so no one else had any reason to worry. Henderson had called. Henderson owned the squalid little dive I called my office, and he thought we should have a conversation about the rent. He was right, but I was pretty sure we'd be coming at the conversation from very different angles. The other messages were from my parents, who were wondering how I was doing and why I hadn't called for a while, and Rachel, a PR I'd had a short thing with a couple of years back and stayed in touch with, because I'm that sort of a guy, and not in any way because when you're trying to get your name out there, it's useful to have a friend in PR. Nothing I needed to deal with right away. No new clients. Not even an old one.

I thought about calling Pierre. He'd been clean a few years now, or so he said, so I wouldn't be getting any business off him. But I had the feeling his friends were still stealing and dealing. He was a good guy. He'd spread the word, if I asked him to, remind them there was a good lawyer out there who had their back. I didn't like to ask for favours, but Pierre still thought he owed me for getting him off, and I wasn't going to tell him otherwise.

I'd almost finished the kebab, and decided I would give him a call, when the Samsung rang.

"Hello," I managed, through a mouthful of minced lamb.

"Sam Williams?"

"Speaking."

"This is Olivia Miles from the *Sun*. I gather you were at Dovesham yesterday."

"Yup." I swallowed the final bit of the kebab.

"It must have been terrifying."

The line was supposed to be sympathetic, but the voice was bored and I hadn't even said anything yet. I guessed this wasn't her first call of the morning.

"I wouldn't want to do it again, that's for sure."

She could quote me on that.

"I was wondering whether you had anything to add, unique angle, something to offer our readers, the whole experience."

I thought, for a moment. A journalist calling me up and asking my opinion was precisely what I'd got into the whole mess for in the first place, and now there was one on the other end of the phone and I couldn't think what to say. I hadn't spotted anything out of place, not before the riot, hadn't even been in there long enough to make up something reasonably convincing. I could give a spiel about the room, the shooting, the fire, a bit of human interest, it would be better than nothing. I'd opened my mouth, ready with a line full of darkness and terror, when I realised I did have something else to offer after all.

"Yeah, I've got a unique angle all right."

"Really, Mr Williams?"

If she was trying to sound intrigued, she wasn't doing a great job of it. Came out more like sarcastic.

"How about this, Olivia: there's still a prisoner out there."

"Say that again."

Now *that* was intrigued.

"There's still a prisoner out there."

"Go on."

Olivia Miles was a pro. She slowed me down when she needed to, but interrupted only briefly, prodding, prompting, seeking out more detail or a confirmation of something she'd already heard. I gave her everything from yesterday, plus the calls I'd had that morning with Connolly's minion, Connolly himself, and Roarkes. She was silent for a moment when I'd finished.

"Connolly wouldn't speak to us. Roarkes just gave us the same useless quote he gave the TV people last night."

"Right, well, you've got something different now, haven't you?"

She paused, again.

"If it checks out."

I didn't understand.

"Well, it won't, will it? I mean, I've just told you. Everyone's denying it. But I'm not making it up."

"You're sure? You couldn't have imagined it, maybe remembered it wrong?"

"I've been through all that with Roarkes and Connolly. I don't forget things. And I don't imagine people pointing guns at me, either. Trust me. It happened."

"Hmmm."

"What does that mean?"

"It means I probably believe you, Sam – it's OK if I call you Sam, isn't it?"

"Fine."

"Yeah, well, I think I do believe you, but that's not

enough to run it straight."

"So?"

"So I'd like to run it anyway. But it won't be straight."

I didn't like the sound of that.

"What does that mean, precisely?"

"It means I'll have to make it clear you're on your own here and so far we haven't found any evidence to back up your story."

"So you'll make it look like I'm a nutter who's made the whole thing up?"

She laughed.

"No, Sam. Like I said, I believe you. If I didn't believe you, I'd still run it, using the nutter angle. But with you, I think I can nudge it the other way."

"How?"

"It's all about the little phrases. Like just now. I said we haven't found any evidence *so far*. Makes it sound like we're still looking, so don't write this thing off too soon. And Connolly and Roarkes, I can make it clear they've refused to comment."

"But you haven't even asked them about it yet."

"I didn't say what it was they refused to comment on. Our readers can make that deduction for themselves."

I was starting to feel a little less uncomfortable.

"We can describe it the same way you did, just now. The way you tell it, no one else *could* have seen these guys unless they'd been outside the choppers looking around. And who'd be doing that? If there was anyone left outside the choppers, they'd have been looking *at* them, running towards them. You're the one person who had the chance to see what was going on in the woods. It's hardly surprising no one else spotted it."

"You're very convincing."

"Thank you. Now, is there anything else you'd like to add?"

She went back through her notes, made sure I still agreed with everything she'd taken down. I did.

As soon as the call was over I started to worry I'd done the wrong thing. This wasn't the *Guardian*. It wasn't even the *Times*. I had no more reason to trust Olivia Miles than she had to believe me. And if she didn't really believe me, I shuddered to think what kind of idiot she'd have me dressed up as in tomorrow's edition.

I called Claire. She answered on the first ring, and once I'd told her what I'd done, she made sure I knew I was an arrogant, ignorant fool. But a lucky one, too, because Olivia Miles was, apparently, a decent journalist with a reputation for digging out news rather than hammering members of the public. Real news, too, not, as Claire put it, *Big Tits and Celebrity Weight-Loss News*. That made me feel slightly better, but only slightly, because Claire, who'd actually been there with me and knew that whatever else might be going on in my head, I wasn't just making the whole thing up, even Claire wasn't prepared to run with the story herself.

Claire wasn't the only journalist. The *Sun* and the *Sentinel* weren't the only newspapers. If I was going to get slaughtered in the *Sun* I needed something to balance it out. So I spent the next two hours calling the rest of the broadsheets and trying to tell them the same thing I'd told Olivia Miles.

None of them were interested. None of them believed me. None of them even pretended to.

I called Pierre. He couldn't help me out of this mess, he probably wouldn't even understand what the problem was, but I needed something to take my mind off it, something else to worry about, and one thing I *am* good at is worrying about the state of my career.

"Hey, man, how's it going?"

Pierre was always pleased to hear from me. In the early days that was something else I'd worried about, how he couldn't really like me that much, there must be something else to it, he had to be setting me up or getting ready to beat the living crap out of me.

But I'd been wrong. I'd torn apart a case so weak the prosecution should never have brought it in the first place, I'd got Pierre out of what wouldn't have been more than twelve months low security anyway, out in six, and ever since he'd behaved like I'd taken a bullet for him.

"Not good, Pierre."

I never lied to Pierre. There didn't seem any point. Whatever you said, he took it the same way. He knew how I'd got him off, how the police had made so many basic procedural errors that at the time I'd thought it was a shame they'd wasted all these cock-ups on the one case. He knew how I'd found it out, too. Didn't matter to him.

"I'd get you some good stuff, but you know, I don't do that no more."

He laughed. Possession with intent to supply, that was the charge he'd beaten, guilty as hell, too, as he happily admitted the first time we met.

"You know what I'm doing nine to five these days, Pierre?"

"Nope."

"Nothing. Nothing at all. I need some clients. So do me a favour."

"Whatever you want, man."

"Just spread the word, OK? Any of your guys needs help, you know where to get it, right?"

"I do that already, man. You know I do. But these guys, they've all got their own briefs now. I say your name, they say tha's a white guy's name. So I tell them white guys make good briefs, fuck, their own briefs are white anyway.

But you can't talk to them half the time anyway, Sam."

"Why not?"

"The stuff they're on, shit, man, it's strong. Nothing like I used to sell. There just wasn't stuff like that on the streets, just two, three years ago. It's a new world, man."

"It's just weed, Pierre. Come on."

"You don't know, man. You don't know."

I hadn't really expected Pierre to have anything for me, because I already knew that whenever one of his friends got busted, he'd be whispering my name in the guy's ear. These days Pierre ran security at one of the Camden clubs where he'd once pushed dope. He knew who was who and what kind of trouble was going on outside. He made damn sure nothing happened that might bring that trouble inside. And I hadn't heard from any new dope-pushers in Camden in a while.

And yes, before you ask what the hell a so-called human rights lawyer's doing defending small-time drug-dealers from small-time charges they deserve, you're right. I might as well have been negotiating corporate takeovers. Would have paid a lot more, too. But there's three things you've got to bear in mind. One, the little guys need someone in their corner too, looking out for the mistakes and the deliberate omissions that can make the difference between the cell and the street. And if someone's being screwed and it's not by the book, that's an infringement of their human rights (your honour). Two, if I had to choose between the Camden dope-pushers and the Surrey twenty-something millionaires with powder all down their faces and their smashed-up cars and smashed-up girlfriends, I'd go for the dope-pushers every time. They don't pay the same, and any lawyer who won't work for people he doesn't like is going to end up poor. But you can still have a preference. Three, the Guildford Four and the

Birmingham Six have been done. I'm not getting any tortured Iraqis or Guantanamo Brits hammering at my door (the Guantanamo Brits would struggle, to be fair). I'm not even hearing from wannabe-famous whistle-blowers from the police or MI5. The big stories go straight to the big names, and if the big names are busy they carry on down the list, past the likes of Mauriers, if they won't take the case, until they hit someone who will. When you're going down that list, it takes a long time to reach Sam Williams, even with Jayati Mehta (top ten, probably) out of the picture, and this time I can't blame the alphabet. I can blame David Brooks-Powell, and I usually do, but it doesn't do much good.

So "human rights" can mean a lot of things to a lot of people. In my case, it means the kind of criminal work I wouldn't have touched when I'd first started out. And now I couldn't even get that.

I took a shower. I'd got lucky the previous night, in every way, we'd both been drunk and still half in shock. I'd need to up my game tonight if I was going to get anywhere with Claire. Not smelling of cheap kebab would be a start.

Six o'clock. Just enough time to head into work, see if any good news had turned up in the post. The office was on the first floor upstairs from a twenty-four hour convenience store halfway between Highbury and Dalston. It wasn't much, but given the clients I had (when I had them) the convenience store was a useful touch. Chocolate, crisps and fags on tap. I hadn't been in for three days, but that wasn't unusual. I hadn't had any real reason to be in for a month. Dovesham had been all about changing that. Maybe it still would.

There was a letter waiting for me, but I knew it was the usual letter before I even opened it. Marcella, who ran the place downstairs, had shaken her head at me and mouthed "Henderson" as I walked by. Henderson was her landlord, too. Marcella hated him, but at least she wasn't getting the letters I was getting on a monthly basis.

I was wrong, as it happened. It wasn't the usual letter, or at least not quite, because as well as the standard statement of how much I owed there was something new, a line in bold type at the bottom demanding payment by the end of the month. I counted in my head. Next Friday. There was a handwritten note beside this demand, and it said *"A colleague will be visiting in advance to discuss payment"*. I didn't think there was much to discuss. Unless half a dozen millionaires who didn't mind paying large advance retainers wandered in off the street in the next few days, Henderson was out of luck.

I couldn't blame him. I hadn't paid a thing in three months, and nothing on time for the six months before that. I'd given up bothering to make up excuses or tell him the cheque was in the post.

It hardly mattered, anyway. It would take months for him to get me evicted, and by that time I'd either have some new clients, or I wouldn't need an office any more.

Marcella caught me on the way out with the letter in my hand.

"Is it bad?"

"You tell me."

I passed it to her and watched her mouth fall open. It didn't look good, all those months of unpaid rent, all those extra fees, all that interest. Most of the fees and interest would have to be written off when he kicked me out. But still.

"This is bad."

"I know. Guess you'll have a new neighbour in a few months, right?"

She looked at me like I was joking.

"Aren't you worried?"

"How often have you seen me here in the last few months, Marcella? I don't have any work. It's not like I really need an office."

Now she was looking at me like I was mad.

"Not that. I mean Henderson."

I stared at her, confused.

"Henderson. He's not a nice man, Sam."

"Landlords rarely are."

She didn't laugh.

"I don't mean like that. Why do you think he's let you build up this kind of debt?"

The thought had occurred to me over recent weeks, as it happened. If I was in Henderson's shoes I'd have started the eviction ball rolling months ago.

"Be careful, Sam. Henderson's bad. And his friends are worse."

I tried not to think about it. I had a date, after all.

At least, I thought I did. I got there early, five to eight, managed to snag a decent table by a window but not too close to the door. Thought about ordering wine, decided Claire might have her own views. Looked through the menu. I hadn't taken a girl out for a meal in a while. I hadn't realised how expensive it had got.

Ten past eight, and the place was starting to fill up. Quarter past, and I ordered a coke. She couldn't be much longer. I drank the coke way too quickly and asked for some flat bread to keep me going. The bread came twenty seconds later, slapped down on the table by an angry-looking woman who could have been anything between eighteen and fifty and clearly didn't think anyone was joining me this evening.

I was starting to worry she might be right. Twenty-five past. I'd give it another five minutes, I thought, and then glanced out of the window and saw her walk by, stop at the door and enter. I stood, smiling. It wasn't her. Another tall blonde woman.

Half past. I picked up the phone and realised I didn't have her mobile number. Still. There was a slim chance she'd be at work.

I dialled the number. It rang a couple of times and then, "Hello?"

Claire.

"Where are you?"

I hadn't meant to sound like that. Hadn't meant to ask that at all. And not just because I knew precisely where she was.

"You just called me, Sam. Take a guess."

"Sorry. I'm sorry. I just thought we were having dinner tonight."

There was a short pause. I could hear voices in the background, and typing, and when she spoke again, I thought she sounded distracted.

"No, I'm sorry Sam. Listen, something's come up. I've got a deadline and I'm really up against it. I'm not going to be able to make it. Look, I really am sorry. I'll give you a call, OK?"

"Yeah, OK."

I'll give you a call. She hadn't said when. Christ alone knew what I'd done wrong, but it didn't look I was going to be seeing much more of that smile.

I'd hardly put down the phone when the waitress was back. With the bill, and an apologetic smile. *Sympathy*, I thought, and then I picked up the bill and realised what she was apologising for. Twelve pounds. Bread and a coke. I started to get up, ready to argue it down to something sensible, but before my legs were straight I realised I wasn't going to bother. It hadn't been a great day. Just your usual, everyday kind of grey, with a dash of more exotic black thrown in. I'd got nothing done, got nowhere, gone backwards. The sooner it ended, the better. *Nothing*, I thought, dully, repeatedly, all the way back home. *Got nothing done.*

If I'd known what I'd set in motion, I'd have welcomed nothing with open arms.

7: Fame

I was up at six next morning, which was unusual, and my head was clear, which was close to historic. I'd been home by nine and too tired to think. My usual solution to that particular problem would have been alcohol, but the part of my brain that keeps me from chucking it all in and joining the dealers kept me away from the bottle. That and the fact that I'd been through all the good stuff with Claire, which left a bottle of Bulgarian red that had been staring at me across the kitchen for the best part of three years, and a half-litre of low-grade Scotch Marcella had pushed into my hands as I'd shuffled out of the office earlier. No hangover. Clear head.

The nearest newsagent was across the road from the kebab place, so by seven I was sat on the sofa with a cup of tea and half a dozen newspapers. I started with the *Sun*.

The article was on page fourteen, past all the naked celebrities and communist politicians, but the spot didn't matter. The words were what counted. It took up the top third of the page, and apart from a fingernail headshot of Olivia Miles herself (late forties, I guessed, black hair, serious expression) and an old press shot of me (Trawden, as usual), the rest was a well-phrased summary of what I'd said. The spin was spot on, too. Just when the facts might have you thinking this Williams chap was just another nutter or a publicity-hungry liar, Olivia would nudge you back in the right direction with her little conspiratorial hints. Various important people had "declined to comment" or "been unavailable to answer these allegations". The incident itself had been "mysteriously" absent from the official briefings provided by the police and HMP Dovesham. She'd done me proud.

I went through a couple of other papers. Nothing. Dovesham was yesterday's news. Except that wasn't quite true. Always the first with a different angle, the *Guardian* had tracked down a disaffected former security man at Dovesham who claimed he'd been warning about the dangers of a riot there for years. He didn't have a lot to add, and when I compared the treatment he'd got to the write-up Olivia had given me, I couldn't help feeling pretty pleased. There was Sam Williams, champion of the oppressed, concerned citizen, convinced he'd seen something strange and unreported and wondering why nobody seemed to be doing anything about it. And then there was Mr Derek Thurwell, forty-six, of Horsham in West Sussex, still bitter over losing his job two years ago and not exactly bringing anything new to the table. "I told them there'd be trouble. It was always too easy to get hold of things they shouldn't have, not in a maximum security prison." It might have been dynamite, if Thurwell had a single example of what these "things" might be. But he didn't. Not exactly Pulitzer stuff. I didn't think the *Guardian* would be running with Mr Thurwell for long.

So I'd got myself in the papers. Not the paper I'd have chosen, and not exactly front page, but it wasn't a bad start to the day, especially considering how poorly the previous one had ended. I toyed with the idea of going for a run. I hadn't been for a run in a few years. I looked out of the window, saw the rain and the cars and the blank-faced pedestrians and the angry cyclists, and remembered why. I made myself a coffee instead.

While I was sipping on my espresso, feeling more pleased with myself than I had done in a while, I picked up the *Sentinel*. Claire might not have run with my story, but she'd certainly been doing something when she could have been picking the stones out of overpriced olives with me.

It wasn't till I got to page fifteen that I saw what she'd been doing, and then all that *pleased-with-myself* vanished faster than the little zip-lock bags when the blue lights appear.

It was on the bottom right, half page, two columns. Typical *Sentinel* American-style headline, spread across four lines. This one was *"Controversial Past Of Human Rights Lawyer Who Claims To Have Seen Unidentified Dovesham Gunman"*. Underneath was the byline: "By Claire Tully".

I felt suddenly sick. Something warm and wet landed on my leg, and I realised my hands were shaking. In my left hand was a cup of hot, strong coffee, the very same coffee that had made the world seem like a half-decent place just five minutes earlier. *Calm down*, I told myself. It's probably OK. The article can't be as bad as the headline.

If anything, it was worse. It started with a statement of my "allegations" – which had been checked with a number of sources at Dovesham and the police and found to be "entirely without substance". No other witnesses had reported seeing the mysterious gunman or the guards who had, "according to Williams", been shot at. No mention anywhere of Claire's own involvement or testimony. A couple of bland, scene-setting paragraphs. And then the real dirt:

A brief review of Mr Williams' past reveals a colourful career and a number of controversial incidents. A self-proclaimed "human rights lawyer", Mr Williams appears to specialise in defending his clients against a variety of low-level charges including street dealing, driving offences and domestic violence.

That hurt, the domestic violence one. Once. It wasn't like I made a habit of it.

Mr Williams currently works alone, following an acrimonious split from West End firm Maurier & Co. in 2005. A source at Mauriers told this newspaper that Mr Williams had left in difficult circumstances, following accusations of payments to police officers involved in the case of Pierre Studeman. The case against Studeman, accused of possession with intent to supply Class A drugs, collapsed when Mr Williams brought to the attention of the court a number of procedural errors made by the police during Studeman's arrest and the subsequent search of his home.

A source at Mauriers. Not difficult to guess who. Bastard.

Just one year earlier, Mr Williams had been considered one of the shining lights of a new generation of brilliant young human rights lawyers, following his part in unearthing the evidence that overturned the conviction of Edward Trawden after twenty years in prison for murdering a nine-year-old child. But whilst Trawden's innocence is now established beyond doubt, questions will always remain over Samuel Williams' starring role in the case.

That was too much. The Pierre stuff I could live with. I mean, it was hardly great publicity, but the kind of client I was after wouldn't give a damn how I got the evidence, as long as I got it. And at least it was true. But the line on Trawden was so wide of the mark it was landing on the wrong continent. I'd dragged that stuff up to the surface all on my own, and back then I'd been so clean you could have stuck me in a convent and called me Sister Sam. The dirt didn't start till after Trawden. And no one called me Samuel.

I read the whole thing three times, trying to work out why the hell Claire had done it and whether there was anything there I could call an outright lie. There wasn't. Plenty of insinuation, sure, but she could get away with that and she knew it. Or her lawyers did.

The phone rang, and I picked it up without thinking.

"Sam?"

It was Rachel. I'd never got round to returning her call. It hadn't been top of my agenda before. It sure as hell wasn't now. I sighed.

"Don't you sigh at me, Sam Williams."

I started to say something, and stopped. Best let her get on with it.

"You should have come to me in the first place. Might have avoided all this mess."

I sat up. She was right, of course. I was an idiot. I'd been so caught up in Claire, and then Olivia Miles, I'd forgotten about Rachel. This was her field.

"So you've read today's *Sentinel*?"

"Sam, I read every paper cover to cover every morning while you're still dreaming about Buffy the bloody Vampire Slayer. It's my job, remember?"

I laughed, in spite of everything.

"So imagine I'm coming to you now, Rachel. For help, I mean. Am I too late?"

"Depends. Give me the background."

"Where do you want me to start?"

"Wherever you want."

"OK. I did see the guy, the prisoner. It happened and he was there, even if no one wants to believe it. And he did point a gun at me. It all happened."

"Uh-huh," she said. I couldn't tell whether that meant *I believe you* or *you're a liar*. It was probably neither. "Carry on." So I did.

"The Pierre stuff's true, but you knew that."

I'd been quite open with Rachel when we'd been seeing each other. No point in hiding anything. She's the kind of girl who finds it all out in the end.

"Trawden?"

"That's bullshit."

"I thought so. That was the old Sam, right?"

"What, the one who believed in doing the job straight? Doesn't sound likely, does it? But I did, back then. I really did."

There was a silence, during which I could almost see her sitting there, pen tapping gently on her lower lip, trying to work out an angle from which Sam Williams didn't look like a self-obsessed liar. The silence lengthened.

"So, this Claire Tully."

"Hmmm," I said, like I'd never heard the name before.

"Looked her up before I called. She doesn't seem much of a journalist. I certainly haven't come across her before. Most of her previous work's local."

"Right." I didn't see how that helped.

"She doesn't seem to like you very much, Sam. Done something to upset her?"

"Well, I did sleep with her."

I heard a sharp intake of breath, followed immediately by a high-pitched cackle.

"Well, gosh, Sam, I've had better myself, but I didn't take it so personally."

She didn't wait for me to reply.

"Look, I don't usually work for free but you're a charity case."

I started to interrupt, but I should have known better.

"Shut up. I'm just going to make a few calls. The other papers, the journos who covered Dovesham. Make sure no one else is running with *Samuel Williams is a liar*. If they're planning to, I'll see what I can do to put them off. But there's one call I can't make for you."

"Olivia."

"That's right. You don't want to get on the wrong side of the *Sun*, Sam, and right now Olivia Miles is probably working out how to get you back for making her look stupid. Convince her not to."

Rachel was right, Olivia Miles was a call I had to make myself. Didn't mean I wanted to. I sensed I wouldn't be top of her list of friends this morning.

The laptop was still on from yesterday, and as it

groaned into life I tried to work out what Claire was doing and why she was doing it. Had I done something to offend her? She'd seemed fine when we'd spoken yesterday, until she'd stood me up. For her article. For *this* article.

I looked her up. Rachel was right, she hadn't written much. A royal visit to a stately home. A fundraiser for a hospital. Council funding crises and cutbacks. It was in the *Sentinel*, but it was local newspaper stuff, really. And now, suddenly, she had a scoop on me. Page fifteen, granted, but that was still better than she'd managed till now.

I looked at the pile of newspapers on the floor and picked up the *Guardian*. I'd missed Claire's article in my first run through the press this morning. Might have missed something else. It struck me that I was making up jobs to put off calling Olivia, but right now I didn't care.

Nothing else in the *Guardian*. I read the Thurwell article again, feeling a lot less smug second time round. No doubt Thurwell would be sitting at home having a cup of tea and a good old laugh at poor Sam Williams, the idiot who'd tried to get his name in the papers and wound up branded a liar.

I put the paper down and went to pick up the *Mail*. And then I stopped.

Something wasn't right. Something I'd just read.

I picked up the Thurwell article again. Third time round, it jumped right out at me.

It was always too easy to get hold of things they shouldn't have.

Nothing concrete in the article itself, but there was something familiar about that line, and I sat there sipping cold coffee for a couple of minutes until I had it. Detective Inspector Roarkes, back at the police station, at the debriefing. Something about guns in the prison. *Firearms*, he'd said. Firearms where they weren't supposed to be. And yet – not a word about these "*firearms*" in the newspapers, the television, the radio coverage. Nothing online, either – even the news outlets with a circulation that made my legal practice look healthy hadn't mentioned guns being smuggled into the prison.

His card was right in front of me, beside the laptop. I dialled, it rang half a dozen times and he answered.

"Roarkes."

"Hello, Detective Inspector. Sam Williams here. How's the cress."

Roarkes didn't laugh.

"What do you want, Williams?"

Didn't sound so pleased to hear from me this time. No doubt he read the *Sun*. If the friendly approach wasn't going to work, I thought I might as well play it straight.

"Remember when you interviewed me? You said something about guns in the prison, firearms being where they shouldn't be?"

Roarkes gave a noncommittal grunt. It took a little imagination to interpret it as a *"Yes"*, but I went on anyway.

"I was just wondering why this little fact hasn't made it into any of the news coverage."

There was a short pause, and then his voice, weary, still, but with an edge of anger I hadn't noticed before.

"Listen, Williams, a couple of things for you. When an incident's just happened, there's a lot of confusion, right? Things get said, might not be true. You should know all about that. And second, I don't remember saying anything to you about guns in the prison. You sure you haven't imagined it?"

"I didn't imagine it."

"Because you're quite good at imagining things, aren't you, Williams?"

I knew what he'd told me. There didn't seem much point in carrying on with the call.

"Goodbye, Detective Inspector."

I put the phone down and picked it straight back up again. No point wasting more time. I put it back down again when I realised I didn't have Olivia's number, and it started ringing straight away. I stared at it.

"Sam Williams?"

"Sam. Olivia Miles. We need to talk."

There was a lot of noise in the background but I could tell she wasn't pleased and wasn't going to bother hiding it.

"I was just about to call you."

"Sure you were."

"Really. Listen, it's rubbish, all this stuff in the *Sentinel*."

"What, Pierre Studeman?"

I couldn't tell if she was teasing me.

"No, that's true. But there was nothing dirty in the Trawden case. And everything I told you yesterday –"

She cut me off.

"Yeah, yeah, it's all true, you'd swear it on your mother's grave, save it, Sam."

"But it's true."

"Do you think that matters, now?" I started to interrupt, because surely even a journalist – even a Murdoch journalist – would understand that whether something was true or not was actually quite important. She carried on talking over me.

"Listen, Sam, interesting as your shoddy little history might be, that's not what I wanted to talk to you about. Have you heard the news?"

"Depends what you mean."

"I'll take that as a no. It's Ilic. The guy who was injured in the recovery op. He's dead."

I was speechless for a full ten seconds.

"Are you there, Sam?"

"Yes. How?"

"No one knows. Or if they do, they're not telling me. But you said he'd broken his ankle."

"That's what they told me."

"First time I've ever heard of anyone dying of a broken ankle."

"I don't understand."

It might have been the understatement of the year, but it was all I could think to say.

"You're not the only one. Last we heard he was in hospital. Royal Free. Under guard, they said. Injured whilst escaping, nothing serious."

"And now he's dead."

"Announced about five minutes ago. It's all over the TV. Here you go."

I heard her put the phone down, take a few steps, and then the background noise got louder and clearer. A news report.

"…more serious than was first thought. Medical staff worked through the night to save Mr Ilic, but ultimately the internal bleeding resulting from the original injuries was too severe. This is Amy Allington, outside the Royal Free Hospital, for Sky News."

Internal bleeding? From a broken ankle?

"I don't get it."

"Nobody gets it, Sam. But I'm the one with an editor who seems to think I'm an idiot because I didn't write up this guy's death before it happened."

"That's not very fair."

"Who gives a damn about fair? The way he sees it, I told everyone I had the inside scoop and the inside scoop turned out to be the other side of London in the Royal Free Hospital. Doesn't matter that nobody else saw it coming either. Doesn't matter that it makes your comments even more interesting than they were yesterday, despite your girlfriend calling you a liar."

"Claire Tully isn't my girlfriend."

"Whatever. Can you give me anything or am I going to have to get off my arse and head down to Belsize fucking Park with the rest of Fleet Street?"

I'd spent enough time with journalists to know how they spoke. Olivia Miles wasn't playing games. She needed something.

"I've got nothing," I said, and then before she had the chance to start up again, something struck me.

"What about the others?"

She paused.

"Which others?"

"The brother, and the other one. Stankovic. What's happened to them?"

"How the hell should I know? They're back in high security."

"Dovesham?"

She laughed. "Dovesham looks more like a barbecue than a prison right now. But no, I don't know where they are."

"Don't you find that a little odd?"

Because it *was* a little odd. When someone was sent down, it was standard practice for the press and the public to know precisely where they were doing their time. There was so much else going on around the Dovesham story that details like that had slipped by without anyone asking all the important questions. But I couldn't remember anyone saying where Stankovic and Marko Ilic had been taken. "Behind bars". That was all.

"Maybe. But why the hell does it matter?"

"Because if there's anything strange about Pedrag Ilic suddenly dying – and I reckon there is – then Stankovic and the brother should be watching their backs right now."

I could almost hear her mulling it over across the phone. I was surprised she hadn't thought about it herself, but not everyone was as obsessed with Dovesham as I was. Finally she spoke.

"Might be something in that, Sam. I'll make some calls."

8: The Surface of Things

There was still nothing in the fridge and I didn't feel I'd sunk low enough to eat kebab for lunch two days running. Not yet. I decided to head into town, get something to eat. Maybe visit an old colleague or two.

Mauriers had moved on since I'd been their rising young star. They'd hit the big-time, doubled in size, relocated closer to the Royal Courts and the Old Bailey. On the bus into town, squeezed into half a seat by a gigantic white guy with a sweat-stained T-shirt and a baseball cap who reminded me uncomfortably of Che, my phone rang three times. Each time it was a journalist I'd spoken to the day before, a journalist who hadn't been interested when all I had was my own no-doubt imaginary gunman. The mysterious death of Pedrag Ilic had changed all that. I gave them the same story I'd already given Olivia, the story she'd already printed. I didn't mention my theory on the other two Serbs. She deserved a head start on that.

I tried to call Claire. She owed me something, an apology or an explanation. Someone else answered, a male voice, said she wasn't around, offered to take a message. I hung up.

The bus stop wasn't far from Mauriers. Still closer to Kings Cross than Chancery Lane. No need to be smug. Kings Cross beat Dalston, and I doubted David Brooks-Powell had the landlord on his case the way I did. There was a sandwich place right across the road and nowhere convenient to cross, so I checked both ways and crossed anyway.

That was stupid. There was one car, coming fast, I hadn't seen him, and he hadn't seen me either, so I ended up throwing myself the last couple of feet onto the pavement as he streaked past in a blur of grey, unaware that he'd missed a top human rights lawyer by inches.

A woman in a suit helped me to my feet.

"You alright?"

"Fine. Thanks."

"Fucking idiot. Could have killed you."

I looked back at the road, but the car was long gone.

"Nah. My own fault. Wasn't looking."

She shrugged in a *fine, if that's the way you see it* sort of way, and marched south towards the river.

I hadn't seen the new office before, and it wasn't really new, they'd been there eighteen months already. I didn't have much call to visit Mauriers these days. I wasn't sure how welcome I'd be, but the receptionist didn't recognise me when I asked to see David Brooks-Powell.

It wouldn't have mattered if she had. David Brooks-Powell was in court, expected to be there most of the day, but I could see one of his associates or leave a message for his secretary if I wanted.

I didn't. What I wanted was to get three hundred copies of that fucking article, wrap them round David fucking Brooks-Powell's greasy fucking head, set fire to the lot and watch the bastard burn. It would be the best thing anyone at Mauriers would ever see, a far greater contribution to the cause of justice than all their attention-grabbing cases put together. I didn't have any matches, or a single copy of the article, or David Brooks-Powell's greasy fucking head, but a man can dream, right?

It wasn't till I was almost home I realised I'd forgotten to get myself a sandwich, which meant the whole trip had been a pointless waste of time, but time was one thing I wasn't short of. I got off the bus two stops early and picked up that kebab I'd been trying to avoid. As I was standing outside the front door picking my keys out of my pocket, my mobile rang and I dropped the kebab. I tried to retrieve it and dropped the phone, which landed in the kebab. It sat there, face down in a puddle of minced lamb and chilli sauce, and as I bent to pick it up I tried not to see it as a metaphor for my life. I laughed to myself, which was good, I thought. At least I could still laugh about it.

It had been Paul trying to get hold of me, and when I'd cleared up the mess on the pavement and wiped my phone clean, I called him back. He'd managed to clear some work and was on for a drink tonight. He wasn't the only one.

We met up four hours later in a pub round the corner from Paul's place and a hundred yards from a filthy little dive where I'd just spent eight quid on a large haddock and chips. The fish was greasy and the chips were fat, pale and flabby, but I didn't care, because I was hungry and there was a lot of it. Paul had a four-storey townhouse in a leafy bit of West London, with a wife in it, and an eighteen-month-old son. Most people with young kids, they can't talk about anything else, but the great thing about Paul was he knew what to talk about and who to talk about it with. With me, that meant there wasn't much family conversation, and that suited me fine. I liked his wife. More than liked, really, I'd been with her before she'd hooked up with Paul and if things had been different – but they weren't. And the kid was cute, no doubt. But the way things were going for me right now, I didn't think I could handle someone else's domestic happiness.

It wasn't until we were onto the third pint that I realised Paul was trying to get me to look seriously at my situation. Something needed to change. He was right, I needed to get a grip on myself, and he could probably help me, but he shouldn't have waited till the third pint to get started. He'd get nothing from me like this.

Of all people, Paul should have known that. We'd been friends nearly twenty years, met in the first week at Oxford, him a street-smart Manchester lad who wasn't thrown by anything, me an ignorant grammar school boy from Reading with a second-hand guitar, a bad haircut and a little party trick that had me thinking I was better than I really was. I didn't know what I wanted to do once I'd finished my degree, but I was convinced that whatever it was, I'd end up changing the world.

The party trick was quite simple, really. I had a photographic memory. Still do, when I'm sober, fully awake, and paying attention. For a modern history student a trick like that was more than just convenient. It meant I didn't have to bother looking under the surface. The facts were right there, glittering in front of me. All I had to do was scoop them up and sit back while everyone else dug into the mud, into people's minds and obsessions and motives. Under their skins. Sod that, I thought. I had history in the palm of my hand.

I was right, too. I spent three years drinking, gambling and screwing, and I still managed a first. My tutors told me I should get a job in the City. My friends said the same thing. Two well-known financial institutions actually sought me out and offered me the kind of money any sane person would have killed for. But arrogant little sod that I was, I thought I was better than that. Because of the trick.

So I went for law. Human rights law, because I was cool, cutting-edge, Mr Bloody Unimpeachable. If I couldn't make it from drunk student to top lawyer in ten years, the cabinet ten years later, and Prime Minister by fifty, then I wasn't the man I thought I was.

I wasn't.

Sure, law school was fine, articles were easy, the first year or so as a junior solicitor went as smoothly as I could have hoped. Most of what I was doing was research for the partners in the firm that had taken me on, Mauriers, a specialist human rights outfit in the wilderness between Kings Cross and the Inns of Court. And when you don't forget a single word you've read, research isn't exactly challenging. The more senior lawyers – the *older* lawyers – they called me Sam Spade, and laughed. I was doing the spadework, the idiot-work, they thought. I didn't. The way I saw it, I was scooping the gold off the surface again. I was God's gift to the legal profession. David Brooks-Powell disagreed.

David Brooks-Powell had started at Mauriers three weeks before I did, and never bothered hiding his disdain. Brooks-Powell was Knightsbridge, St Paul's School, tall, blonde, good-looking, reasonably clever, very smooth and extremely arrogant. Malfoy with a slimline leather briefcase. David Brooks-Powell had his own handy degree from Oxford, just like me, but David Brooks-Powell had spent his three years running the Union and the Law Society and all the things you were supposed to do instead of just drinking, gambling and screwing. I might have been to the same university, I might be working at the same firm, but as far as Brooks-Powell was concerned I was from another planet, and the sooner I went back there the better. David Brooks-Powell thought he was better than me, a better person, certainly a better lawyer. So you can imagine how he felt when it was me instead of him that landed the junior solicitor gig on Trawden.

Trawden was the biggest case Mauriers had ever handled. He insisted he was innocent, like they all did, but he was convincing enough to have mobilised a campaign that would have been the envy of a mid-sized political party. Over nearly twenty years he'd been through half a dozen law firms, and each one had found the usual tiny clues, miniscule inconsistencies, the fool's gold that's enough to get you hoping but not enough to get you over the line.

If he'd owned up at the start, he'd have been nearing the end of his term, but he'd never admitted a thing and there was no way he was going anywhere. Mauriers was his last throw of the dice. I was his snake-eyes.

So we set to work. We looked at all the evidence everyone else had already looked at, and started trying to find some more. And the problem wasn't that there was nothing out there. The problem was that there was too much. It turned out little Maxine Grimshaw was a collectors' item among the murderers, paedophiles and rapists that infested the nastier corners of the penal system. There were a dozen of them serving time who'd tried to claim her while Eddie Trawden was out there shouting he knew nothing about it. Trouble was, every time anyone looked closer it turned out the claimants had never been anywhere near her. Trawden was a drug addict and a drunk with a penchant for turning violent when he wasn't getting his way. And he happened to be her next-door neighbour.

Of course, as everyone who'd ever represented Trawden pointed out, violence is a far cry from paedophilia. That wasn't a bad hand to start with, but it wasn't good enough when you put it next to the half dozen witnesses who had him talking to her the morning she disappeared, and him insisting he'd been in Carlisle.

But you've got to play the hand you're dealt, and pray you get something decent off the top. So on I went, through the witness statements, the forensics, the claims and counterclaims, looking for the one big thing someone else had spotted but not considered important.

After four days and three nights of staring at the papers I had it.

A mistake. A simple mistake.

Robbie Evans had done horrific things to a toddler on a cold, deserted beach stuck like old gum on the side of a bit of Wales nobody cared about. Robbie Evans had as much chance of making parole as I did of making the England rugby team. He'd appealed his sentence and got nowhere, but it turned out he needn't have bothered, because he hadn't lasted six years before he was stabbed to death by a gangster who took exception to sharing a prison with a paedophile. Thing was, there was a nasty little rat of a man called Hussein Akadi who'd been the closest thing Evans had to a friend inside, and Akadi insisted that Evans had claimed Maxine Grimshaw.

Akadi was a liar. No one doubted that. He'd made a criminal career out of lying, lied his way through court, and pretty much everyone who knew anything about the guy guessed he was just offering up another lie to cut his time. But it was another card. It had to be turned over.

The usual checks were done. Maxine Grimshaw had been murdered in Warrington on 18th October, 1983. Evans was from Bangor. His movements had been reconstructed as carefully as they could be, all those years later, but there was nothing to put him east of Chester on the day in question. Evans had been filed away on the discard pile.

I flicked through the Evans data, knowing it was leading nowhere but determined to lodge every detail in my brain, just in case. 1983. December. November. October. September. Nothing.

I kept on going. Right back through the year. And the year before, which seemed pointless, but it wasn't like I had a pile of clues calling me away. And that's what you want. No distractions. No options. So when your ace turns up, you'll know it.

For a month or so towards the end of 1982, Robbie Evans had worked for a local glazier. Now, a normal person might say that rang a bell, and they'd flick through the files to try to find out why, and eventually they'd give up, because it was a year before the murder so what use could it possibly be?

But I'm not a normal person. I knew precisely which bell it rang. Casey Donohue worked at the Ford showroom at the end of the street the Grimshaw house backed onto. She'd been interviewed by the police because she'd come running to the house when she heard Eileen Grimshaw screaming. She'd heard the scream because she'd taken a long walk that afternoon, and she'd taken a long walk because she was having an extended lunch break, and she was having an extended lunch break because the whole showroom was shut for three hours while some Welsh bastards fitted a massive new glass front and no one had bothered telling her a bloody thing about it or she'd have organised a lift home.

I pulled out Casey Donohue's witness statement and reread it and knew this was the ace. This was it, the thing, the detail that would clear Eddie Trawden. And I was the one who'd found it.

By this time I was the only person left in the office and it was nearly nine o' clock but I wasn't thinking of going home. Austin Glass of Bangor didn't exist any more, but it didn't take me long to track down a phone number for Gareth Austin. I explained who I was and what I was doing and yes, he remembered that bastard Robbie Evans, he'd said a prayer of thanks when the bastard died and he felt sick every time he remembered he'd put money in the bastard's hands.

"Do you remember precisely when it was Robbie Evans worked for you, Mr Austin?"

"Clear as day, me lad. Took him on when Alun married our Sian. I gave him a month off, Alun Davies. A month off, and let him marry my daughter, and all he ended up interested in was screwing the babysitter."

I had to interrupt. Compelling as the Austin family saga might be, now wasn't the time to be hearing it.

"And when did the wedding take place, Mr Austin?"

"October 1st, 1983."

"You're sure?"

"I'll never forget it."

It was easy to see what had happened. A tired cop on a pointless task, late at night, useless files on a dead man. Hears 1983. Writes down 1982.

After that, it was simple. Even the forensics matched. Until the moment we'd been waiting for – the moment Eddie Trawden had been waiting for for twenty years. It was a closed session, just four pre-selected journalists, court officials, lawyers, the Grimshaws. And I punched the air.

I certainly didn't whoop or shout. I think I hissed between my teeth, a long, quiet, "Yesssss", not loud enough for anyone else to hear. But I punched the air, and Bill and Eileen Grimshaw turned and saw me celebrating the release of the man they'd spent twenty years blaming for their daughter's brutal murder, and their faces were the faces of people going through the whole thing all over again. I'd got under their skin, and I can't say I enjoyed what I found there.

Nobody knew. Nobody saw, not even Elizabeth Maurier, who was sitting two empty chairs away armed with a serious expression and the gentle nod of someone who knew justice had been served, however painful that might be for the innocent. We spent the afternoon celebrating with Trawden, and I didn't know if he'd always been like that, or prison had done it to him, but he was about the nastiest individual I'd ever come across. "Here's to Robbie Evans," he said, a glass in each hand, and I tried to catch Elizabeth Maurier's eye, but she looked away in time. I couldn't believe *this* was our victory.

I saw the Grimshaws in my sleep for the first time ten hours later, and they hadn't missed a night since. I used to wonder, sometimes, whether I should try to contact them, to apologise, to explain, but once five days had gone by I knew I never would, because the truth was the Grimshaws didn't know who I was, couldn't give a damn who I was, had probably forgotten me already. The only person who remembered was me.

Trawden should have been the start of a glittering legal career – Claire had got that right enough. Instead, it was the high point. I could have married my clever little trick to my even cleverer new insight – that these cases weren't solved by the raw facts glittering on the surface, that more often than not the key was the fallible memory of a random human being, someone peripheral, a Casey Donohue, a Hussein Akadi, a Gareth Austin. If you wanted to unlock these memories you needed more than just a trick, you needed a trigger, to understand, to get under a person's skin. I'd had my flash of insight, and it burned.

So I decided I didn't care any more. Whatever spark of interest I'd had in my legal calling, it died and stayed dead. My nightly visits from the Grimshaws put it out. The trick had made me lazy, made me live on the surface of things. The burn made me even lazier. I didn't bother trying to get under anyone else's skin, because after Trawden I didn't want to know what I'd find there. As for my own skin, I reinforced it with wall after wall of fact and detail and made damn sure nothing was getting through, and if anything did get through, it wouldn't matter, because as far as I was concerned there might be organs and pumping blood and a bit of heat, but there was nothing in there that was really alive. Everything else was numb.

Everything else was dead. I didn't know if Trawden had killed it, or it had just burned clean away, but that wasn't the point. The point was keeping it like that. Keeping things out. Staying dead. It was an art. I was good at it.

And I didn't mind it, either. I preferred it that way.

I'd served enough time to have my own clients, and I started instructing Paul, now a hotshot junior barrister in Kings Bench Walk, whenever I got the chance. But I was still a junior myself, and the clients I was getting weren't the Trawdens, they were the Pierre Studemans, the clients no one else wanted. I couldn't pull the same trick twice, and even if I had done, no one would have noticed because getting a street dealer off isn't going to be news unless you can prove it was the Prime Minister that fitted him up.

After a while, I only knew one way to win a case: find out where the police had screwed up. And not long after that I couldn't even find their mistakes, because I couldn't be bothered to look through the bottom of the glass at the papers underneath. So I did what I thought everyone did, I paid a few cops, I got some information, I won the case, Studeman walked free, I thought at least the firm would be pleased with me. It wasn't like Elizabeth Maurier knew how I'd done it.

Except she did. Brooks-Powell had hated me even more after Trawden and I hadn't been as subtle as I'd hoped when it came to my dealings with the police. Someone told Brooks-Powell. Brooks-Powell told Elizabeth Maurier. Elizabeth Maurier told me if I left now, quietly, without a fuss, she wouldn't feel obliged to tell the police and the Law Society. And thus was born Samuel Williams & Co.

Early on, I didn't do so badly. There were a few clients who followed me from Mauriers, not the kind of clients Mauriers would miss, but good enough for Samuel

Williams & Co. Paul would mention my name, when he could, and I got a little work that way. Pierre spread the word. So did Maloney, at first, after I swung his acquittal through the kind of lucky break I'd once thought was down to talent and brains. But it wasn't enough. I was paying people to tell me about mistakes, and I was OK with that, until it hit me that I might be paying them to make the mistakes in the first place. So I stopped doing it, which might have been a good thing, but doing good things wasn't going to win any cases, and losing cases wasn't going to bring me any more clients. Mauriers might not have told the police or the Law Society but people still knew: Sam Williams was only as good as his last bribe, and he wasn't even doing that any more. Pierre's friends weren't interested. Maloney had said *anything you want, pal, you just ask*, but I didn't want Maloney's help. I wasn't that far gone, I thought. I wasn't desperate enough.

It wasn't like I cared. It wasn't like I let it get to me. And even if I did care, and even if it got so deep it sometimes stopped me sleeping two, three nights at a time, it wasn't like I let anyone see it. Even myself, when I could help it. I might not have facts, and I might not have clients, but I had enough one-liners to throw at the fear and the failure, and the Grimshaws, and anything else I didn't want to look at.

The things I didn't want to look at was a long old list. And it was growing by the day.

9: Same Eyes, Same Face

By now I was drunk and Paul had given up trying to get me to talk seriously. Instead we were discussing Brooks-Powell and what a piece of work he was. I was far gone enough to convince myself that Paul meant it, that he was on my side, that it was me and Paul against Mauriers and Brooks-Powell and all their bloody friends, and that the fact that Mauriers threw work at Paul on a weekly basis and he'd been in court that very day on a David Brooks-Powell case was completely beside the point.

Paul had read the *Sentinel* that morning but waited until I'd mentioned it before admitting to the fact, something I'd have been grateful for if I'd noticed it at the time. Claire Tully joined the list. Mauriers, Brooks-Powell, Tully. *Mauriers* comprised every smug arsehole of a lawyer that worked there or ever had, from the grande dame herself right down to the latest batch of up-themselves trainees fresh from law school. Of course that meant Brooks-Powell got on the list twice, but if anyone deserved such an honour, it was him.

I forgot about Brooks-Powell for all of five minutes while I laid into Claire Tully, but something stopped me crossing the line and bragging about the other night. Instead I told Paul I needed the toilet, headed straight outside and phoned the bitch.

Nobody was answering her desk phone and I had no other number for her. *Lucky girl*, I thought, for a moment, and then decided she wasn't. The last four digits of her phone number were 7376. I dialled again, replacing them with four zeroes, and got rewarded with a *"Sentinel,* how can I help you?"

"I'd like to speak to Claire Tully, please."

"I'll see if she's available. Who's calling?"

I'd already thought of this. Even drunk, I'm capable of using my brain when I really don't need to.

"She doesn't know me, but I'm with her brother."

Thirty seconds of silence followed, during which I fervently hoped nobody had picked up the ringing phone on Claire's desk and informed the receptionist that Claire was an only child. They hadn't – the receptionist was apologetic when she returned, but there was nothing she could do.

I knew it was wrong, but I couldn't help myself.

"Oh. Right. Is there any way you could find out where she is or how I might reach her?"

"Can't her brother tell you?"

"Well, that's the problem. There's been an accident, and I need to let her know as soon as possible."

I was hoping I'd struck the right balance between desperation and courtesy, without too much slurred drunkenness creeping in. I must have managed it, because the receptionist disappeared again for a minute and when she came back, she had a mobile number that she *really* wasn't supposed to hand out but *in the circumstances*, and she *very much hoped* she'd done the right thing and more importantly that Miss Tully's brother was OK. When she asked if she needed to repeat the number I managed not to laugh, thanked her and hung up.

I glanced back at the pub. The table we'd been sitting at wasn't far from the window, and I could see Paul there, sipping slowly on a glass of what I was beginning to suspect might not be gin and tonic after all. He put the drink back down and looked at his watch, then back up in the direction of the toilets. Maybe I was just being paranoid.

Claire answered on the second ring. There were noises in the background, voices, laughter, by the sound of it she was enjoying herself. Wreck Sam Williams' life, go out and celebrate.

"Hi, who's this?"

"Why the fuck did you do it?"

It wasn't precisely what I'd meant to say. There was a carefully crafted script, phrases, insults, a whole vile bestiary of nouns and adjectives I'd had floating around my brain since I'd read her piece that morning. Didn't matter. It would do.

"Sam?"

"Yes."

"How did you get this number?"

I didn't want to go down that route.

"That doesn't matter. What are you playing at? Do you really think I planned all this? Get stuck in a riot, rescue the journalist, screw her, feed her the story?"

"I —"

I was in full flow now. She wasn't getting in my way.

"Seriously, why the fuck would I make something like that up, Claire? And I'm not trying to make out you owe me anything, but for fuck's sake, Claire, after what happened, I didn't think you'd stoop this low. I didn't think anyone could stoop this low."

I hadn't meant to bring that up. Hadn't meant to play on gratitude or sympathy or anything like that. I'd meant to stick to the facts, the logic, the total lack of any purpose in what she'd accused me of doing. I hadn't really even wanted to swear at her. It was supposed to be subtler, cleverer than that. But having a photographic memory doesn't help when you're as drunk as I was. I'd forgotten where I was going. I stopped.

"Look, Sam, what did I write that wasn't true?"

I opened my mouth to say something about Trawden,

and then I realised that if I defended *that*, it would be all the more obvious I wasn't defending anything else. She was still talking, and I could smell something horrible, something old and meaty that didn't belong. My phone. It still stank of lamb and chilli sauce.

"I'm sorry if you think you haven't been treated well, but everything I've seen points to you making this whole thing up."

She didn't sound very sorry. She didn't sound like the Claire Tully I'd met the other day.

"Why were you even there, Sam? I've been through the lists. You weren't supposed to be there, you took someone else's place. Paul Driver. Now Paul Driver's a barrister, and I could see why a barrister might hand something out to a solicitor. But only a solicitor who might be able to refer work to him. And a solicitor would have to have clients to do that, wouldn't he, Sam?"

Part of me was thinking *bitch*, part of me was reeling, trying to think of any way back into this conversation. Part of me was thinking she was wasted in journalism, the way she was going she'd have given Paul a run for his money in court.

"So drop the injured puppy act and be straight with me, right? You were only there to get yourself a bit of exposure, weren't you? And what better way than a fake man with a fake gun?"

So there was a way back in, and she'd just given me it, because it was true, I'd only gone to Dovesham for the exposure, but what was wrong with that, and hadn't everyone else?

Including Claire Tully?

"Of the two of us, Claire, it wasn't me who was there under false pretences."

"I beg your pardon?"

Instant defensive. I felt a little better.

"Well, let's look at this, shall we? Dovesham wasn't exactly your usual bag, was it? No royalty, no D-listers with a giant pair of scissors and a big cheesy grin. So what were *you* doing there?"

"You're barking up the wrong tree, Sam."

"Am I? What *were* you doing there, Claire? Desperate for the front-page spread, were you? And if you couldn't get that, maybe the only thing left was slamming some poor bastard whose only crime was picking you up when you fell over. Right?"

There was a silence. The background noise had faded, I guessed she'd moved away from her friends, closed a door, gone outside. The silence grew and I started to think I'd done it, I'd got to her, she was going to apologise after all. Take the whole thing back in tomorrow's edition.

"Look, Sam. Don't get me wrong. I *am* grateful for what you did. It was frightening, we were all in a rush, terrified, and it was a kind thing to do."

I couldn't tell yet where this was heading but it didn't sound like the unreserved apology I was hoping for.

"But let's not pretend there was anyone else there, because we both know there wasn't. There were no wounded guards, no armed prisoners. Don't make the whole thing more than it was. I'm sorry if I've hurt you, Sam, but I've only told the truth."

There was a click. She'd hung up. I hit redial, but she'd already switched off her phone. I glanced back at the pub. Paul was looking straight at me, shaking his head, putting on his jacket.

When I finally slumped down on the sofa and swallowed the last mouthful of the kebab I'd picked up on the way home, it still wasn't half past ten. Some grinning little imp had been waiting for me outside the door, it had only been five minutes ago but all I could remember was a pair of round glasses and a bit of curly brown hair. He was an *associate* of Mr Henderson, he'd said. He hoped there wouldn't have to be any unpleasantness about the money. *So do I,* I'd replied, and then, for good measure, *and you can fuck off, too.* I wasn't feeling particularly friendly. The grin hadn't shifted from his face. He'd be back, he told me. *Suit yourself,* I'd replied, as I let myself in and slammed the door in his grinning face.

I switched on the TV. A gig in Hyde Park. A gameshow. A documentary that sounded serious. I was about to try something else when a word caught my ear.

Mirandano.

I hadn't heard that name for years. I looked back at the TV, there was an image there, a hut, a collection of huts, or what had once been huts, burning, burnt, the smoke still rising, footage from, what, thirty years ago? And then a modern shot, a different place, different huts, but it might as well have been the same. The same fires. The same burning. The same death.

Mirandano. They hadn't called it that for years, decades, maybe. The Republic of Surtalga, these days. I'd skimmed the edges of the war there while I'd been at Oxford. It was Freddie's obsession, Freddie Harmsworth, our tame genius of a professor, this little-known war in an African backwater. When it came to the choice I'd opted for Nicaragua, a war with a whole world of data and documents I could just scan into my brain without the complications of dealing with real people. But if Freddie was your tutor, you couldn't help knowing something about Mirandano and those six years of bitter conflict in a bit of the world no one cared about. There was no oil and too few diamonds, and those that had the diamonds used them to buy guns and make sure the money stayed with the same families, and everyone else could live or die with nothing but mud and scrubland and a handful of sick cows. It was no wonder there'd been an insurgency, a bunch of guerrillas who called themselves communists but really just wanted anything other than what was already there. It was no wonder it turned brutal, turned a country into a giant rutted killing field. The only surprise was how long it lasted, six years, before the men with the money and the guns and the diamonds finally forced the rebels to a ceasefire that was little more than an admission of defeat.

I wondered drunkenly why this was on, why a major terrestrial television channel would show a documentary about something so old and remote when there were even worse things happening even closer to home this year, this month, this week. Then I remembered.

After nearly thirty years, the United Nations were on their way out. The truce had called for the permanent stationing of thousands of international peacekeepers in Mirandano, or the Republic of Surtalga, as it became the day the war ended. Thousands dwindled to hundreds, but there was still work to do, still mines to clear.

And now they were leaving. Their job was done, they said, even though the men in charge and what was left of their enemies said *no it isn't, please stay*. There were no mines left to clear.

But there was something else. It had started with a few villagers fleeing over the borders, from the Congo, from Gabon, then from further, from hundreds of miles to the north, from as far as Nigeria. When they got to Surtalga there was nothing there for them, just the same old mud and cows as there had been forever, but they hadn't expected anything else. Whatever they were running from, starvation was preferable.

What they were running from followed soon after. They, too, came from Nigeria, and they made Boko Haram look friendly. Frentoi, they were called, which didn't make sense in any language anyone had ever heard of, but the rumour was it was the word they shouted as they severed limbs from their victims, as they beheaded them and boiled them and burned them alive or set them on stakes to shrivel and die on the roadsides, their friends and family forced to walk by, too afraid to cut them down or even to help them die. They called themselves Islamic, but no other Muslim acknowledged them. Frentoi had done great things further north, if greatness can be measured in numbers of dead. But their power had begun to wane, and Nigeria, after all, had oil, and governments in richer continents couldn't let it fall to such savages. The public beheadings were OK as long as they stuck to the locals. But severing an American head was stepping over the line. Troops were rallied, coalitions were built, bounties were paid, and Frentoi were driven from Nigeria. And everywhere they went, if there was oil, or diamonds, or fertile fields, or tourists, western soldiers with clean uniforms and helicopters would drive them on again, before they had killed enough or taken enough limbs to assuage their strange notion of divinity.

But in Surtalga there was no oil and not enough diamonds, there was nothing for the West to protect. The international peacekeepers who remained from the Mirandano conflict had run out of mines to clear, they said, even though everyone they were leaving behind knew they weren't leaving at all, they were running, as fast as they could, because the whole damn country had been written off, and anyone who was left in it when the lights went out might as well scream themselves bloody into the darkness. No one outside Surtalga would hear them.

The image now was of Frentoi fighters, a convoy of Jeeps streaming through featureless plains, children with the faces of men. The voice behind the screen was talking about their weapons, replenished from remnants of the old conflict. The rebels had kept their guns. So had the mercenaries and militias who had changed side whenever it suited them. They had hidden their weapons, or buried them, and now they were being found, dug up, sold or surrendered under torture. A conflict that had died nearly three decades earlier had returned to haunt its survivors.

There was a photograph on the screen now. Black and white. I squinted. A band of rebels, the only surviving image of the leadership of the People's Army of Mirandano before they were killed or captured, one by one, and finally broken. In the middle I recognised Hurtado – the Captain, he'd called himself. Freddie Harmsworth had found Hurtado fascinating, had teased out and endlessly analysed his reasoning, his tactics, his motives, his tragic end. Standing either side of Hurtado were another four men – all men, the leadership was entirely male, but that was hardly unusual in Africa in the eighties. It was an informal shot, smiles, arms on shoulders, fists raised.

I squinted again, stood, walked closer to the television. The image was panning out, and more men were coming into view, five on either side, now six. Now seven.

I froze. The remote control fell from my hand.

It was him.

Three decades earlier. Hair dark, not grey. In uniform, but a uniform thrown together out of other bits of uniform, the uniform of a volunteer, not a conscript. Smiling at the camera, one hand shielding his eyes. But these were the same eyes. This was the same face. I was sure of it.

The last time I'd seen that man, I'd been standing on the bottom step of a helicopter. And he'd been pointing a gun at my face.

PART 2: Dead Men Walking

10: Is It Worth It?

I was up at six next morning, two mornings in a row, which was unheard of. I'd slept about three hours, on and off, pictures bouncing around my brain, the photo, the man in the woods with the gun and the metal disk, the Grimshaws, of course, and – for some reason – David Brooks-Powell's smug, smiling face. The first thing I did, once I'd let my brain filter out the rubbish and remind me who I was and what was going on, was stagger naked into the living room and stare at the image on the television screen.

I'd paused it there, last night, frozen it, because I didn't know what to do about it and I thought maybe, just possibly, I was so drunk I was imagining the whole thing. I'd gone to bed, and fifteen minutes later I'd jumped out of bed and taken a photograph of the screen, just in case there was a power cut and I lost the image forever.

There had been no power cut. The image was still there, fifteen men in one black-and-white photograph. At the far right hand side, second from the end, was a man in glasses, tall, unsmiling, his uniform less ragged than the rest of them. His arm rested on the shoulder of the seventh man, who was a foot shorter and had a smile and a hand shielding his eyes and hair that was thirty years younger than it had been in the woods outside Dovesham. It was less than eight hours later and technically I was probably still drunk, but it didn't matter. It was the same man. I was sure of it.

I made myself a coffee and tried to work out what the hell I was going to do, which was half an hour throwing ideas around inside my head and seeing what stuck. Nothing did. Talking to the press wasn't an option. I didn't have the facts. All I had was a disputed sighting of a non-existent man who I thought looked like a thirty-years-older version of someone else I couldn't name but had seen, whilst drunk, on TV. Even Olivia wouldn't touch that. I needed some facts.

Half an hour with Google reminded me of something I already knew: no one had any facts on the Mirandano conflict because no one cared. You wanted anything on Mirandano you had to go to the source, that was what Freddie Harmsworth had taught us. One of the reasons he was so fascinated by it, something so fresh yet almost unrecorded, something you had to speak to real people to learn about, get under their skin, let them get under yours. "Real history," he'd say, "is the story of real people," and we'd nod away like we knew what he was talking about.

I'd never had much interest in real people and their skins, and most of the real people were dead, anyway. The rest, who knew? Rotting in some prison, probably, or fighting another unknown war in another half-heard-of country. I had nothing. I made myself another cup of coffee and prepared myself to give up on the whole thing. I'd do it. I looked at the clock on the oven. Seven-thirty. I'd give myself until eight and if the answer hadn't come to me by then, that would be it. Goodbye, mystery man. Goodbye, Mirandano. Goodbye, Claire Tully.

Half an hour. I pressed play and watched the rest of the documentary, but there was nothing there. Mirandano was just a footnote, the real news was Frentoi, and that was only because of the reputation they'd made for themselves in other, richer countries and with shiny-toothed American hostages. I opened the laptop again but I couldn't think of anything to type. 7.54. Just six minutes.

Might as well call it now. I closed the laptop. No one knew a thing. No one could help me. Outside the mind of Freddie Harmsworth, Mirandano was hardly even real.

Of course.

Freddie Harmsworth. I hadn't seen him in years. I wasn't even certain he was still alive. But if he was – well, it might lead somewhere. And if it didn't, then I'd know there was nowhere else to go.

Freddie was alive, after all. Alive, and still teaching history at St Edward's like nothing had changed in all those years. He could see me today – he'd be delighted to see me – of course he remembered me, he'd followed my career with interest, particularly that murderer fellow. Except of course he wasn't, was he? Anyway, tea and cake at three, if I could get to Oxford for then, how did that sound?

It sounded excellent.

I felt a twinge of guilt for forgetting him so easily, and then I remembered what he'd told us as we filed out of his rooms for the final time. *To forget*, he'd said, *is a luxury only the young can afford.*

I wasn't far off forty. I wasn't so sure I could allow myself that luxury any more.

Three o'clock gave me time to kill and not a lot to kill it with. Chances were Mirandano was nothing, chances were I was wrong – no, I wasn't wrong, that was the one thing I was certain about, the man on the photograph on my television screen had pointed a gun at me nearly thirty years after that photograph was taken. But chances were that was all I'd ever know about it. The only other thing I had, the only other thing that made anyone other than me think I was anything other than a liar or a lunatic, was Pedrag Ilic, and Pedrag Ilic was dead.

I hit Google for what felt like the hundredth time that morning, and started typing in words I knew every journalist in the country had already typed in twenty-four hours earlier. There was plenty on Ilic, most of it the worst kind of conspiracy bullshit, and one recurring theme, a rumoured connection with a gang of British mercenaries who'd trained the three Serbs to kill in the Balkan wars and helped hide them years later in London. These mercenaries, it was suggested, were men of some influence. After London they'd supposedly smuggled the Serbs out to Iraq in 2005, briefly, to make use of them there, not long before they were finally arrested. There were a few grainy photos, a few code names – *Vlad, Rasputin, Osiris, the Scourge* – a little spice, no substance. It all seemed ridiculous, almost childish, no relevance to the real world. But that didn't mean it couldn't be true. The last few days of my life hadn't borne much resemblance to the real world.

The Oxford bus hadn't changed. Same crowd of people huddling against the rain under a tiny shelter while a thousand cars a minute threw puddles at them. Even the majestic hotels to the south looked somehow shrunken, shrivelled, dreaming of different and sunnier skies. I'd forgotten to bring an umbrella, which was stupid. If it wasn't raining in London, it would be in Oxford. And the bus itself – same foggy windows, same narrow seats, same faint pencil of light from overhead, same broken air conditioning. I thought I might have travelled on this bus before. I cleared a small circle on the window and fell asleep to visions of flyovers chasing aeroplanes and traffic lights advancing on London.

I didn't wake until we'd reached Oxford, nudging gently through a Summertown that, unlike the bus, seemed to have changed beyond recognition, larger, brighter even in the rain and murk, cleaner and more expensive-looking. Words were racing through my head, numbers and letters, nonsensical, inexplicable but insistent. *ROS*. That was obvious enough. *Republic of Surtalga*. The rest could have come from anywhere.

By the time we'd reached the bus station the rain had thinned to a fine mist and there were hints of blue above. I was early, so I sat in one of the new cafés on Cornmarket and tried to clear my head. The numbers and letters didn't want to go. A double espresso helped chase them out.

Professor Harmsworth – *Freddie, please, dear boy, when have you ever called me Professor Harmsworth* – was more like the bus than the city. Older, but otherwise unchanged. The room didn't show any obvious signs of further age, but two decades wouldn't have made a great deal of difference to the centuries it had been there or the hundreds of books piled vertically and horizontally into every possible space. Even the paintings were the same. *Modern history, classical art*, he'd always said. Modern might have moved on. Classical never would.

Something had changed, though, and I noticed it the moment I settled in the same threadbare armchair I'd read my essays from all those years ago. I had a glass of red wine in one hand. But Freddie had nothing, or rather, he had water. And no pipe. I asked why before my brain kicked in and cursed me for a tactless idiot.

"I'm not as young as I was, Sam", he said, and the smile didn't shift, but I knew to leave it there. Now was as good a time as any to get on with things.

"Do you still teach Mirandano?"

He shook his head.

"Can't. The economics don't allow it. Students want racier wars now, and the human race has been generous enough to provide them with plenty over the last few decades. They've no interest in a conflict they've never heard of."

"That's a shame."

"For me, yes. For them, too, because Mirandano's very obscurity encased it in an objectivity so often missing from the subject."

It was like I'd jumped back eighteen years. He'd used the same words, or ones similar enough, back when he'd introduced the conflict to us. Same language, high-flown but clear, same aura of modest authority.

"I hope you don't mind me asking, Sam, but why the sudden interest in Mirandano? From what I recall you rather resisted the allure when you were here."

I realised I'd been staring at him, lost in memories. I had a line for this.

"Client, Freddie. Can't say a lot, but between you and me, he says he was tortured back then, and he's got a fairly convincing case that Her Majesty's Government knew a thing or two about it."

"Hmmm." He sat back, frowning. "That's not inconceivable, although after all this time I can't imagine how you'd go about proving it. Why's he waited so long?"

I hadn't thought about that. It was the obvious question to ask, and it hadn't even crossed my mind. I shrugged and said the first thing that came into my mind.

"He's only just arrived. Been in Nigeria."

Freddie looked at me, silent, for a moment. It was plausible enough, I thought. Some people had made it to Nigeria, if they had the money and the friends.

"Well, as I say, Sam, it's not impossible. We're being sued over here for things that happened in the Middle East five years ago and Kenya sixty years ago. And it's not like they all behaved like gentlemen in Mirandano."

This surprised me. I couldn't recall him mentioning British Government involvement before. He wasn't mentioning it now, as it happened, but he wasn't denying it either. I waited.

"It was an awful war, Sam. Horrible and bloody, like they all are. And it's not over."

"What do you mean, not over?"

"What do you think it was, Sam? The war, I mean. Why was it really fought?"

I sat there and tried to remember what he'd said to me, nearly twenty years ago. What was it? A struggle for survival, a battle against a hierarchy who believed they were fighting for their own existence, too, a vanity project for Western-educated twenty-somethings who wanted to be Africa's Che Guevara, a proxy war for corporations and national interests over strategic routes they'd lost interest in before the conflict was six months old? I didn't know what to say, but that didn't matter, because Freddie hadn't really expected an answer.

"It was a phase, Sam. Just a phase. There were the slave wars, and the colonial wars, and then the liberation wars. After independence there were military coups and family feuds that enveloped whole nations. Then came the political insurrections and civil wars, like Mirandano, and then the tribal wars, which had always been there in the background, erupted again. Now there are religious wars, but the older I get, Sam, the clearer it becomes that they're all the same war, with the names changed to suit the times."

I shifted, uncomfortable. I couldn't tell if he was right or not, it was an interesting theory, certainly, but too abstract to be any use to me right now. I felt in my pocket for the bit of paper I'd printed from my phone that morning, the picture that had brought me here, and wondered where it would lead.

"And Sam, for all we hear about these savages, these Frentoi, let's not pretend the ones doing the killing and the kidnapping now are so very different from the ones who did it thirty years ago. Villages were burnt back then, too. People were massacred and raped, mutilated and starved."

He tailed off, for a moment, and I thought maybe now was an opportunity to bring him somewhere more relevant.

"Yes, I get that, but it wasn't us, Freddie, was it? I mean, the place wasn't a British colony, the big companies out there weren't ours, they were Dutch and American." I was guessing here. But in that particular little corner of West Africa, Dutch and American was a likely guess.

He frowned, again, realising I was steering him, and shrugged.

"We could have stopped it, Sam. Or at least slowed it down so much it was no more than a ripple on the surface of everyday life. There were British mercenaries out there, lots of them, and they were allowed to keep those wars running, because there were people in Westminster who thought they were useful, whatever that meant."

He lingered on that *"useful"*, wrapped it around his tongue and then spat it out like it hurt. I didn't think he shared the opinion of those people in Westminster. He'd started to get somewhere interesting, at least. I sipped at my wine and waited, but it seemed that was all I was getting. It was time to prod, again.

"What do you know about these mercenaries?"

"Lies and rumours, for the most part. History's two parts lies and three parts rumours anyway, Sam, you know that. It's just that in this case most of the rumours are lies too, and there's truly no way of knowing which ones aren't."

He sat back, pleased with himself. *Mercenaries.* It wasn't much, but there was a possible connection, at least.

"Any names?"

"Not real ones, Sam." He was still sitting back, running his finger around the rim of his glass and staring into nothing. I needed to bring him back. I remembered the words I'd read that morning.

"Vlad?" I asked. Nothing. "Rasputin? Osiris? The Scourge?"

He sat up so suddenly I thought for a moment he might be having a heart attack.

"The Scourge, did you say?"

I nodded. Forehead creased, he sat back into his chair, lost in thought.

"No. No, it can't be. It was just a myth, I thought."

"What was?"

"The Scourge."

I waited. The silence lengthened, Freddie still half-supine on his deep old armchair, staring at nothing. I was starting to think he'd forgotten I was there, and then he spoke.

"Nobody really knew what it was. The Scourge. A man? A group of men? On the Government side, certainly. But brutal. Even by the standards of the day."

He paused, briefly, and went on.

"People would vanish, villages would go up in smoke, and all anyone would know about it was *The Scourge had been*. Nobody knew who, or why, or where, or if it was even true. I tended to think not. A bogeyman to frighten your children and your enemies. Quite effective, really."

He'd lapsed again, sitting back, looking at the wall behind me. I waited. Nothing. Maybe he really did think he was alone. I reached into my pocket and brought out the image I'd printed from my phone earlier that morning.

"Do you recognise this man?"

He sat up, gently, apparently unsurprised by my presence. I reached across and passed it to him, pointing with my thumb to the right-hand side of the picture. He squinted. Again, I waited.

He nodded.

"Ah, yes. Familiar faces, Sam."

I continued to wait.

"And these people – this person – has some relevance to your case, does he?"

Something about the way he said the word *case* and the way he peered into my face over the top of the photograph told me he hadn't been taken in by my cover story. He didn't seem to mind. He looked back down and went on.

"The man with glasses, the tall man at the end, that's Olufemi Gueye. Femi, they called him. He ran their science projects, which meant adapting weapons, repairing weapons, designing bombs. Went to university in Europe. Netherlands, I think."

I waited. I didn't say *"and the man next to him?"*, because I knew Freddie would get there his own way. He always had.

"The smaller man Femi has his arm around, that's more of a problem. I can tell you what he did – money, diamonds, that kind of thing. Sold assets for the People's Army. Financed the war. I can tell you he was also university-educated, also probably in Europe. They called him Chima. But I don't know if that was really his name."

"Is there anything else?"

He sat back again, the photograph held in front of him, gazing at it, frowning.

"Great pals with Femi, I thought. I seem to recall seeing other photographs, during the war and before it, and those two were always together. But there isn't anything else. Not in here" – he pointed to his head – "or in here" – he waved his hand at the books and journals.

So that was it. A name, or a hint of a name. A role. A friend.

"What happened to Femi?"

Freddie shrugged.

"He died, Sam. Like everyone else in that photo."

Except one.

"Executed after the war?"

"Femi? No, I don't think so. Died during it. Bomb, I seem to recall. Might even have been one of his. Chima died too. Same bomb."

I nodded. Olufemi Gueye might have been a certified bomb-making genius for all I knew, but he'd have needed people to work for him, and he'd have taken whoever he could get his hands on. That's how wars like this one went. So no great surprise if one of those recruits got clumsy, screwed up, blew himself to hell and his comrades with him. Olufemi Gueye could be in a thousand decomposing pieces across Surtalga.

But Chima wasn't.

I was staring at my own hands, trying to work out whether this was worth mentioning. Chima was alive. Freddie seemed pretty certain Chima was dead. I wasn't sure he'd be able to help me figure out why he wasn't.

"Sam."

I looked up. Freddie was holding the photo out, passing it back to me, eyes narrowed, suddenly alert.

"Listen to me, Sam. I don't know what you're doing, and I don't want to, so don't bother carrying on with this charade about a case."

I started to argue, then realised there was no point. Freddie had his hand up anyway, forestalling interruption.

"Just hear me out, Sam. These people" – he gestured at the photograph I was holding – "they're dead. They can't do anything to you, or to anyone else. You can forget about them. But listen to me, Sam. Don't get involved."

If everyone was dead it sounded like there wasn't much to lose by getting involved, even if there wasn't a great deal to gain, either.

"Ask yourself, Sam. Is it worth it? There are other people left. On both sides. And you know what they did."

I knew, all right. Freddie had shown us. Photographs, home videos, voice recordings, the kind of thing that you wouldn't have found on the internet even if the internet had existed back then. Enough skin for everyone to get under together, if you really wanted to. *We had to see for ourselves*, he'd explained. Reading about it wasn't enough.

There were four of us in that tutorial group, the ones who weren't even supposed to be studying this particular war. One boy had run out of the room to be sick. He hadn't come back.

"They're ruthless. They're brutal. Mirandano might be thirty years ago but what they did, it'll be with them and the people they did it to until the last memory has faded. For you, for me, though, it's history. Just history."

I looked at him. I knew what he meant. I just couldn't do what he was asking me to.

"Try to keep it that way."

The blue sky had disappeared back into rain and gloom by the time the bus was ready for us, after fifteen minutes crammed in another tiny shelter among the backpacks and the tight, knowing student smiles. The bus was full, I had someone sitting next to me, but I hardly noticed her. *Try to keep it that way*, he'd said, and the odds were he was right. Dead men and a dead war. Nothing to gain from raising them all back to life. Glasses, smiles, bits of old clothes. Words on a page, burning in the wind. Six charred fingers climbing from a crater. Three severed hands pointing guns at my head.

I woke with a start. London. Darker, still raining, lights tearing round Marble Arch like gigantic bumper cars. This was the real world. Everyone keeping their distance, just, everyone safe inside their own metal skins, and it was enough. Enough not to make contact. Enough not to get involved. Enough not to get hurt.

Freddie Harmsworth was right. It was just history. It had already brought me enough trouble.

The rain had intensified by the time I hauled my way off the bus and onto the pavement. I started out towards Marble Arch station and hadn't gone more than ten steps when I sensed a car coming to a halt beside me. What kind of idiot would stop in the rain to ask directions from the one man in London without an umbrella?

The window nearest me slowly opened. I turned towards the car. It was big. Expensive. It was a Bentley, that's what it was.

The face at the window was smiling at me and it took me a moment to place it. A tall, middle-aged man with a carefully-sculpted sweep of hair who said he was "from the military". Dead, I'd assumed, at Dovesham. But lately the dead seemed to have an awkward habit of coming back to life.

"Mr. Williams," he said, for all the world as if we'd met for tea and cake at Claridge's. I nodded at him. Even if I'd been able to speak, I wouldn't have known what to say.

"I think it's time you and I had a little chat."

11: Urbane

Major Ballantine (he turned and introduced himself as I slid into the back, next to a large, bald, unsmiling gentleman in a black suit who stared straight ahead, unblinking, as if he were suffering from shell-shock) wasn't just alive. He was alive and in possession of a Bentley and, as it turned out, a large suite of rooms in a smart, anonymous building not five minutes' drive from Marble Arch. Apart from the introduction, the journey had been silent. Ballantine seemed to be waiting until we got wherever it was we were going, and I still couldn't think of anything to say. The man sitting next to me certainly didn't invite conversation.

The driver stayed with the car but the large bald man came with us, a looming presence behind me as we entered the building and wound through a handful of bare corridors, two staircases and several doors. I didn't feel threatened – quite – I sensed I could leave if I wanted to – but they wouldn't be very happy about it. Still, I kept an eye on the keypads at each door as Ballantine typed in the entry codes. He didn't bother shielding the input from my casual glance. Fourteen digits each time – why would he?

Finally we came to what looked like a particularly well-appointed dentists' waiting room. A profusion of armchairs of varying styles. Magazines. Carafes and coffee tables. I tried to remember which direction we'd gone in and realised we weren't a million miles from Harley Street. A demure young lady in a white blouse and black pencil skirt appeared and the impression was solidified. I glanced at the walls, finding standard reproductions, half-expecting medical degrees and hygienists' diplomas.

"Tell Jenkins we've arrived, will you? He can meet us in my rooms. And tell him to bring tea." He turned to me, asked "Tea alright, Sam?" and I nodded, noting that I was no longer "Mr Williams". I couldn't tell whether that was a good thing or not.

Ballantine's "rooms" were a singular room, in fact, plushly-carpeted, mahogany-desked. Jenkins, a quiet white-haired fellow with creases round his eyes and a nervous smile, was waiting for us, sat beside a light wooden coffee table with a notepad and pen and a tray loaded with cups, cakes and biscuits. Miss Moneypenny was probably waiting outside with Q, I thought, and started to laugh, and then remembered I wasn't here by choice, or at least not *entirely* by choice, and stopped.

Jenkins poured the tea. Ballantine sat behind his desk and waited. Then the three of us were sitting comfortably, sipping tea, and again I had to resist the urge to laugh.

Ballantine did the talking. Jenkins took notes. He'd asked whether I would like milk, or cream, or sugar, but once the tea had been served he was silent.

"Mr Williams. You've been causing a little controversy lately, haven't you?"

I shrugged. It wasn't really a question, after all.

"And if I'm honest with you, your controversy has caused us some difficulty."

I wasn't letting that one go. "It's not exactly been a bed of roses for me," I snapped, and he nodded.

"I understand. I'm sorry about that."

Well, Claire Tully wasn't exactly his fault, I thought, but I'm not one to knock back an apology. I gave what I hoped was a gracious nod.

"What I propose is this. You tell us everything you know. I'll tell you everything I know. After that, hopefully you'll understand what's been going on the last few days and you'll agree to keep quiet about it all."

"Why should I do that?"

He scratched his chin, and looked me in the eye, and waited until I was almost ready to get up and walk out, and then he said "Because if you don't, a lot of innocent people will die."

Well, when he put it like that.

It was a long and complicated story but the gist of it was this:

I was right.

The man I'd seen at Dovesham was Chima Nwosu.

"He's supposed to be dead," I pointed out.

"Yes. The bomb was real enough. Took out their entire weapons design facility, which for a pathetic little scrap in the back end of Africa was years ahead of where it should have been. It was probably the only thing keeping them in the war. Once it was gone" – he made a gentle popping noise with his mouth – "the dominoes started to fall."

"But Chima wasn't killed?"

"No. His friend was. Gueye. Chief scientist, they called him, but basically he made bombs. Good ones, too. Gueye was identified by a bit of his face and the fact that half a dozen people had just seen him walk in with Nwosu, and everyone just assumed that Nwosu had bought it, too."

But he hadn't. Chima Nwosu had left before the explosion and gone about his business completely unaware that his best friend was dead. His business, as Freddie had already told me, was finance.

"He'd retrieve the diamonds from wherever it was he'd hidden them, get on a plane to Antwerp, sell them for the best price he could, and come back with a suitcase full of cash."

I was confused. Why didn't he just go to South Africa? It wasn't like they didn't know their diamonds down there.

The answer was distance, it turned out. No one in South Africa was going to touch a Mirandano diamond. It wasn't like they had better-developed consciences down there, more that it was a smaller world. Buy the wrong thing off the wrong man and that man's enemies might decide you were safer dead. They didn't have the same reach in Europe.

"And anyway, Nwosu knew Antwerp. He'd studied there."

Which made sense. Mirandano had been a Belgian colony, even if the Dutch and the Americans had all but taken over in the decade or two after independence.

"And that was where we picked him up."

I had to ask. He was practically begging me to ask.

"We?"

He smiled.

"The less you know, the better. Let's just say we're a Government agency and you could count on the fingers of one hand the number of politicians who know we exist."

I wasn't getting any more than that. It would have to do.

"So how come you were involved?"

He shrugged.

"Before my time, really. But like everything else, Sam, it was all about stability. There was a danger the war was going to spread. It needed to be brought to an end, with as little damage as possible. Drying up the finance was a useful angle."

"Did you bomb the weapons facility, then?"

He shook his head.

"No. That wasn't us. That was just war. Government got lucky. Had to happen eventually. They'd been looking for years."

So Ballantine and his people had arranged for Chima

123

Nwosu to be taken in Antwerp and brought to Britain in secret, and hidden here so well that even the people who were hiding him in Dovesham didn't know he was there.

"But the war ended decades ago. Why didn't you let him go?"

Ballantine shrugged.

"We would have done, of course. Do you really think we relished the cost and the trouble of keeping him here, in secret, all this time? But he wouldn't tell us about the diamonds."

Nwosu, it turned out, hadn't just been the man who sold the diamonds. He'd been the man who got hold of them in the first place. And since he hadn't told anyone else where he was getting them from – a habit which had probably been the one thing that had kept him alive so long – the moment he disappeared, the People's Army had started to run out of money. No money, no clever bombs: the war fizzled out in months.

"And meanwhile our fellow Nwosu's sitting there in – well, you don't need to know where, but this was before we moved him to Dovesham – and every time we ask him about the diamonds, he just smiles at us. If we hadn't seen proof that he'd arranged another drop – a particularly large drop – for a few weeks later, we'd have convinced ourselves there weren't any diamonds left. Heaven knows, it would have been more convenient for us. And a sight cheaper. But there were more diamonds, and once we knew that we couldn't just ignore it."

It was all starting to become clearer.

"So at the end of the day, you just wanted the diamonds, right?"

Ballantine looked shocked.

"Certainly not. If we'd found out where those diamonds were we'd have told the new government in Surtalga at once."

I raised one eyebrow, a trick I'd learned from Rachel when she found herself doubting the claims of my more disreputable clients.

"Sam, really. We're a Government agency, not some kind of *bank*. Our only interest in the diamonds was in ensuring Nwosu didn't use them to start the war again."

It might be true, I thought. Freddie would have believed it. Back in the eighties a boxful of diamonds was more than enough to start a war in Africa.

So for thirty years Chima Nwosu had languished in various secret locations, the last ten at Dovesham, and no more than two people in Her Majesty's Government had ever known a thing about it.

"And then, what, the day you happen to turn up at Dovesham, after thirty years, he escapes. Hardly a coincidence, is it?"

Ballantine shrugged, again. This time I wasn't buying it.

"People died there, Major Ballantine. People who had nothing to do with your war or your diamonds."

The shrug turned into a nod, an apologetic sort of nod, a reluctant acknowledgement.

"Things didn't go quite as we'd planned, Sam."

That was the understatement of the year.

It had all been planned, the escape, set up meticulously so that Nwosu would think he'd managed it all by himself. A couple of long-dormant People's Army's contacts in London had been tracked down, cajoled and threatened, and were ready to receive their old comrade and help him in whatever way he asked. Chima Nwosu would be in Surtalga by now, and he'd never know it was Ballantine that had set him on his way.

"Why? And why now?"

"You watch the news, Sam?"

I nodded.

"Of course you do. So you know about Frentoi. You probably know they're getting weapons from all sides of the old conflict. What you don't know is that there are cells from the People's Army still active in the region."

I couldn't help a frown. That didn't seem likely. Freddie thought they were all long-gone. Ballantine didn't seem to notice.

"These cells, and Frentoi, they're working together. They know about the diamonds, and we have reliable intelligence that they're not far off tracking them down. If they get hold of them, it'll make Syria look like a picnic."

I could see that. Frentoi had done enough damage through violence alone. Violence and money would make a particularly unhealthy combination.

"We need to get to the diamonds before they do."

I nodded. It did make a kind of sense. The plan was to get Chima out of Dovesham, get him to Surtalga, pray that he'd lead Ballantine to both the operative cells and the diamonds.

"So what went wrong?"

"We miscalculated."

I waited.

"The plan was a small riot, contained within one area of the prison, something that could easily be brought under control once the escape had been managed. We didn't expect it to spread so quickly."

"You brought the guns in."

He shrugged again, saw my expression, and quickly nodded. He needn't have bothered. I was starting to understand Major Ballantine.

He'd made a mistake, and people had died. Jayati Mehta had died. But the thing was, I could see why he'd done it. He had an impossible job. I wasn't going to make it any harder. I just had one further question.

"What about Pedrag Ilic?"

He looked me in the eye again, hard, clear. He needed me to understand what he was about to say.

"Mr Ilic became a liability."

I nodded. I'd guessed as much. Too close to the outside world. That wouldn't do.

Something sparked in my brain. An old article. A dead soldier.

"And Major Dawes?" I asked. "Did he become a liability too?"

I looked up. Ballantine's expression had changed. He was staring at me, frowning, and for the first time it seemed like the mask had slipped, the suave urbanity, the genial comfort. I saw shock, and a hint, I thought, of anger. And then I thought perhaps I'd imagined the whole thing, because a split second later the mask was back on.

"I'm impressed, Sam," he said. "You've been doing your research. But no. That wasn't our doing." He shook his head slowly, sadly. "He was a good man, Dawes, but he couldn't take the pressure. In over his head. A sad case."

I waited, but there was nothing more. In for a penny, I thought.

"And the others?" I asked. "The brother? Stankovic?"

Ballantine shrugged.

"They're alive. They're safe enough. Nobody can get to them."

I nodded, again. As long as they were kept away from anyone who might ask an awkward question, they'd be allowed to go on breathing. The Royal Free Hospital had been just a little too public for Pedrag Ilic's safety.

There was a long pause. I was suddenly conscious of myself, my body, the blood in my veins and the hairs on the back of my hands. I felt calm, which didn't seem quite right, because I might not be in the middle of a prison riot but I was still a long way out of my comfort zone. I was in

the eye of the storm. I figured the calm would pass soon
enough. Ballantine had been leaning forward, looking me
in the eye, making sure I understood everything he was
saying. Now he sat back and smiled.

"Your turn, Mr Williams."

I should have been prepared. I'd known from the
beginning this was coming. I had moments to decide – tell
all, tell nothing, do what I always did and tell just enough
to get what I wanted. I'd heard everything I was going to
hear, I was "Mr Williams" again, suddenly, and I still
didn't know what to say. I wasn't ready. I needed more
time.

I had no more time.

I went with everything I knew. It wasn't much, I
realised, as I told it. Ballantine nodded as I spoke. Jenkins
scribbled furiously. I was surprised there was enough
material to justify writing it down at all.

Ballantine and Jenkins left me in the office alone while
they arranged for me to be taken home. I couldn't help
looking around.

The bookcases were filled with modern biography and
military history. The fireplace was decorative, the flowers
fresh. The whisky in the decanter on the mantelpiece
smelled old and expensive, cigar smoke and chocolate.
The desk drawers were locked. The window overlooked a
courtyard I hadn't suspected. The rain had lifted, and with
it the clouds, but it was getting late and the murk of earlier
on had been replaced by dusk. There was a car in the
courtyard.

Jenkins had left his notes on the coffee table but his
writing was illegible. They'd been gone nearly five
minutes, Jenkins and Ballantine, which was longer than I'd
expected, but it was always possible something important
had come up. Something more important than getting me

home on time to grab another kebab and watch whatever happened to be on TV. Yes, it was always possible.

There was a car in the courtyard.

There was no overhead light in the room, just a pair of standard lamps and an old-fashioned green-glassed banker's lamp on the desk. The coffee table was on wheels. I hadn't noticed that. There were no curtains, just a dark, velvet-lined vertical blind, turned at forty-five degrees so you could look out of the window and feel like nobody was looking in.

There was a car in the courtyard.

I'd looked at it down there in the courtyard three times before I noticed it, and then I noticed it like it had driven at me at fifty miles an hour and hit me in the face.

It was a grey Volkswagen, and the number plate read KG63 ROS.

It had been parked outside my flat when the courier from Dovesham had turned up with my phone.

It had followed me to Oxford and back.

I replayed a scene in my head from the day before. Slowed it down. Noticed the little things.

One car, coming fast, not so fast now, a fraction of a second at a time, *hadn't seen him, he hadn't seen me,* except he had, there was a face, looking right at me, and I couldn't read the expression on it but it wasn't surprise, *throwing myself onto the pavement.* The streak of grey came into focus, became a car.

It was a Volkswagen. The number plate read KG63 ROS. The driver was the large, bald, silent man in the black suit.

The door was locked. There was no modern electronic keypad, just an old-fashioned keyhole without a key in it. I put my eye to the door and silently thanked Pierre for teaching me a number of things I'd been certain, at the time, would never be of the slightest use to me.

As well as his notes, Jenkins had left all the tea paraphernalia on the coffee table, which meant a butter knife for the scones. I had the door open within a minute, quietly, because although the corridor looked empty when I poked my head outside, I could hear a voice. Ballantine. His voice, then a pause, then his voice again. It sounded like he was on the phone.

I wanted to know what he was saying and who he was saying it to, but not as much as I wanted to get out and a long way away. I was out of the eye and into the storm. I felt sick, felt the bile rising in my throat, felt my body rebel against the calm I was forcing on it, the instructions I was issuing like this was just a normal kind of event on a normal kind of day. The only way out I could see was straight past the open door through which his voice was coming, so it looked like I was going to be hearing a little more whether I wanted to or not. I could run down the corridor, I thought, past the door, even in the shape I was in I'd be there in a couple of seconds. I put one foot onto the bare wooden floor of the corridor, gently, just to test it. No doubt I was oversensitive, but the creak sounded like the whole building was coming down. I decided not to run. Keeping as close as I could to the edge furthest from Ballantine's open door, I started slowly down the corridor.

"*Yes, he's in Surtalga.*"

"*No. It seems he's gone to ground.*"

"*We'll have our own people out there shortly. There's no problem.*"

"*I just told you. There is no problem.*"

I was level with the door now, and glanced in as I crept past. Only a portion of it was visible, a small square of carpet, a chair, the edge of a table. The carpet was the same as the one in Ballantine's other room, I noticed. I couldn't see Ballantine. Good. He couldn't see me. I could still hear him, though, and I tried to time my steps to the sound of his voice.

"*We'll have it within a week, I'd imagine.*"

"*I don't really care if this is making you nervous. We have a deal. There are plenty of buyers out there, but I don't think the Colonel would like it if you decided to drop out now. It might be interpreted as bad faith.*"

"*Thank you. I'm glad you see it that way. I'll be in touch.*"

I heard footsteps and cursed myself for choosing stealth over speed. Faster, now, I walked to the end of the corridor and the closed door, and prayed that the code to open it from the inside was the same as it had been from the outside.

It was. I pushed it open, walked through into a stairway, and pulled it shut behind me. I still felt sick, but alongside the nausea was the faint, growing outline of the notion that I might just get out of this. Each door Ballantine had taken me through had been opened with the same numbers, and it looked like these people, so professional in every other way, had made no distinction between entry and exit codes. As Pierre always said, "overconfidence is the burglar's best friend".

Two more corridors, one more door. As I entered the final digit it opened away from me and I found myself staring in the face of the woman in the white blouse. There was a smell of meat and raw onion. In her left hand was a white paper bag. I looked at the bag. So did she. After a moment I recalled something else Pierre had told me, and arranged my face into a look of controlled concern.

"Where's Ballantine?" I asked. She looked from the bag to me, but didn't say anything.

"The Colonel?" I said, hoping like mad I hadn't misheard Ballantine's phone call.

She shook her head, which I took to mean she didn't know.

"Go and find Ballantine and tell him there's a problem. I'll see if I can contact the Colonel."

She nodded and came in past me. I watched her walk to the end of the corridor, turn, and look at me, frowning. I twisted my mouth into what I hoped was a reassuring smile and pushed the door closed behind me.

Thirty seconds, maybe a minute. That was all I had before she found Ballantine. He might be able to disable the exit codes. He might have his large, hairless Volkswagen driver – or someone less obvious – waiting outside for me. I sprinted down the stairs and the next corridor, and there was the final door.

The thing about a photographic memory is that it doesn't just wipe away all the other little failures we're cursed with. There I was, at the final door, fingers on the keypad and fourteen digits right there at the front of my brain ready to be transmitted to those fingers, and suddenly there were noises behind me, the slamming of a door, a raised voice, loud footsteps. I couldn't think of the numbers. I'd had them a minute earlier. I'd had them sat there ready and waiting since the first moment I'd seen them. But they were gone. I had Serbian names and number plates and the history of the People's Army of Mirandano. What I didn't have was the code to get me through the final door.

Seconds ticked by. I leaned against the door, breathing hard and trying to clear my head. The footsteps were getting louder. I closed my eyes and blocked them out and forced my way back, to Freddie, Oxford, the bus, the car, the driver, the building. Ballantine's hand. Ballantine's fingers.

There it was. Fourteen digits. The last one went in, the door clicked open – so Ballantine hadn't been able to change the codes yet – and I was out. It was getting dark. I ran for the corner of the street, turned, and there was a busy main road, cars, streetlights, people.

I didn't know where I was going, or why, but it hit me when I saw Marble Arch ahead. The bus stop was a couple of hundred yards further, and there was a bus there, waiting. I didn't stop running until I was on it.

12: Rock Bottom

I hadn't had time to think about why I was back on a bus heading for the one place Ballantine knew I'd already been that day. As somewhere to hide it was nothing short of stupid, but I was on the bus and I couldn't think of anywhere else right now, so it would have to do.

This time round there was no chance of sleep. Too much had happened. The sickness had gone, and as the Edgware Road slid past in a blur of fast food joints and shisha bars I realised suddenly that I was hungry. I played back in my head what I'd heard Ballantine saying on the phone. He was selling. Someone was buying. His interest in the diamonds wasn't the selfless thing he'd said it was, and I had the feeling there was more to this than a handful of rough stones covered in African dirt. I was certain, now, that he'd tried to have me hurt, killed maybe, by the Volkswagen. All those people who'd died at Dovesham. And Pedrag Ilic, who'd become a "liability", had been killed in cold blood, in hospital, inches from the eyes of the press. Given everything else, it didn't seem all that likely that Major Dawes had pushed himself off that cliff. You didn't need to know much to become a liability. I'd become one myself, and I hardly knew a thing. The sickness might have gone but the fear was starting to burrow in alongside the hunger and make a little home for itself, and there was nothing obvious I could shout at or laugh at or swear at to make it go away.

This time of night the journey was quicker than earlier. It had been clear in London but it was still raining in Oxford, rain driven sideways in that bitter Oxford wind I remembered so well. I picked up a cheese and tomato sandwich from the first place I saw open outside

Gloucester Green, hunched down and forced myself on towards St Edward's.

The main door was closed, but a handful of students were approaching, laughing and already half-drunk. Some things hadn't changed. It wasn't difficult to slip in among them. Freddie's rooms were in the second quad beyond the main lodge, watched over by statues of sixteenth century benefactors, clerics and kings.

The door to Freddie's staircase was open. I tried to remember if that was the way he usually left it. We'd always just filed in unthinking, papers in hand, chattering nervously amongst ourselves. I'd walked straight in this afternoon. But we'd been expected. I'd been expected. It was just like Freddie to pop downstairs and make sure the door was open for his guests. Was he expecting someone this evening?

Voices. I froze, one foot on the bottom stair. There were footsteps approaching from above, two voices, quiet but clear in the cloistered silence.

"Old bugger practically welcomed it."

"Shut up. Did the fire take?"

"Yes. Don't be a fool. No one can hear us. They're all fucking and reading Shakespeare."

I stepped back, and sideways, down the darkened passage which lead to Freddie's private bathroom. The footsteps drew closer, creaking on the wooden floor and ringing suddenly louder as they descended the stone staircase. I ducked down as they reached the bottom, but it was too dark to see anything. I could just about make them out as a slightly different shade of black. No chance they'd see me.

I waited thirty seconds while the footsteps faded into nothing, and sprinted up the stairs. Freddie was sitting in his armchair, his favourite armchair, the one he'd been sitting in that afternoon, head to one side.

Even from here I could see his neck was broken. The bookcase beside him was on fire. I heard a noise and turned to my left, to the other side of the room. Books were burning there, too. There was a crash as a bottle of wine exploded.

There was nothing I could do. I turned and ran back down the stairs, stopped between quads to hit the fire alarm, and fifteen minutes later I was back, again, on the bus.

I stared at the back of the seat in front and thought about how I'd like to watch Ballantine die. Fire, I decided. Fire, without any means of escape, knowing his death was coming, watching it close in. I'd like to speak to him as it approached, to explain why he had to die, why it was fitting, how he might suffocate before he burned, but only if he was lucky.

"Excuse me, are you OK?"

There was a tiny Japanese woman sitting in the seat across the aisle from me. I hadn't noticed her. I hadn't noticed anything. I must have looked confused, because she pointed to my face and I put my hands to my cheeks. They came away wet. I hadn't realised I was crying. I nodded, and tried to get back to Ballantine and fire, and the things I'd say to the bastard as I watched him burn, but it was no use. All I could see now was Freddie. Head to one side. *Is it worth it?*

No, Freddie. It wasn't.

I was most of the way into London and swinging wildly about between fury and grief and terror when it hit me. I'd hit rock bottom. I couldn't go home. I could try the police, but the way Ballantine had things covered I didn't think they'd believe me. Paul, maybe – but they hadn't hesitated to kill Freddie, and it didn't take a genius to figure out why. They'd know all about Paul. They'd know who my friends were, what they looked like, where they lived. Who they lived with. There weren't many people I could trust, and I was too dangerous for any of them.

But it was just possible there was someone else.

I knew the office, everyone in London knew the office, with its huge glass orange-lit lobby and camera crews loitering outside hoping for the sniff of a second-hand story. I was still trying not to think about Freddie and what Ballantine would do to me if he got hold of me, to push the fear away and concentrate on doing what I had to do to stay alive. I'd ditched my phone on the way over, on the tube, just left it on the seat like it had fallen out of my pocket. I knew how easy it was to trace a mobile phone. As soon as I got back to street level I found a payphone. They still existed. I called her desk, and when she answered I hung up. She was there. The fear was starting to push its way out of the little corner I'd shoved it in. I pushed back, thought about what I needed to do. She was there. That was the only thing that mattered.

There was a small crowd outside, protesting about something or other, press intrusion, corruption, there was always an issue, always a target. All polite and softly-spoken, no attempt to stop the employees coming and going as they pleased. A very middle-class protest. I merged with the group, kept my eye on the main door, and waited.

After fifteen minutes she emerged. Walked straight through the crowd. She looked tired, stressed. Easy enough to follow, she wouldn't think to look behind her. And I knew where she was heading.

I was right. I stood across the road while she waited for the bus and hopped on just as it was about to leave. Headed North. My street, ten minutes later. She was at the front of the bus. I was at the back. It was full. Past my street, back on the main road. I took a risk and shuffled forward, hoping there would be others getting off at her stop. I was lucky. She was off first, then half a dozen noisy teenagers, then me. She paused for a moment and I caught a glimpse of her face bathed in pale yellow streetlight. She still looked tired. And unhappy. I hadn't spotted that, at first, but now it was clear. I'd been wearing that expression myself for the last couple of years, an expression which said *I don't know how the hell I ended up here, and I don't much like it.* Claire Tully might have bagged her big story, but it didn't seem to have brought her what she wanted, yet. That was good. It might make her more likely to help me. Or I might be reading way too much into a momentary relaxation of a bunch of facial muscles, but I was here now. And I couldn't think of anywhere else to go.

The rain had hit North London. I still had nothing useful, like a coat or an umbrella, and I'd only just dried off from Oxford. Suddenly the bile was back in my throat and I was shivering so hard I didn't think I could carry on walking, and without realising it I started to count off the problems I was trying to deal with, the *Sentinel* story, Ballantine, Freddie, the state of my legal practice. I stopped. Wallowing in misery wasn't going to help. I forced my head up and looked around.

The teenagers had drifted off into the night and we were alone, Claire and I, no one else on the street and she twenty yards away, oblivious, lost in her own thoughts. I could do this, I thought. She'd started off up the street, and I followed, still shivering. Most of the apartments seemed to be lit; it was turning into a foul evening, and North London wanted to be at home, in the warm and the dry, with the television and the oven and the kettle. I couldn't blame them.

I looked ahead – I'd forgotten to stop and check and I was almost upon her. The sound of the rain had masked her footsteps. Mine too, I saw, with relief. She hadn't noticed a thing. I stopped again, let her pull ahead a little way, started walking and then saw her stop and look up and down the street. I was still close enough that if I'd stopped now she'd have noticed, but her eyes just slid over me as I approached. She crossed the road. I carried on walking, past her now, and glanced over my shoulder to see her rummaging in her bag for something. A key. A large, white, anonymous building, nineties by the look of it, probably thirty or more flats. She didn't have an umbrella either, I suddenly realised. Her blonde hair was slick and dark with rain. She turned and looked up and down the street, again, but by now I was no more than a distant figure, heading away. She was gone.

OK. I knew where she was. I knew where she lived. I could get in, or try to get in, demand some answers, demand some help. Or I could go home and wait until it stopped raining. I thought back over the day, I didn't want to, but every time I tried to turn my mind to what I was going to do now it insisted on looking the other way. Ballantine. Freddie. My rage, white-hot as I'd boarded the bus back from Oxford, had subsided. I hated Ballantine, that was still there. But on top of it was layer after layer of shock, sadness, guilt, disappointment, confusion, images and words piled ton upon ton like ancient silt. Freddie's broken neck. *Did the fire take?* A Volkswagen coming so fast I hadn't even seen it. Chima Nwosu pointing a gun at my head.

I crossed the road. Up close, the building was older than I'd thought, weather-stained, people-stained, ugly. Not that I was doing a whole lot better. At least she could probably afford the rent.

The rain had settled into a fine drizzle, which couldn't

make me much wetter than I already was. I stood by the door staring at the buzzers. *Griffin. Turner/Alexander. Mhali. Jacobs/Singh. Tully.* So she lived alone. That made things easier. But I still didn't know what to say. *It's Sam. Who? Sam Williams.* Would she even let me in? If she didn't, what could I do? Wait outside until she called the police and the police called Ballantine and I wound up on fire with a broken neck under the wheels of Volkswagen?

I was reaching for the buzzer when the door started to open, and I turned away, instinctively, hunched down a little, hands in front of my face as if I were holding something there and looking at it.

It was Claire. She'd changed her clothes, but it was her. She was walking away. I could speak to her right now. I stood, frozen. She was six feet away, eight feet, ten. I didn't want to chase after her. She might scream. The door was falling closed beside me, and without thinking I stepped forward, got a foot in the gap, turned again. She'd crossed the road. She hadn't even noticed me.

I slipped inside and let the door fall shut behind me.

Flat seven was on the first floor and even with a credit card instead of a butter knife, the door was easier to open than Ballantine's office. I needn't have worried about the state of my place the other day, I realised, as I took in the clothes on the floor and the plates piled up next to the sink. It wasn't filthy, but it was a mess. It was also tiny, a kitchen not much bigger than the round table squeezed into its centre, and a single room for sleeping and living. A sofabed. A miniature bathroom to the side, sink, toilet, mouldy shower. There was a big old glass-topped table in the main room, a laptop, a pile of papers. I sat down and started to read, realised I probably shouldn't, then remembered I probably shouldn't have broken into her flat in the first place.

Notes on top, about me. A short bio, basic facts, no glaring inaccuracies. Underneath, something indecipherable, shorthand or code, comments from David Brooks-Powell, the same comments she'd printed in the *Sentinel*. Below that, some printed information on the Serbs. Nothing I didn't already know. A sheet on something called the Anglo-African Relief Foundation. I carried on through, but nothing seemed to make much sense or have much logical connection with anything else. Serbia, yes. Something about Baghdad. More on Pierre and the bribery allegations, some notes on the Trawden case.

I was about to give up when I caught sight of something, a single word on a page that otherwise meant nothing at all. The word was "Colonel".

I picked up the page and read. Colonel Poulter. Chief Executive Officer, Bor Platinum, Belgrade, Limited. A report into mining operations for a six month period in the mid-nineties. Something else that might fit in, might not. I put the page back down. *"I don't think the Colonel would like it"*. That's what Ballantine had said, on the phone, as I skipped gracefully down the hall to make my escape. *Colonel*. Just a word. There were hundreds of Colonels. Thousands. It was probably nothing.

I sat back down on the sofabed and closed my eyes. Within a minute I was asleep.

"You look like shit."

I opened my eyes. I'd rolled onto my side and my face was pressed into a pair of discarded jeans. Above the jeans stood Claire, black dress, expensive-looking shoes, hair still wet. She didn't seem surprised to see me, but she might have been staring at me for half an hour for all I knew. I twisted myself into a more suitable shape, sat up, blinked at her.

"Well?"

My head hurt. I felt like I'd been drinking all day. I looked down to see how long I'd been asleep and remembered I'd forgotten to put my watch on that morning.

"What time is it?"

"Just before midnight."

Christ. She'd been out for hours. I'd been asleep for hours.

"Are you going to tell me what you're doing here, or am I supposed to guess?"

She wasn't smiling, but I couldn't blame her. You go out, for a drink with friends, a date, whatever, you come back a couple of hours later and there's a lying dirty-looking lawyer asleep on your sofa. She frowned at me. She hadn't called the police yet. Hadn't even threatened to. Or maybe she had called the police, while I was asleep. Shit. I stood up, too quickly. My head hurt even more. I sat back down and the room seemed to move around me. When it came back into focus, she'd gone. If I'd been capable, I'd have gone too. I wasn't capable.

A couple of minutes later she was back, with a cup of tea, a glass of water and a Dairy Milk. I took all three.

"So how'd you get in?"

I showed her my credit card, mimed sliding it along the door. She looked unimpressed.

"Why?"

"Nowhere else to go."

My voice sounded strange, detached, deeper than usual. The chocolate and the drinks had helped, but I still didn't feel right. I sat there looking up at her, opening and closing my mouth like a goldfish, but the words wouldn't come. She smiled, which was positive, I thought, bent down and rummaged in the handbag she'd dropped on the coffee table, and came up with an item in each hand.

"Do you know what these are?" she asked.

One of them, quite clearly, was a watch. A small, old-fashioned silver watch on a silver chain. The other was a bit of plastic with a lump on it, hanging from a length of elastic. It might have been the key to Fort Knox for all I knew.

"That's a watch," I said. "That one, I don't know."

She continued to smile as she spoke.

"This is a rape alarm, Sam."

She waited a moment for her words to sink in. She needn't have bothered.

"So here's what's going to happen. I'm going to start the timer on this." She raised the watch to my eye level. She was still smiling, but I was starting to realise that smile wasn't always good news.

"Once I've started the timer, you'll have thirty seconds to convince me not to push the button on this." Now she raised the rape alarm. "If I don't like what I'm hearing, I push the button. If I don't believe what I'm hearing, I push the button. If I do believe what I'm hearing, but I'm still not happy you broke into my flat, I push the button. If I feel like pushing the button, I push the button. Have you got that?"

I nodded, still speechless. There was a gentle click. She'd started the timer. I closed my eyes and waited for the words to come.

There's a scene in one of the old Spaghetti Westerns where the bad guy faces off against his victims with a watch in one hand and the other hanging like a malevolent pink-grey spider over his gun and the music rising as the seconds tick by. All I could see was that hand, that gun. Nothing useful. No words.

"Fifteen seconds, Sam," she said, and I opened my eyes. The hand was gone, but there was Claire, in that dress, hair still glistening from the rain. My thoughts wandered. It wasn't helpful.

"Five seconds," she said, and I blurted out the first thing that came into my mind.

"They're trying to kill me!" I shouted. "It's Ballantine. And the Colonel."

The moment I said "Colonel" her expression changed. The smile was gone and the frown was back. The same frown she'd worn at my place, when she was trying to work out what I'd seen and how it might fit in with the official line. The smile made my spine tingle, but right now I preferred the frown.

"Go on," she said. She put the watch back in her bag and the rape alarm on the table. Still within easy reach. I decided to throw it all at her and hope something stuck.

"I haven't met this Colonel. But there's a bloke. Ballantine. He was there, at Dovesham. And the whole thing, the prison, the riot, it was all them. Him. It's all true."

I stopped for a moment. I'd been looking down at the table, at the rape alarm. The glass was scratched all over. I glanced up at her face. The frown was still there. She nodded for me to go on.

"There's a guy there, at Dovesham – *was* a guy there, called Chima Nwosu. He's the guy I saw. The whole thing was engineered so he could escape. He's got diamonds. In Surtalga."

She'd stopped nodding. I was going too fast. I was losing her.

"Look, Claire, they've killed already. I swear it. And I didn't make it up. Dovesham. I didn't make any of it up."

She nodded at me, still frowning, and said "I know," and for the first time in what felt like days I thought I might, somehow, get out of the mess I'd landed in.

We both had a lot to say, and Claire started, which suited me fine because my head still felt like it was attached to someone else's body.

"You were right," she said. Good, I thought. She finally believes me. But that wasn't what she meant.

"You were right, about the royalty and the D-listers. Dovesham wasn't my usual thing."

I nodded. Claire's particular journalistic tendencies weren't really the point right now, but it was her flat, and her rape alarm, and it wasn't like I was in a hurry to be somewhere else.

"Fact is, Sam, Dovesham was a diversion. And now it's turned into a pain in the arse."

That wasn't what I'd been expecting. I stood up fast, too fast, again, and sat back down with my brain turning big, slow circles inside my head.

It had seemed a little odd, Claire's record in print, because the *Sentinel* wasn't that kind of newspaper. As she continued, it all started to fall into place. She was working on something big, much bigger than supermarket openings or library closures or even a deadly prison riot. An investigation. A long-term project.

I asked, but she wouldn't tell me what it was. She'd only taken the Dovesham story because she had to keep writing, and this looked like a good opportunity, in and out fast and slightly more heavyweight than her usual "diversions". A rookie hack running a major investigation was about as plausible as Ballantine acting for the greater good, but I had the sense not to say so. Still her flat. Still her rape alarm.

"And then the Dovesham story turned into the Sam Williams story, and by that time I didn't have any choice."

I didn't understand.

"I was fed the story, Sam, and as far as I was concerned that was great, because it meant I could get on with my real work and the Sam Williams story would write itself. I didn't like it, and I wasn't sure I really believed it, but by the time I got round to wondering why I'd been fed it in the first place my editor had it too, and he was wondering why the finished article wasn't on his desk already."

"Fed the story?" I croaked, and she nodded again.

"The Foundation."

I looked towards her papers.

"Yes," she said. "The Foundation for the Relief of African Prisoners in England. They're the ones who sent me to Dovesham in the first place."

I felt my eyebrows rise. It made sense, but it didn't. I could see why a group like that might have an interest in Dovesham. I couldn't see why they'd arrange for an inexperienced journalist with no particular history in the field to visit on their behalf.

Claire was still talking.

"Sure, it was a little weird, but the paper wasn't saying no, not if there might be a story in it and nothing to pay. And I wasn't saying no, either."

But then, not long after the riot, just when the riot itself had stopped being the big story, an envelope turned up on her desk. There wasn't much inside, but what there was suggested Sam Williams was lying about what had happened at Dovesham. Just in case anyone was thinking about ignoring the whole thing, the same information had been copied to the editor. Right behind it came the rest of the case for the prosecution, personal history, Mauriers, Pierre, the kind of work I was doing these days, if I was lucky.

"You were taking the piss, Sam. That's how it looked. Taking advantage of the situation. Taking advantage of me. I don't like being groomed, Sam."

It was an odd choice of word, but I decided to let it pass.

"And it didn't look good, Sam. Drug-dealers."

She didn't mean Pierre. She meant Maloney. Pierre was just some guy on the street. Maloney had a hundred Pierres on his payroll, and dozens more shifting stuff over borders, dealing with rivals, arranging for people to look the other way and putting some money in their pockets. Maloney had heard about the way I operated, and as luck would have it, one of my twenty-quid-in-the-pocket stabs in the dark worked out for him, too. Twenty quid plus the price of two pints, because it was in a filthy Walthamstow pub I'd found out the guy who'd fingered Maloney had made a decent living pointing that same finger all over Europe. It didn't make him a liar, but it didn't make him look good, and that was enough to kill the case. Maloney walked.

"I take the work that's going, Claire. I can't afford to be sniffy about it. And everyone's allowed a lawyer. You know that."

She shrugged. It didn't matter. I might smell bad, but the way the story had come through smelled even worse, not that the smell was enough to stop it getting printed. Still, between that, and my phone call –

"Sorry about that," I muttered, but she shook her head.

"You were right."

The facts might all add up neatly enough, but something I'd said, or the way I'd said it, had got under her skin, and suddenly adding up wasn't enough. The "diversion" had turned into something real. Maybe it wasn't me that had been taking the piss after all.

So she'd done a little digging. The Foundation, it turned out, had no history at all. No one had ever heard of it. It had been set up a couple of years back and hadn't done a thing since. It was run by a man called Colonel Poulter.

She'd looked into Poulter. He wasn't a Colonel, at least

not in the British Army, but no one seemed to want to call him out on the title. William Poulter was a mercenary. Wars and coups and insurrections all over the world, mostly places she'd never heard of, but the earliest she'd come across the name was in the eighties. West Africa.

She looked at me again, saw something she expected to see, went on before I could interrupt.

After Mirandano, Poulter had disappeared for a while before resurfacing in Serbia, Croatia and Bosnia, providing "advice" and "assistance" to various groups whose affiliations were so tangled as to be utterly indecipherable. And then nothing, until he showed up providing "security" in Baghdad not long after the invasion. She paused. I raised my head, thinking it was my turn now, but she held up a hand and continued.

"The thing is, for all the connections you can see, with your Serbs, with everything else, there's nothing really that unusual here. Until you look at this."

She was holding another piece of paper.

"It's a list of his directorships. Easy enough to get hold of."

I took the paper from her. There were dozens of names there, maybe fifty. Two had been highlighted in yellow. *Bor Platinum, Belgrade, Limited,* and *Iraq Oil Services, Limited.* I thought about it for a moment, and then realised I was thinking clearly again. I spoke slowly, straightening it out in my mind even as the words formed.

"So this Poulter finds himself a war, goes in, does a bit of killing, and cleans up on whatever he can find under the ground."

She nodded.

"And now?" I asked. She looked blank. "What's he doing now?"

She passed me another piece of paper. Nine years of corporate history for William Poulter. The first seven were blank. Poulter had been taking care of business in Iraq, no doubt. Plenty of money to be made out there, in "security" or whatever it was he was really doing. And then a new company in 2011, a random name and some random numbers, just another off-the-shelf vehicle for whatever the buyer wanted to put in it. Capitalised at the usual two pounds, and then, suddenly, two million pounds, which wasn't usual at all. More shareholders followed, more capital, a full, functioning board of directors, accountants in place, debt finance from a bank I'd never heard of, a registered office in Mayfair – I thought back to Ballantine's *rooms*.

A change of name, just two months ago, and as I read it I realised I'd been expecting it, or something like it, *we have a deal, plenty of buyers*, it should have been obvious all along.

Surtalga Resources, Limited.

13: And Then a Little Deeper

Expecting it didn't stop it hitting me like a lightning bolt on a clear day. I sat back and just let it wash through me, and back again, each piece of the puzzle, each detail, each inevitable implication, through, and back, through, and back. There was something missing still, but I couldn't see it, not with my head the way it was, a detail hovering just out of sight. I looked up at Claire. She was standing up, watching me, that concerned look, again. She seemed calm, which was ridiculous, how could she be calm, did she realise what it all meant?

She probably didn't. She hadn't met Ballantine. She hadn't seen Freddie. I opened my mouth to tell her, but nothing came out. There was too much. Claire wasn't there, and then suddenly she was, with another glass of water and another cup of tea and another bar of chocolate. I ate, and drank. I knew it was a temporary fix, but I felt a little better.

Once I'd finished the chocolate I asked Claire to sit down, and told her everything. Freddie. Surtalga. Ballantine. The Colonel. Freddie, again. I waited, and saw her frown. The frown deepened. She started to stand, stopped, slumped back onto the sofa. I knew it was wrong but part of me was pleased it was hitting her as hard as it had hit me. A "diversion", she'd called it. Not so diverting now. I wasn't mad. I was pretty damned reasonable.

All Ballantine had wanted, he'd said, was to stop a war. And for that, it had almost been worth it, the deaths at Dovesham, the stories about me – everything up to Freddie fitted right in, collateral damage in the greater good. No, he'd assured me, no interest in the diamonds at all. All for Queen and Country. All for peace.

Liar.

It was late. Claire was wearing pyjamas and some kind of robe. I was still dressed. She'd insisted I eat something – something other than chocolate. We'd shared half a dozen fish fingers. There was nothing else in the kitchen. We lay on the sofabed, inches apart, on our backs, looking up into darkness. After a few minutes I heard her breathing ease into sleep. It didn't take me long to join her.

She was up before me, up, out and back again, fruit and milk and everything you'd expect on a normal kind of morning on a normal kind of day. And for a few minutes it did seem normal, almost, even though I was in yesterday's clothes and my head still felt like someone had slid a bit of smudged glass between me and the rest of the world. There had been sirens in the night, but sirens were normal, and they hadn't been close enough to keep me awake. But then, while we sat on the sofa with our bowls of cereal like a normal kind of couple, Claire switched on the TV and she gasped and I shouted "What the hell?" because right there on the screen was a picture of my flat – *my flat* – a mile or so up the road, with smoke coming out of it.

The footage was dark, taken during the night. It cut, suddenly, to a daytime shot, same angle, same flat, or what was left of it. Claire picked up the remote control and hit the volume.

" – body recovered from the second floor flat, where the fire is thought to have started. The occupants of the flats below were woken by neighbours and managed to escape before the fire spread. Emergency services were on the scene soon after, but found part of the roof had collapsed and blocked their way into the second floor flat. It wasn't until six o'clock this morning that officers were able to gain safe access to the flat, where they found one body, badly burned and assumed to be the flat's occupant. London Fire Brigades are expected to make a statement later this morning."

The picture switched to the studio and a report on house prices. Claire muted the volume and turned to me. We stared at one another. Rock bottom, I'd thought, on the bus. *I couldn't go home.* At least I'd had a home to go to. I looked down, at my clothes, the same jeans, T-shirt and jumper I'd been wearing yesterday, and saw suddenly a wardrobe full of keen-young-lawyer suits and ties and cufflinks and Church's shoes. Just smouldering rags now, if there was anything left at all. It didn't matter. It wasn't like they fitted me any more, mind or body. I started to laugh.

"What's so funny?" she asked.

"Don't suppose you've got anything I can wear?"

We finished our breakfast and spoke about random, silly things, because there was no point talking about anything else, but eventually Claire put down her spoon and said it anyway.

"This was Ballantine, right?"

"The fire? Must be. But the dead body – no idea. The only thing I'm sure of is it's not me."

"Might be handy if certain people think it is you, though." I nodded. She had that frown on again. "Could it be one of them? Maybe they messed up?"

I thought about it for a moment.

"Pretty difficult to mess up that badly in an empty flat."

She nodded.

"But if it's not you, and it's not them, who the hell is it?"

There she had me.

We slid back into nothing again, silence, TV, clattering about in the tiny space of her flat and trying not to bump into one another. I went to wash my face, and when I came back she was frowning again.

"What are we going to do?"

I'd been wondering the very same thing, but I hadn't got any closer to an answer.

"If you're lucky, Ballantine'll still think he's got you."

"Do I look lucky to you, Claire?"

She lapsed into silence. I remembered something from the past – from yesterday, that was all, even if it felt like history.

"The Scourge."

"What?"

"Have you heard of something called The Scourge?"

She stared, for a moment, and slowly shook her head. I sank back into the sofa. I'd figured out a lot, in the last twenty-four hours, learned a lot of facts, but the fact that stood out clearest of all was me, screwed. There were people who wanted me dead, capable people, people who'd stop at nothing to get me there. They might think I was dead already, but I doubted that would last. There was an art to staying dead and popping back up at the right moment. Nwosu had it. Ballantine, too. Ilic might have thought he had it, but he'd been wrong. If someone like Ilic hadn't mastered it, the odds on me making it into next week didn't look great.

Claire had stood up and wandered over to another pile of papers I hadn't noticed, in the kitchen next to the toaster.

"The Scourge, did you say?"

I nodded.

"I thought it sounded familiar. Look at this."

It was a printout of an article from 2005. A magazine I'd never heard of, politics, current affairs. The Iraqi insurgency. There were interviews with politicians in the US and Baghdad, with soldiers and rebels. One particular group was switching its attention to sabotage – power stations, road, telecoms – but not, apparently, the oil refineries that had just reopened in Kirkuk. They'd tried, half a dozen times, and they'd given up.

"We couldn't get close. Not even within a mile," the rebel leader had said. "The target is too hard. The Scourge controls it. We choose targets that have value, but there is no use dying for nothing."

The Scourge controls it.

"Was there anything else?" I asked. She shook her head. *Iraq Oil Services Limited.* Ballantine, Poulter, *they* were The Scourge. It was too much to be a coincidence, wasn't it? I couldn't be sure. Not sure enough to pin my life on it, anyway.

"We need to put this out there," I said, and I could see her looking at me like she knew what I was about to say and she knew it was nonsense. I didn't pause long enough for her to say it.

"Hear me out, Claire. These guys are killers. We've got all this stuff here, and it might not be enough to swing a jury, but it'll be enough to get the police interested, and the newspapers, and get them thinking maybe someone should look after this Sam Williams and make sure he isn't shot or set fire to before he's had his turn in the witness box."

Claire was slowly shaking her head. I didn't care.

"And bloody hell, Claire, you're a journalist, aren't you? You could do this. You and Olivia Miles and Rachel –"

"Who's Rachel?" she asked, suddenly alert.

"Just a friend. PR. Knows her stuff. But between you and her you could get all this out there. They wouldn't touch me then. They couldn't."

She was shaking her head again.

"That's rubbish, Sam, and you know it."

I started to say something, to ask her what her brilliant alternative was, but she'd decided she had the floor.

"It's too big. There's too much at stake here. They killed Ilic with half of Fleet Street camped outside the door. What makes you think you'll be any safer?"

There wasn't a lot I could say to that. And she wasn't finished, either.

"And what the hell gives you the right to tell me what I should be writing about, anyway?"

This time I wasn't keeping my mouth shut.

"Sorry, Claire. I didn't realise. Only the Colonels and the Foundations get to set your agenda, right?"

It was low and I knew it, but I didn't care. She looked at me like I was something she'd found on her shoe.

"Do you really think this is the only story out there? Just because it's got you in it? Do you think that makes it more important than everything else?"

I shrugged. I did, as it happened, but not because it had me in it. Because it *was* more important than everything else. People had died. People were still dying. Hadn't she been listening to a word I said?

"It's not, Sam. It's not the only thing going on. And it's not the most important, either."

"Oh yes. Sorry. I forgot. Your big investigation. Your long-term project. What was that all about, again?"

This time I couldn't keep the disbelief out of my voice. She stepped back, as if the words had hit her physically, and hurt. And then she turned, walked a couple of steps into the kitchen, ducked down and disappeared into a drawer I'd assumed was full of cutlery or tea-towels or trendy oriental spices.

When she came back up a moment later she was holding some papers. She walked back – stormed, I'd have said, but it's difficult to storm anywhere if you've only got a couple of metres to do it in – and shoved the papers into my hand.

They were photographs. Flimsy, home-made printouts of photographs on poor-quality paper, but that didn't matter. There were five photographs, and each one showed a different dead girl. Each girl was naked, and each looked to have died violently, and even though I'd spent days going through the records of people like Robbie Evans a decade back, and I'd seen Freddie dead, actually dead, in front of me, not fifteen hours earlier, there was something about those cheap scraps of printer paper that put the bodies right there, in Claire's flat on a normal North London morning, scattered among the clothes and the dirty plates.

Claire was talking. I hadn't noticed.

"These girls were all murdered, Sam."

I nodded.

"Five different girls, three different murderers, and they're all behind bars and the chances are they'll die there."

"So – what?"

"The thing is, Sam, they all have something in common. More than just the way they died. They were all brought into this country by the same people, people who lied to them and beat them and then handed them over to the men who killed them."

I nodded again. "People trafficking," I said, surprised at the sound of my own voice. She carried on like I hadn't spoken.

"They knew the girls would die, Sam. They knew it, and they handed them over anyway, and they're still doing it, still luring girls to London and letting them die for a couple of thousand quid. So yes, Sam, I know it's big, what you've found, I know it's important, I know people are dead, but for me, this is bigger."

"So this is your investigation?"

She nodded.

"Why don't you just let the police deal with it?"

A harmless enough question, I thought, as questions go. I was wrong. She exploded.

"The police? The bloody police? Are you joking? The police couldn't give a fuck! They've got the killers. As far as they're concerned, it's job done."

After my recent experience with Roarkes I wasn't inclined to defend the police. I waited for her to go on, and after a moment she did, calmer now, but still filled with an intensity I hadn't seen in her before.

"I gave up on the bloody police months ago. I'm a journalist. I don't need the damned police."

"So, what, you've been doing all this in your spare time?"

She shook her head.

"No. I think the editor likes me. Or maybe he just fancies me. I don't really care. And he's got a nose for a story, and when he thinks he's got a story he's like a dog with a bone, he won't let it go. Hence the Sam Williams article."

She threw in an apologetic shrug.

"He told me to run with it, with these girls, take as long as I liked, keep on digging, and he'd throw a few easy stories my way to keep me on the page."

"Like the D-listers."

She nodded.

"Like the D-listers. And Dovesham."

There was a pause, during which my eyes were drawn back to the photographs, still in my hand, still giving me the same siren song they must have been giving Claire since she'd first seen them. I coughed and looked away and back up at her.

"So did you find anything?"

She shrugged. "A little. Something and nothing. This has been going on more than two years, Sam, and it's only just beginning."

She held out a hand and I gave her the photographs. She was right. Ballantine, the Colonel, Nwosu, it was all big. But it wasn't the only thing going on. Not that that was much help to me.

"So what do you think I should do, Claire?"

She stood there and shook her head.

"Come on, Claire. You've done all this digging. You've dug up the Colonel and the Foundation. You've got to have a plan."

She didn't have a plan, of course, but she did have something else to show me. She walked back to the kitchen – it took about a second – leafed through the pile of papers by the toaster, and picked out a handful. "Look at these," she said, and handed them to me.

"That's him," she said, but I was already staring open-mouthed at the first picture she'd passed me. Old newspaper clippings, going back decades, by the look of it, right up to the month before last. Cabinet Ministers, CEOs, Chief Constables, Managing Editors. They were all captioned, *"Colonel William Poulter with The Minister for X"*, *"Lord Y, Sir Richard Z and Colonel Poulter at the International Conference for Q"*, *"Colonel William Poulter and Adam M at the launch of N Magazine"*. The captions weren't really necessary, these were famous faces with household names attached to them, but what had me still staring, still unable to speak, for a moment, until I let everything out in an enormous gasp, was Colonel Poulter.

I'd seen him before. Over the years he'd moved from beard to moustache to both to neither, and back again, several times, but the creases round the eyes were always there, the same quiet, shy smile, the same air of someone at the edge of things, watching, taking notes.

Colonel Poulter was Jenkins.

That settled it. I couldn't go public, not again, not with Colonel William Poulter sitting there like a spider, spinning away wherever he saw an eye for a killing, figuratively speaking, but if anyone happened to wander into those webs and get stuck, quite happy to make that killing a reality. I couldn't move a leg without getting it torn off. I sat there, Claire sitting beside me, silent, for five, ten minutes, and I couldn't see a way out for the life of me.

When it hit me, it seemed so obvious I couldn't believe I hadn't thought of it already. There was one man who could back me up, not that he'd want to, but he was all I had. He wasn't in England, but that didn't really matter, because England was getting too hot for me anyway. I replayed the half-conversation I'd overheard in my mind. *"In Surtalga… gone to ground…our own people out there shortly."*

I stood up so suddenly Claire thought something was wrong, but it wasn't. It was an idea, an alternative, another shit one, sure, but at least it was something. I told her. She thought I was joking.

"Surtalga?"

"Yup."

"Right, so you're going to leave England and go somewhere you can find Poulter's men, who are trying to kill you, and Nwosu, who's already pointed a gun at you, and the Frentoi, who want to kill everyone?"

I couldn't help myself.

"It's just Frentoi, Claire. There's no 'the'."

She shook her head and gave me that look of disgust usually reserved for flashers or people who let their dogs shit in the park and don't pick it up. "Sorry," I said, and she shrugged.

"You'll get yourself killed."

I pointed to the TV.

"I'm not that safe round here."

London was sewn up so tight that even if by some miracle I stayed alive long enough to find any evidence there, I wouldn't be able to do anything with it. She'd told me that herself. She was nodding now, thoughtful.

"The real story's out there," I said, "in Surtalga, with Nwosu, and his diamonds," and she nodded again.

"I could stay here," she said. "Carry on digging."

I nodded.

"And you could bugger off to Africa, get a bullet in your brain, and I wouldn't have to worry about you any more."

I started to argue, then stopped. She wasn't angry. She was smiling.

"So you'll find this Chima, persuade him not to shoot you, and drag him back to London to testify in court?"

She was still smiling, but she had a point. And I had an answer.

"Maybe, Claire. Better than running around London looking behind me for a fire every five minutes. And if that doesn't work, well, Poulter and Ballantine are out there, or their people are. They'll find Nwosu, get their diamonds. A week, he said. And then it'll all be over."

She was looking at me like I'd just told her I could fly.

"You want Poulter to win?"

I shrugged.

"It's not my war."

"OK," she said, "say he does win. Do you really think he's going to be happy with you walking around knowing everything you know?"

I opened my mouth to reply, but I didn't have anything to reply with. She went on.

"Look, Sam, you're probably right. You probably should go, find this Nwosu, speak to him, try to get him back here, but that's only because between the two of us we can't think of anything else that won't get you killed. But don't you think for one second this is all going to take care of itself, because one thing I am sure of is if Poulter wins, you're dead."

She was right, again. I started to say something to that effect but she wasn't looking at me. She was looking at the TV.

My flat was on, again, the same shots from earlier, burning by night, black and smoking in the morning. Claire turned the sound back on.

" – development in the North London blaze we've been reporting on this morning. Police are now anxious to speak to this man in connection with the incident."

The police had a hundred different photos of me, court and police station ID, the good press shot, the one Olivia had used, from outside court the day we'd freed Trawden, so there was no reason for them to have chosen this particular one other than spite. Standing outside a pub with a cigarette in one hand and a bottle of lager in the other, laughing like an idiot at something someone out of shot had said. It was five years old, at least, more hair and less fat, but you'd know it was still me. No idea how they'd got hold of it. Someone's Facebook account, no doubt. Zuckerberg was doing everyone's work for them these days.

"The man seen in this image, Samuel Williams, is the registered occupant of the second-floor flat in which the fire is thought to have started. We have been told that the body found inside the flat was that of this man, Maurice Harwood."

It took me a moment to place him, because in the photo the hair was shorter and there was no grin. But the glasses were the same. Henderson's *associate*. He'd been waiting outside my flat, when was it, the night before last?

He'd said he'd be back. Must have got inside, it wouldn't have been difficult, I'd never bothered to keep the place particularly secure. And then – then what?

"The police are, we understand, treating the fire as deliberate, and have opened a murder investigation."

Ballantine's men had come to find me, and they'd found someone in my flat. Maybe they thought it was me. Maybe they knew it wasn't. Either way, my guess was the pathologist would be spotting a neck injury sustained before the fire was started.

My face flashed up on the screen again. There was a familiar voice in the background. Detective Inspector Roarkes, of all people, warning the public to be cautious and not to approach me as there were reasons to believe I might be dangerous. I started to object before I remembered Roarkes wasn't there to hear me. And anyway, it was true. I was dangerous. Ask Maurice Harwood. Ask Freddie Harmsworth.

Roarkes had finished and the next story was up. I glanced over at Claire. She was looking at me. The voice of the anchor droned on. A hospital closure in East London. Claire was still looking at me, frowning, chewing that lower lip. Finally she spoke.

"How are you going to get there, Sam? It's not just Ballantine, now. The police are after you. How the hell are you going to get out of the country?"

Anything you want, pal, you just ask. Was I desperate enough now?

I thought I probably was.

I grinned at her.

"You don't want to know."

PART 3: Skin

14: Best-Laid Plans

I wanted to call her the moment I was off the plane, but there were signs everywhere, in a dozen languages, with pictures of mobile phones with big red lines through them, and in case anyone got the impression that the rules weren't there to be followed, there were a lot of bored-looking men lounging around with guns. I waited till the signs ran out.

"Hi Pete," she said, when she heard my voice. "How's everything?"

"All good, all good. Morning classes done, thank Christ. Thinking about when I can get down to London and see you again."

"Well, Pete, I'm a busy girl, you know. But I'm sure I can make some time for you."

Maloney's tech guy – Maloney had a guy for everything, a security guy, a documents guy, a money guy – had assured me the phone was "solid". I'd stared at him blankly until he'd explained what that meant.

"People like these guys what are after you, they'll be listening to everything you say, right?"

I'd nodded. The moment they suspected Claire might be involved, they'd be bugging her office phone. And she couldn't risk giving anything away, because if that *suspected* became any more certain, she'd be waking up on fire with her neck at a funny angle.

"So first thing is, you need a code. You can figure that one out between you. But also, if they see she's got calls coming in from bongo-bongo land or wherever the fuck it is you're going, they're gonna be thinking '*this is a bit fucking iffy, isn't it?*', and if that happens, well…"

He did the thing with a finger sliding across his throat and the usual gurgling noises. It might have been because of who he was and who he worked for, but it seemed quite realistic.

"So," he continued, "we're gonna have to make it look like they're coming from somewhere else, aren't we?"

And he'd given me this phone. Looked like a normal mobile, a bit old-fashioned, but I've never been particularly cutting-edge anyway. And wherever I was, wherever the phone was, it wouldn't mean a thing because it would always look like it was calling from Scotland.

"Edinburgh, to be exact. I forgot the codes for Glasgow."

As it happened, Edinburgh was perfect. Claire had studied journalism there. One of her old friends was now teaching the course. Pete Haslam, he was called, and it wasn't too much of a stretch to imagine they'd met again recently, hooked up, started spending a lot of time on the phone. The tech guy and the documents guy had got into Vodafone's billing network, which really should have been beyond the capabilities of a bunch of drug-dealers working out of a couple of council flats in North-East London, but that wasn't any of my business. They'd rigged it so that if anyone looked, this phone was registered to Pete Haslam. If they looked any closer they'd find the payments were being made in Tottenham, but we hoped it wouldn't get that far.

Maloney was shutting up shop, he told me, going straight, something he'd been planning for years. *Going straight.* I tried to grab hold of that and twist it so I could feel better about the people I was working with. It didn't work. But then, it didn't really matter how I felt about it, either. It wasn't like London was awash with people begging to help me out.

"If you're shutting up shop, what the hell do you need all these people for?" I'd asked, somewhat ungratefully, and he'd looked at me like I was an idiot, which, it turned out, I was. Maloney was king round here. He couldn't just walk off into the sunset and lock the door behind him. There would be war. An orderly transition, he said. That was what he was working on these days. He'd kept just what he needed to wind things down. Hence "all these people".

The operation was still impressive enough. If this was wind-down then full swing must have been quite something. I'd been there two days, waiting for them to sort out my tickets, my passport, my phone. "We can do it quicker, when we have to," he'd said, "but the quicker you are, the more likely you're going to make a mistake. And if the people you're hiding from are half as professional as you say they are, they'll be on you the moment you make that mistake."

I'd been happy to wait. A week, Ballantine had said on the phone. "*We'll have it within a week.*" Another day or two wouldn't kill me. I hoped.

Maloney made things as comfortable for me as he could. He still owed me, and unlike Pierre it wasn't just an overblown sense of gratitude for the right bribe at the right time. I'd got Maloney acquitted, but I'd done a little more than that, too.

The fact was, as Maloney liked to boast, he was a drugs man. He didn't do robbery, or prostitution, or weapons, or anything else, and he made sure the drugs were clean and the dealers were cleaner. He walked around like he was the Robin Hood of N4 and the fact that he was usually surrounded by half a dozen men who made Mike Tyson look like Linus from Peanuts meant no one was going to argue with him. He was proud of himself, was

Maloney, and even though I didn't really buy it, because you don't get to be the biggest dealer in North London without treading on a few toes, still, the nice-guy act made me a bit happier about having someone like him as a client. This, of course, was back when I was still expecting the next Birmingham Six to walk through my door every time it opened.

And then a few months after I'd got him off, I learned something that made me a little less happy after all. A cop I knew – one of my regular sources, but that didn't make him any less reliable than the rest of them – came to me with a story about one of Maloney's people in Blackhorse Lane. This guy – Hassan, his name was – he didn't seem to be following the rules. He was pimping, a dozen women at least, and when he wasn't happy with what they brought in he was expressing his feelings with his fists. The local cops wouldn't touch him because he paid them too well. No one else would touch him because as far as they were concerned, he was Maloney's man, and they didn't want to tangle with Maloney.

I sat on it for a few days. Either Maloney was a liar and the Robin Hood act was just that, or he was for real and Hassan was either very brave or very, very stupid. In the end I decided I believed Maloney, or at least, I wanted to. I called him up, arranged to meet, told him what I'd heard. Maloney nodded and looked serious and, as more of the story came out, increasingly furious. I'd had enough liars sit in my office and tell me they were innocent to spot an act, I thought, and Maloney was for real.

"Thanks," he'd said, suddenly casual and calm as you like. "I'll take care of it." And then he'd got up and walked off. When he was a few yards away – this was in the middle of Finsbury Park, crowds milling around, teenagers, families, locals and tourists – he'd turned to me and said "I owe you one, Sam," and then he'd repeated the thing he'd said back when we'd first walked out of court together earlier that year. "Anything you want, pal."

He looked like he meant it, too.

The whole thing should have had me feeling pretty good about myself, really, and for about five minutes, I did. Hassan was an evil son of a bitch, and something had to be done about him. But that was all it lasted, about five minutes, and then I heard that *I'll take care of it* again, and it didn't sound casual or calm at all. For the next few years, every time a body was fished out of the Thames or dug up in the Essex marshes, I'd feel sick and miserable and certainly not good about myself. Eventually I filed Hassan among the things I wasn't going to think about, and the sickness and misery grew too blunt to get through. Unless something brought it back into sharp relief. Like seeing Maloney.

So that was it, I decided. No more Maloney. There was too much attached to Maloney to get involved again. And now I was sleeping in a camp bed in a box room in a flat and it might not have been his name on the rent book, but it was Maloney's flat all right.

The police were still looking for me, he said, and since the story was as dead as Maurice Harwood I thought it best not to ask him where he was getting his information. The *Sun* had a line on the Serbs – Olivia's line – my line, as it happened – and the fact that she was getting stonewalled everywhere she turned only made the whole thing seem more intriguing. But that was just the Serbs. It didn't involve Sam Williams, which was better for me and certainly better for the *Sun*, now that Sam Williams was considered about as reliable as Baron Munchhausen. Meanwhile, a fire in an obscure corner of a sixteenth century Oxford quadrangle had been marked down as a tragic accident, caused, the authorities presumed, by the persistent pipe-smoking of the fire's sole victim. Freddie's obituary appeared in the Times the day I departed, and I read it thirty thousand feet over the Atlantic. *A giant of a man...self-imposed seclusion...no published work for a quarter of a century...still revered for his unique understanding of modern conflict.* He'd quit the pipe. *Not as young as I once was,* he'd said. And *Is it worth it?*

I'm fine, that's what I'd told Claire, in our hastily-contrived and extremely limited code. *I'm fine, and I've landed.* And in return: *everything's OK here. Nothing significant to report,* which meant she hadn't had any more luck than Olivia Miles on the disappearing Serbs, and nothing out of the Dovesham security man, Connolly, who we both thought might be some kind of route in to the men at the top, and someone Claire could be expected to contact without arousing suspicion. The way we'd said it, it sounded innocent enough, I thought. Again – hoped.

And I was fine, but it wasn't like I had a plan. I had a hotel booked, and a vague idea of where I might go, which was to the offices of the political wing of what remained of the People's Army of Mirandano, which was now known, fairly predictably, as the People's Party of Surtalga. I also had an annoyingly persistent beggar by my side offering the best accommodation, transport and sight-seeing services in excellent English as I wandered through the grandly-named Ybaddli International Airport. I could see why he'd picked me. No one else in the airport looked like they might need his advice. I was in jeans, T-shirt, sunglasses. The other passengers wore suits or uniforms and the air of people who knew precisely where they were going and how they'd get there.

I had a driving licence in my new name, Edward Allinson, but Maloney had cautioned against hiring a car unless I absolutely had to. All the major car hire companies used facial recognition software these days, apparently. So did the airports, of course, but I didn't have any choice there.

I was the only person at the taxi rank, and eight yellow taxis that might have been called "classic" in the eighties lined up patiently as if they'd been waiting there all week. Ybaddli International Airport wasn't particularly busy these days, if it ever had been. Three flights each week from Paris and Riyadh, one from Amsterdam, and flights on alternate weeks from London, Mumbai and Kuala Lumpur. I'd have been surprised if a single one was more than half-full.

The beggar was still with me, still talking, passing something small and grey from one hand to another. I was trying to look like someone who'd been here before, who knew where he was going, but I could tell it wasn't working. I stood for a moment at the terminal exit, just by the front of the rank, expecting the lead taxi to drive up. Nothing happened. I walked the few yards to the taxi and saw it was empty. The beggar was trying to tell me something, pointing back the way we had come, he had a car, he had an excellent car, I didn't want these taxis, and see, there were no drivers.

As if summoned by this slur on their existence they suddenly appeared, four of them, somehow grinning at me and shouting at the beggar at the same time. He held his ground for a moment, started to argue back, thought better of it and retreated. I watched him disappear back into the terminal building with a curious feeling of regret.

Once he'd gone they turned on each other. I'd assumed the car at the front was the one I'd be taking, but it didn't work like that. It took a few minutes of shouting and some complex negotiation before one emerged as the winner. I wasn't going far. I hoped the fare would be worth whatever he'd paid for it.

He was heavy on the horn, the gas, the brakes, anything that could turn a short drive through the near-empty Ybaddli streets into something you might not expect to survive. We were moving too fast to see much, but Ybaddli didn't offer a great deal to please the eye anyway: dust, metal shacks, chickens, men in uniform, men out of uniform but with guns, still, silent women. No children. We were outside the Majestic twenty minutes after we'd left the airport.

The Majestic Hotel was out of place. It didn't live up to the name, but it came a hell of lot closer than I'd expected. Real walls, clean and white, real windows, four whole floors, a man in a uniform (but no gun) rushing out through revolving doors to collect my luggage and doing a decent job of hiding his disappointment when he saw the one small suitcase I'd brought with me. The room wasn't bad, either, a TV with three American news channels that actually worked, a bed, a ceiling fan that turned slowly and didn't move a whole lot of air, but still.

I checked the time and saw it was getting late. The People's Party would have to wait another day. The hotel had food, not the food on the menu, but something I could eat, alone, quietly, in the deserted hotel dining room.

"Is there anyone else staying here?" I asked the waiter, and he grinned, and shook his head, and nodded. *There wasn't*, I figured, but suddenly there was a flurry of activity in the lobby and three men walked in. Two black, the other white, all in suits. They strolled over to the table nearest me as if they owned it, glanced briefly towards me, and ignored me for the rest of the meal.

It wasn't much of a meal. Small gobbets of lean meat. "Lamb," said the waiter, and winked. *Just a facial tick*, I thought. Hopefully. The "lamb" came with an equally unidentifiable starch, fat grains of something that looked like rice but exploded in the mouth like a tiny salty grenade. No alcohol. I'd asked the waiter when I'd arrived. There was, after all, a bar, although the racks behind were all empty. He'd shaken his head, looked out of the window and back to me, horrified, and then suddenly relaxed and touched the side of his nose. The fear I understood. Frentoi. I should never have asked, really.

The tap on the nose finally made sense as I got up to leave. The waiter was standing by the dining room door, comedy-furtive, eyes whipping round the room, which seemed unnecessary as there were only three people in it and they were all sat at the same table. They were eating the "lamb" too, I noticed.

"Here. They have beer. Whisky. My brother he take you."

He passed me a piece of paper with an address on it, and tilted his head backwards, towards a man standing beside the revolving doors and smiling at me. I thought about it for a moment. They could be planning on abducting me, robbing me, killing me, but they didn't really need to take me out of the hotel to do that. And anyway, I'd made a point of tipping well, figuring that would be an incentive to keep me happy. I wouldn't be tipping so well if I wasn't breathing.

Sod it, I thought. I needed a drink. I'd take the risk.

The waiter hadn't been lying, at least. It took five minutes in the brother's car, which had taken longer than that to start, moved like it was trying to go in all four directions at once and felt uncomfortably like the ancient evolutionary ancestor of the taxi I'd taken earlier. The place was just another shack, dark inside, half a dozen men drinking alone, no women, no conversation, just pointing, and paying, and drinking. It was humid enough outside, but inside it was even worse, dank and heavy with an air of misery and desperation and men who knew they shouldn't be here but couldn't be anywhere else. I needed a drink. The rest of them looked like they needed it more. The whisky was alarmingly clear and didn't look like the kind of thing I'd have picked at home. The beer was brown and thick and I didn't need to try it to know I wouldn't like it. Whisky was the better choice, and I tried not to flinch when the man doing the pouring called it Scotch.

It wasn't as bad as I'd expected, or at least it went down smooth enough for me not to worry too much what it tasted like. I nodded to the barman and he poured another. There wasn't a bar, really, just a few tiny round tables, half a dozen chairs, a man at the back with a long table and twenty or so bottles lined up on it. I looked around, my eyes finally adjusting to the gloom. There were only four drinkers now, all black, and two of them in suits. No one was looking at me, no one was looking at anyone else, at anything at all except whatever it was he was drinking. That suited me. Everyone I'd come across so far seemed to speak English, and I didn't want to talk.

Except, after the fourth "Scotch", I decided I did want to talk after all. I felt in my pocket and stood up. It wasn't as straightforward as I'd thought it would be. I held onto the table and tried again. I was tired. The whisky was stronger than I'd thought. I stepped outside and dialled the number. She answered on the fourth ring.

"Claire," I said. It was just one syllable, but even I could tell I'd slurred it.

A moment's silence. Could be the delay as my voice travelled from West Africa to London, and hers made the trip back, I thought. Could be her trying to figure out what the hell to say to a drunk on the phone in the middle of the night. I thought it was the middle of night. I wasn't sure. Could be her trying to figure out who I was.

"Pete?"

"What?" I said, and stopped for a moment, trying to remember what was familiar about "Pete". That was it. I was Pete.

"Yeah, yeah, that's me. I'm Pete," I said. I wondered briefly why she'd called me, and then I remembered I'd called her.

"Are you OK, Pete?"

"Yeah, yeah," I said. "Fine. The shit I have to drink here, Claire, and they call it Scotch. Fucking liars. And don't get me started on the food."

"Are you sure you're OK?"

She sounded concerned. I couldn't think why, I'd just told her I was fine. I'd forgotten why I'd decided I needed to speak to her. It couldn't have been about the whisky.

"Yes, I told you. I'm fine. I'm just drunk, OK?"

"OK, Pete," she said. "Let's talk in the morning."

Now she didn't sound concerned, she sounded annoyed. Well screw her.

"Yeah, fine," I replied, and killed the call. It was all fine for her, sitting there in London with pubs and proper food and whatever she wanted just a phone call away. She should try being out here. The thought passed through my mind, hazily, that I'd already dragged her further into this mess than either of us had wanted to, but it didn't make me feel any kinder. Screw her.

My head was starting to hurt and I didn't think I wanted another drink. There were two bright lights beside me, a car, the brother, I thought, maybe. It wasn't, it was someone else, but he said "Taxi?" hopefully, and I said "Majestic Hotel, please," and he opened a door. As I slid into the back I caught a glimpse of something lying on the passenger seat, a small, grey metal disk, and something stirred in my brain, briefly, something woke and tapped me on the shoulder and whispered something in my ear, but whatever it was, I was too tired and too drunk and too angry to care, and thirty seconds after I heard the key turn and the engine fire up at the first attempt, I was asleep.

15: Back in the Metal Box

I came to as the car shuddered to a halt. I opened my eyes. It was still dark, I was lying across the back of the car and my head hadn't stopped hurting. I closed my eyes again. I heard a door open and close, and some more thuds around the front of the car, and felt a slight movement in the air as the door to my left opened. I tried to move. My body didn't want to help. Hands reached across, pulled me sideways, dragged me out, took my weight, heaved me slowly and painfully towards the hotel entrance. I wondered if the man in the uniform was still on duty at this time of night, of day, whenever the hell it was. I opened my eyes. There was no sign of him, which was a shame because I could tell the man currently taking most of my weight would have liked some help, and I certainly wasn't in a position to provide it. There was no sign of anything, actually, but this was Surtalga, there was a war on, or at least a bit of a war. Even somewhere like the Majestic would struggle to maintain twenty-four hours electricity. They should have a generator, I thought, a generator would help, plus the man in the uniform, because if there was light and another pair of hands the guy half-carrying me would have spotted the ditch or pit or pothole or whatever it was that caused him to stumble, wouldn't have had to let me go to stop him hitting the ground without his own hands to protect him, wouldn't have left me lying there with my eyes open for just the right number of seconds to realise this wasn't the Majestic after all.

"Where are we?" I asked, but his only reply was to haul me back up and get on with the business of dragging me towards – towards wherever it was he was dragging me, I hadn't seen a thing except stars and a glow on the horizon and closer at hand, some low structures that could have been just about anything bar the Eiffel Tower or the Majestic Hotel. I tried to shake his arm off, but either he was stronger than I'd guessed, or I was drunker. He carried on dragging, and after a minute I gave up trying to fight him, because even if I got the guy off of me, where the hell would I go?

I don't know how long it took. Two minutes, twenty minutes, step after painful step with the pain in my head gradually turning to fear and the whisky mixing with lamb into a horrible, volatile compound that felt heavy enough to stop me moving at all and light enough to explode out of my mouth the moment I stopped concentrating on keeping it down. However long it was, I could tell it was coming to an end when my left foot finally came down on something solid and smooth rather than sliding on dirt. My right shoulder brushed up against something cold. Metal. The arms holding me up suddenly weren't there, without any kind of a warning, and I was on my back on something soft, a sofa, maybe, or a bed, and grateful at least for that.

I opened my eyes. Orange light, battery-powered lamps, probably. A low, corrugated roof, another one of those shacks. Maybe I'd been right after all, about the waiter and his brother, they'd just decided to let me have a few drinks before they got hold of me and did whatever it was they were going to do to me.

To me. Whatever it was, they were going to do it to me, and I couldn't just lie back and let it happen. I closed my eyes, again, because if I didn't I thought I'd pass out, pushed my elbows down, tried to force the rest of me up. Whatever I was pushing against was too soft. Something was going to happen to me, almost certainly something bad, and there wasn't a thing in the world I could do about it.

I opened my eyes again. I wasn't going to be sick. It shouldn't have mattered, really, because I was in some shack in the middle of nowhere in a country where life wasn't worth much more than your next meal, and nobody knew I was there (except Claire, and Maloney, and his people, but no one else, none of my real friends or my family or anyone like that, all of whom would have seen my face on the news, and the fire, and wondered what the hell was going on), and I was helpless, and I'd been brought here by someone who clearly didn't want to buy me breakfast and discuss current affairs or classical music, so whether or not I was going to be sick should have been so far down my list of priorities that it didn't register at all, but bizarrely, the fact that I was now confident the whisky and lamb were going to stay in place sent that same shock of energy through me that I'd always felt when I'd switched off my brain and raced past a speed camera or a police car, back in the days when I'd bothered driving anywhere, and looked in the mirror and seen just darkness, no flash of white or bolt of blue light, or when I'd sat down tired and hungover in some high-ceilinged hall full of shivering students and looked at the questions and felt the answers bursting through the veins in my arm to the fingers holding the pen, or when I'd said the wrong thing to the wrong person, in a pub, or a club, or just on the street, drunk and stupid until the moment I realised I was going to have the shit kicked out of me, and then seen that person turn away, having misheard or not heard or just not really cared.

I was invincible.

I wasn't going to be sick, so there was nothing stopping me from levering myself up and barging past whoever might try to get in my way and out of the shack and into the open air where I'd just run and keep running until I found myself at the Majestic Hotel, Ybaddli, where I would be greeted by a man in a clean, white uniform, take a shower, switch on the TV, and collapse into a satisfied, invincible sleep under clean, white linen on a comfortable bed.

I closed my eyes and prepared myself for all this. I opened them again, and there was no roof and less light. Instead, there was a face, inches from mine, breath smelling of mint, dark skin, a beard, grey hair.

"What do you want?" he said, in clear, unaccented English, and it struck me as an odd thing for him to say, since he was the one who'd brought me here when I'd clearly and unambiguously asked to be taken to the Majestic.

"What do *you* want?" I replied. I was trying to sound tough, unafraid, nonchalant, but even as the words left my mouth I realised I sounded like an idiot who couldn't do anything more than repeat what had just been said to him.

"Do you know who I am?" he said, and for just a second, that was even stranger, because how the hell was I supposed to know who this stranger was who'd just picked me up outside a bar somewhere in the middle of nowhere and driven me somewhere else in the middle of nowhere?

Just a second, though, because that was how long it took for everything to come together, the grey hair, the eyes, the metal disk.

I nodded, and said, "Yes, you're Chima," and something in my face must have made it obvious what was about to happen, because he stood up and stepped away.

I looked down, and back up at him, and was violently, painfully sick.

Being sick was over fast, and all the tiredness, all the

stupidity, all the drunkenness took its leave at the same time. I was standing up, leaning against one corner of the shack while Chima Nwosu cleared up my half-digested lamb with a bucket of water and a couple of unidentifiable rags.

I was in trouble, I wasn't invincible, and no amount of one-liners were going to fix this one.

I couldn't get a fix on Nwosu. He hadn't killed me yet, but it didn't mean he wasn't going to. If I'd wanted to make a good impression, vomiting all over his shack probably wasn't the thing to do. But I couldn't let him go on, cleaning, his back to me, the silence growing. If he was thinking of killing me, I needed to remind him I was a real person. I needed to get under his skin. I didn't have the faintest idea how.

"You were the beggar."

He looked up, confusion on his face.

"At the airport."

He nodded, walked to the entrance and threw the water and the rags out into the darkness. He didn't care if I was a real person. The People's Army of Mirandano had killed plenty of real people in their day. I doubted three decades as Colonel Poulter's guest had softened him. He pointed to the sofa, which I'd somehow missed when I'd redecorated the floor. I sat back down.

"What do you want?" he said, again, and my brain did one of those *clicks*, those moments where it feels like you've shifted track, subtly but significantly, and everything you were thinking before was almost but not quite right. What I was thinking before was that Chima Nwosu had got hold of me and might well kill me, and that was it. What I remembered now was that Chima Nwosu was the reason I'd come to this godforsaken shithole of a country in the first place, and the fact that he'd found me before I spent all my money and starved or had to go home and got killed by the Colonel, the fact that he'd found me before the Colonel had found him, was a stroke of extraordinary good fortune. The fear was still there, of course. I pushed it back down, under the good fortune.

What do you want, he'd asked. I thought about it for a moment. Safety, from Poulter, who wanted me dead, from the police, who wanted me for the fire. From Henderson, who probably wasn't best pleased about his burnt-out associate, but I doubted Nwosu could do much about that. Vindication, proof I wasn't a liar, that the stories going round about me weren't true, or not completely true. I thought back to the beginning. Exposure. Success. Right now exposure and success were the last things on my mind. Funny how your priorities change when you find out people want you dead.

But it was a good enough place to start, the beginning, Dovesham, who I was and why I was there, because it led neatly and irrevocably to everything else.

So that's where I began.

Chima Nwosu nodded a lot. That's what I noticed, as I told him everything that had happened to me since Dovesham. He nodded when I told him about Ballantine, about Freddie, everything I'd heard about Nwosu himself, he nodded when I told him about Claire and Olivia Miles, although I didn't see how he could know anything about them. He gave nothing away, no sense of whether he believed me, whether he was surprised or impressed or contemptuous or just disappointed. The story took me to Surtalga, to the airport, and after that there wasn't much point going on, because it was at the airport he'd found me, even if I hadn't realised it at the time. There was no grand conclusion. I tailed off, shrugged. That was it.

He nodded.

"It it true?" I asked, but he turned away, his back to me, silent. Motionless. I didn't know whether he was thinking, or praying, or just preparing to smash my face in with whatever happened to be at hand. I repeated the question and he turned again to look at me with the slightly distant gaze of a man thinking about something else.

"Yes, it is true, I am Chima Nwosu. Yes, it is true, I was the treasurer for the People's Army of Mirandano. Yes, it is true, I was captured by that man you call Colonel Poulter, and held for many years, and yes, it is true, I escaped. Is that what you want to hear?"

I opened my mouth to say something, to appease him, because he didn't sound too happy with me and at the moment the balance between my living and dying was determined by how happy he was – I opened my mouth, but I didn't get a chance to go on because Chima Nwosu had started talking, and I imagined that he hadn't done a great deal of talking in secret custody for all those years.

"And they say they let me escape, on purpose, they made me escape, and I did not see that at all, but I think now you are right, this also is true. It was easy."

It hadn't looked easy from where I'd been standing, but these things were all relative, I supposed.

"And they say they do this for diamonds, to stop the war, but they kill your friend and they try to kill you and really, they do not act very much like people who are trying to stop a war, do they?"

I shook my head, and Chima Nwosu suddenly smiled, teeth gleaming in the orange light, and I had a glimpse of a man who hadn't fought a brutal and fruitless war, who hadn't been captured by his enemies and tortured (I assumed) and held for half his life alone, friendless, far from home. It was just a smile, I knew, it meant nothing, Ballantine had been all smiles and biscuits while he was arranging to have me killed, and the last time I'd seen Nwosu he'd been pointing a gun at me. But Nwosu's mood had changed, it appeared, from suspicion or impatience or general dislike to something approaching friendly, and that, I thought, was definitely better for me.

"Why?" I asked, deliberately vague, because although he'd paused he still had the air of a man with a lot to say (with three decades worth of things to say), a man who just needed a nudge in the right direction. I didn't care what that direction was right now.

"What is strange, when I look back, is that at the time we did not care for the war at all, me and my friends – me and Femi."

The name was familiar. Freddie had mentioned it. The man in the picture, the man with his arm thrown round Nwosu's shoulder. Femi Gueye, the weapons expert. Femi and Chima, the weapons expert and the treasurer for the People's Army. Unlikely roles for people who didn't care for war. I was aiming for a sympathetic look, but a hint of disbelief must have crept in, because Nwosu went straight on like he was trying to justify himself.

"We had no interest in it. And back then, you know, it was hardly a war anyway. We knew our rulers were selfish scum who cared for nothing but themselves and their own power and money, but everybody knew that. We knew somebody should get rid of them, and again, everybody had known that for decades. Still, throwing bombs around the market places didn't seem the right way to do it."

He paused again, and stared at me, so I nodded, the way he'd nodded throughout my narrative. *Why?* I'd asked, and I hadn't known what to expect in response. It sounded like I was going to get a life story.

"And why should it concern us? We were getting away, me and Femi. We were students. In Europe! We were the brightest in the village and then it turned out we were the brightest in the whole province, so when the men came with scholarships to send students to Europe we were the ones that went. And Antwerp was wonderful, it was so different, we could forget about poverty and corruption there, and bombs, and we felt bad, both of us, because we both knew we would make our lives in New York or London and become rich and fat, and all the time our country would be poor and dangerous, but what could we do about it?

"And Femi, he was a chemist, and I was an economist, and these skills were needed in Mirandano," (he used the old name, I noticed) "that was why we had been sent away to acquire them, but what could two people do against all that?"

He paused, again, and I nodded, but it didn't seem enough. He was looking down, lost in his own thoughts. I took a chance.

"What changed?"

He looked back up at me and smiled again, but the smile was different. There was nothing companionable, no sense of friendliness or happiness or anything like that. I'd known Chima Nwosu for minutes and even I could see he was bitter.

"Well, we did come home. We came once every year, there was no money to come back more often, and we would come back and see our families and friends and show off, a little, and get used to Mirandano again just in time to leave it. That happened once, that happened twice. The third time was different."

He stopped. I waited. There was a sense, with Nwosu, that he had so much to say and no real sense of how to say it. There were times when he might need prompting. This wasn't one of them.

"We had a lift from Ybaddli, we had arranged to meet a man from our village there. Just the three of us, travelling back, and although the distance is not far the roads are terrible."

He stopped, again, and nodded, to himself, and went on.

"Yes, they were terrible, and I can see they still are. So it took some hours, and when we were just ten miles away we saw coming towards us a convoy."

He looked up at me, to make sure I understood what he was saying. I nodded.

"The army. I told you, we had no interest in that, then, the war, we had heard it was worse now than when we had last been home, but we had no idea how much worse. Our driver, he knew. There were some trees – you know, that is an unusual thing here in Mirandano – and the moment he saw the army our friend drove his car off the road to these trees. We asked him why and he told us to shut up, and we were stupid, arrogant boys but we could see he was afraid and so we were afraid, too."

Nwosu was no longer looking at me. I wasn't sure he was even speaking to me. He went on.

"Even from there, from ten miles away, we could hear them. Screams. At first I thought maybe it was the birds, but there were no birds. Even the birds had left our country by then. Then we heard the army drive by, and our fear grew, and we heard them laughing and singing, but they did not see us and soon they were gone and all we could hear, again, were the screams. There was smoke far away. We could not push the car back onto the road so we had to leave it there, in the trees, and walk to the village, even though we knew what we would see when we got there."

He stopped again and when he looked back up at me there were creases on his face, signs of struggle. He didn't want to tell this story, and it wasn't for my benefit he was telling it at all. I didn't really want to hear another burning flash of someone else's tragedy, either. But that made no difference. He had to go on.

"They were dead. Everybody there was dead. Some they had shot. Some they had burned. Some had fled, and returned only hours later. Some had been away, or at the river, or in another town, and when they returned they found their homes burned and their wives and children butchered. And they were the lucky ones. They were at least alive."

"Why?" I asked, again, and this time I knew what the question meant and so did Nwosu.

"Nobody knew. Somebody said rebels had sheltered in the village, but nobody in the village knew about it. The Government said it was rebels that had done the killing but we had seen the men, the uniforms, we knew. My mother and father and my three sisters and my baby brother. They all died. For Femi it was worse. Femi's father had escaped, but he could not escape for ever. A week after the attack he drowned himself in the river."

His face had cleared. He had answered the question. Not my question, perhaps, but another, more important question, one that was always with him.

"And so you see."

"Why you joined the People's Army?"

He nodded.

"And you know, we might have been no use to the country, two men, me and Femi, but to the People's Army, men like us were everything. Without us, they were some men and guns that did not fire and bombs that exploded while they were still being built. But I got them money and Femi made them bombs that exploded when the murderers were right on top of them, bombs that killed the murderers by the hundred. To the People's Army, we made a difference."

I hadn't noticed, until he started passing it from hand

to hand, but Nwosu was holding that disk again, the metal object he'd had at Dovesham, at the airport, and this evening in the car. He saw me looking at it.

"This was theirs. My mother's. A gris-gris, her people call it. It binds us to our ancestors, they say, and even though we do not believe things like this any more, still we keep them, out of love, out of respect."

He looked down at his hands, at the gris-gris.

"My mother had five of these, and she gave them to her children. Four of those children died, and their gris-gris were never found. This is all that is left."

I don't know what made me say it. After all I'd just heard, it seemed, vicious, even as I spoke, unwarranted, unfair. Stupid, too. But I said it anyway.

"The war's over, Chima. But if you get these diamonds, if you give them to the people who want them, it'll start again, all of it. All that fighting. All that burning. All that killing."

He looked back up at me. His face was blank, now. This was a man who'd suffered, and fought, and been imprisoned. We'd lived our lives in different worlds. There was no reason to expect him to understand me.

He smiled, suddenly, put down the gris-gris on a small round table beside the entrance to the shack, and picked up something that had been lying beneath the table. I hadn't been able to see what it was, in the shadow, but now I could. It was a gun.

He gestured to the sofa. I'd been leaning forward, but he meant me to sit back, or even to lie down, and he had a gun, and whatever had built up between us was gone so completely it might never have been there at all. He waved the gun at me.

"You need to sleep, Mr Williams," he said. "Tomorrow will be a busy day."

16: Choices

The sofa wasn't so bad, I decided, after the first hour or two lying there trying desperately to get to sleep. The angles weren't quite right, so however I tried to position myself, my head was too low or too high or my entire body tilted slightly too much in one direction. *Adverse camber*, I thought, and smiled to myself in the darkness. But it was soft enough and not too soft, and all in all, I'd spent the night in less comfortable places. So it wasn't the sofa that was stopping me getting to sleep.

All sense of tiredness had vanished the moment I'd been sick, suddenly and completely, and although it had been creeping back, throughout the conversation that followed, it still wasn't enough to beat back the terror I'd felt since I'd seen Chima Nwosu pick up the gun. Up to then I'd had a sense we were building a connection. I'd probably been right, too. What I hadn't counted on was that connections can be broken far more easily than they're built, and that someone who'd been through what Chima Nwosu had been through might not be the most reliable individual to connect with.

Beside the round table was a small wooden chair, and Nwosu was sitting in that chair, his left hand by his side, his right hand resting on the table and curled round the grip of the gun. It was a small handgun that looked like it might have seen service in the days when the Belgians still ruled this bit of Africa, but that wouldn't stop it doing more damage than I wanted to think about. He'd killed the light, but there was no door to close, just a short absence of wall, so his shadow was still visible against the faint glow from outside.

The shadow hadn't moved for half an hour.

I'd bought myself a cheap watch at the airport to replace the expensive one that had gone down with my flat and Maurice Harwood, but there wasn't enough light to see it by, so I didn't know how long I'd been lying here waiting for sleep or morning, whichever came first. But when I'd realised Nwosu wasn't moving, wasn't even twitching, when I'd concentrated on listening to what was happening underneath the rumbles and the occasional disconcerting screeches outside and convinced myself that what I could hear was the slow, steady breathing of a man in deep sleep, I'd started silently counting the seconds. I'd counted for thirty minutes, and Nwosu hadn't stirred.

Back when I'd reached three hundred, unconsciously holding my breath for the last twenty seconds as the five minute mark drew near, I'd made a deal with myself. Thirty minutes. If Nwosu didn't move for thirty minutes, I could be sure he was really asleep, and if he was really asleep, and I was sober and stealthy enough, I'd get out of the shack and over to the car which, I hoped, couldn't be more than a few steps away, and then I'd drive in whichever direction seemed brightest in the hope that I'd stumble across Ybaddli and somewhere I could hide from Nwosu and Poulter until I figured out what to do. Because I'd realised, in those breathless twenty seconds, that I'd made an enormous, and enormously stupid, mistake. I should never have come to Surtalga in the first place. Out here the fear was everywhere, it was fear I'd seen in that bar and got it down as misery, fear in the eyes of the waiter at the hotel and the taxi driver tearing through Ybaddli like it was Monaco because he didn't want to be in any one place for a second longer than he had to be. Here even the empty streets might be hiding something that could kill you. And there was fear here, of course, in Nwosu's shack, fear so thick and so deep there wasn't a spade in the world that could bury it. Even with Ballantine and Poulter after me, and the police referring to me as a "person of interest" in connection with the death of Henderson's "associate", and Henderson himself none too pleased with me, I imagined, even with all that, London had to be a safer place than here.

Thirty minutes had gone by.

I raised my head, slowly and carefully. There was no sound. I shifted my weight over to the left and gently pushed, lifting myself into a sitting position. The sofa creaked, quietly. The shadow didn't stir. I decided to wait another few minutes, just in case the creak had penetrated Nwosu's sleep and lifted him a little closer to the surface.

Three hundred beats went by. Nwosu's breathing remained steady. Moving so slowly I could feel my muscles fighting to explode into action, I swung my legs round and onto the floor. I waited. Thirty seconds. Nothing. I stood, waited again, prayed the pounding I could hear wasn't audible outside my own head.

One step, another pause, another step, another pause, then four long, fast steps to take me past Nwosu and outside. It was darker than I'd expected and I came close to falling the moment my foot touched the ground outside. I stumbled, steadied myself, risked a glance back. I couldn't see Nwosu, I couldn't really see anything there, but I was guessing if he was awake he'd be outside already and I'd be learning what it felt like to get shot. Since neither of those things had happened, I was in the clear.

I was standing in the middle of a courtyard, or compound, or just a bit of scrub set off the road. There were half a dozen shacks, including Nwosu's, and no light or sound coming from any of them, although since the others had actual doors that were actually closed, anything could have been happening inside. There was one car, no more than twenty metres away, an ancient blue Ford that looked like it could do with a long, quiet rest. I couldn't remember much about the vehicle that had brought me here, but I thought this was probably it.

Behind the car was the road, and as I was watching a car passed by, moving fast, headlights on, illuminating a smooth strip of asphalt that wouldn't have been out of place in a London suburb. I felt sick again, and this time I knew it wasn't the meat or the whisky, just the fear, but I fought it back down and kept my eye on the headlights. The road seemed to be straight, as far as I could see, and the car was heading out into complete darkness. Back the way it had come, though, there were lights. Lots of them. Lights grouped together in lines, like streetlights, lights up high, all bathed in that dull orange glow that told me I was looking at Ybaddli, and right now Ybaddli felt more like the promised land than a filthy, violent, disease-ridden hovel clinging to the edge of a permanent war zone.

If I had to, I'd walk it, but I didn't have to because a dozen more steps and a crouch told me Nwosu had left the keys in the ignition. I looked behind, again. Nwosu's shack was silent, the shadows around it motionless. I reached for the door handle and pulled.

There was a faint *clunk*, and the door swung open. The interior lights blinked on, which I should have expected but didn't. I straightened up in surprise – I'd already bent down ready to get in – and smashed the back of my head on the door frame. It felt loud enough to wake the dead, but still no sound or movement from Nwosu's shack.

I stared at it for a moment. A single room, a metal roof, no door. Nwosu was screwed, I had no doubt about that. He might be resourceful – he'd escaped, got out here, got himself a car and a shack – but most of those resources had been handed him on a plate by Poulter and Ballantine without him even knowing about it. He'd be dead, soon enough, and Poulter would have his diamonds, and the only way I could see myself staying alive was by convincing Poulter that I'd keep his secret – all his secrets – as long as I lived.

That was what it came down to. Convince Poulter. I pictured him, timid-looking, pink in the face. I pictured Ballantine, smooth, rational, relentless. And then, without meaning to, I pictured Freddie Harmsworth with his neck broken and his room on fire, and I realised that I had no more chance of convincing Poulter and Ballantine to let me live than I had of persuading the sun to rise a couple of hours early in the morning.

I was still looking at the shack. Nwosu hadn't killed me. I'd told Ballantine everything I knew, and he'd tried to have me killed – more than once, now I thought about it. I'd told Nwosu everything I knew and he'd waved a gun around a bit, but he hadn't locked me in or tied me down, and he hadn't gone to any great effort to stay awake and make sure I stayed put. He was a killer – he'd been a killer, even if he hadn't said much about what he'd done with the People's Army I had little doubt he'd killed – but with the story he'd told, I could see why he'd turned into one. And – here was the other difference between Nwosu and Ballantine – this story was one I believed. He'd seemed to believe me, too, although the way the evening had ended I couldn't be sure, and if he *did* believe me, then we were on the same side, sort of. Except, I remembered, the bit about him using the diamonds to restart an old, brutal war, but, it occurred to me, I only had Ballantine's word for that.

I looked back down, at the car, the lights, the keys. It was a choice between Nwosu and Ballantine. It felt like a choice between running and standing my ground. I'd been running for ten years. I was tired.

I backed away, closed the door, and made my way back to the shack as quietly as I could. As I lay back down on the sofa, nausea still nudging at me and the blood racing around my system like an Ybaddli taxi driver, I heard a gentle laugh, and Nwosu's deep, clear voice.

"A good choice," he said. "I disconnected the battery when we arrived."

Nwosu shook me awake a few hours later. The shack was filled with light, my head hurt and it took me a moment to remember where I was and why I was there.

"Get up," he said. "We have to go."

I didn't think to ask *where*, or *why now*, or anything at all except to get up and follow him out to the car. He spent a few seconds hunched over the bonnet – reconnecting the battery, I guessed – and within a couple of minutes of waking I was back in that battered old Ford, with dents in places that looked like they'd have needed a hammer to put them there in the first place, and we were bouncing towards Ybaddli at a speed the car didn't seem too happy about.

"Where are we going?" I finally remembered to ask.

He turned to me and grinned, the real grin, not the bitter one, and said "equipment," and turned back to the road before we could smash head-on into an oil-tanker coming the other way.

I was wearing jeans, still, from last night. Not the ideal choice in this climate, in the daytime, even this early in the morning, but it didn't look like we'd be stopping at the Majestic for a change of clothes. I hadn't even thought to feel in my pocket, but after five minutes I did and there were my passport, my wallet, my mobile phone. So he hadn't killed me, and he hadn't robbed me either.

As I held the phone I remembered something I'd done the night before and despite the heat I felt suddenly cold.

"Do you mind if I make a call?" I asked.

Nwosu shrugged, which I took as consent. I glanced at my watch. She'd have been at work an hour or two by now.

The line rang for a while, then paused, then rang again, and was eventually answered by someone from the main switchboard.

"Claire Tully, please."

"Putting you through."

This time there was just half a ring before the phone was snatched up and a strangely familiar voice barked "Yes?"

"Is Claire Tully there, please?" I asked, puzzled.

"I'm afraid not. Who's that?"

For a man with a photographic memory I'm a lousy liar. I was less than a breath away from saying "Sam Williams" before I remembered and turned it into "Ah – Peter Haslam, Pete."

There was a short pause, during which I tried to figure out who I was talking to, and then he spoke again.

"Do you know where Miss Tully is, Mr Haslam?"

I hadn't met any of Claire's colleagues, and this man wasn't saying the kind of thing I'd have expected one of her colleagues to say. The cold and the sickness returned, along with a growing certainty that something awful had happened and that it was probably my fault.

"No," I said, "isn't she there?"

This was probably the right thing to say. It was what the real Pete Haslam would have said, I thought.

"No, she isn't," came the reply. "My name is Detective Inspector Roarkes, and I'm sorry to tell you that Miss Tully hasn't been at work at all this morning, and we have reason to believe something may have happened to her."

My stomach fell about a foot.

"What do you mean?"

"I can't go into that now, Mr – what did you say your

name was?"

Roarkes was clever, but I wasn't an idiot. Not a complete idiot, anyway. "Haslam," I replied, without missing a beat.

"Can you come in and talk to us, Mr Haslam?"

Claire was missing and Roarkes was involved and now it was obvious he suspected something. Maybe he recognised my voice.

"Mr Haslam? Are you there?"

I opened the window, held the phone out for a moment, pulled it back in and muttered "losing you" into the mouthpiece before killing the call. It was an old trick and it rarely worked, but I didn't have much else right now.

I sat there for a while just staring straight ahead, at the road. If Ballantine had got hold of Claire I didn't like to think what would be happening to her. At least she'd know what she was dealing with, but I wasn't sure how much use that would be. And Roarkes. That couldn't be coincidence. Roarkes was miles off his patch, although now I thought about it I didn't really know where Roarkes' patch was. Not Dovesham. But prison riots and missing London journalists weren't an obvious fit, and the only thing I could think of that linked them together was me. He'd run the press conference after the fire, I remembered. He was narrowing in on me. And I was in the middle of Africa and there was no one I could trust to tell me what the hell was going on.

I took a deep breath and tried to calm down and think rationally. I was in Africa, so Roarkes wasn't really a problem, or at least, not an immediate one. The problem was Ballantine. He'd got to Claire. I cared more about that than I wanted to admit, and not just because it was all my fault. Maybe she'd got to me, too. Right under my human-proof skin.

Nwosu was silent. After a while, I looked to the left and was surprised to see the depressing low-rise mass of Ybaddli falling gradually behind.

"Where are we going?" I asked, again, because even a non-conversation with Nwosu was better than thinking about Claire stuck in Ballantine's rooms, waiting.

"Here," he replied, and suddenly veered off the main road onto a dirt track. I winced, and the car groaned, clearly no more comfortable with the new surface than I was. Nwosu eased off the gas and we jolted along slowly and slightly less painfully. The world outside was flat, red, nothing to see except dust and the occasional wooden post draped with wires. After a few minutes, during which I asked again where we were going and he acted like he hadn't heard me, twenty or thirty shacks appeared, clumped together to the right of the road. Nwosu drove to the edge of the village, if that was what it was, cut the engine, turned to me and said "Wait here."

"What?" I asked, but he was already gone, out of the car, strolling towards the shacks and looking like he'd just popped out for milk and cigarettes.

Now the engine wasn't running – he'd left the keys in the ignition again, I noticed, and this time I knew he hadn't done anything to the batteries – but now the engine wasn't running, I could hear what was going on outside, and what was going on outside was nothing. Absolutely nothing. Silence. It couldn't have been any quieter out there if it was a ghost town, if everyone that had ever lived there had left centuries ago, or just died, suddenly, and nobody had been back since. Maybe that was exactly what had happened, I thought, suddenly cold again, like I needed something else to worry about. Maybe Frentoi had been and gone and left the usual number of survivors behind. Maybe the killers had just popped out for a few minutes and were on their way back right now. An image flashed through my head, Pompeii, the dead buried in the dust. This would be worse. The sun was beating down and I was cold and trying to think about Claire to distract myself from what might be going on right in front of me. No herds of wildebeest roaming the savannah, no campfires and sentries and exotic bush-meat stews, no piano bars or double-dealing aristocrats in private railway cars. This wasn't Buchan's Africa, or even Bogart and Bacall's. It was the Africa of hunger and murder, a bit of Africa the rest of the world had forgotten about and left to stumble alone and friendless into the twenty-first century, and I didn't like it. I couldn't see Nwosu any more, I'd taken my eyes off him for just a few seconds as he passed one of the shacks and that was it, the earth had swallowed him up like he'd never existed and it was just me and the car and the horrible, heavy silence.

I looked at the phone, still in my left hand. It occurred to me, suddenly, that there was someone I could trust to tell me what was going on. Maloney. I lifted it up to find the number, glanced out of the window, and there was Nwosu, standing two feet away, shaking his head, one finger at his lips and the other pointing at the phone. I got the message.

He opened my door, quietly, and, just in case I hadn't understood, quietly muttered "Quiet" as I climbed out, my knees creaking like I'd been sat in that car for a decade. I put the phone back in my pocket. There was no signal anyway. I wanted to ask what we were doing, where we were going, but if Nwosu hadn't been in the mood to answer me twenty minutes ago he wasn't likely to share now.

He walked back towards the shacks, still quiet, but with no attempt to hide, almost strutting, in fact, like he knew he was being watched and didn't care. I stood by the car staring at him until he turned and beckoned me towards him, so when he rapped on the metal door in the fourth shack I was in a prime position to see the face of the man opening it, see the features fall into a smile, a laugh, the arms open in joyful welcome.

And from where I was I could see clearly enough the look that preceded the smile, the moment the eyes fell on Nwosu and for the instant before the brain behind them clicked into gear and sent the message out to smile and look happy.

Pure, abject terror.

17: Old Friends

The two men spoke for a moment in the doorway, and then stepped inside. I followed them in. It was dark, not black, but the contrast with the intense light outside was so strong that for a moment I couldn't see a thing. And I couldn't get that look out of my mind. I didn't like it. I'd just got myself to a place where Nwosu was about the only thing in this country that didn't terrify me. If he terrified this guy, maybe that was the wrong place to be.

The room we were in slowly came into focus. Nwosu and his friend were at the far end, talking quietly. The friend looked a little younger than Nwosu, a little slower, a little fatter. It made sense. Three decades in secret high security prisons isn't going to make a man flabby. The smile was still there, the head nodding, the hands rubbing gently together. I didn't know this man and I'd seen him for the first time seconds ago, but I didn't trust him.

Nwosu was gesturing towards me. They both turned, looked at me, and then Nwosu said, in a louder voice so I could hear him clear as day, "Speak English, Iffy."

Iffy. If I'd had to choose a name for the man, that would have been near the top of the list.

The two of them walked towards me. Nwosu spoke, again.

"Sam, this is Ifeanyi. He is an old friend."

Ifeanyi held out a hand. I shook it. He was still smiling, and the grip was firm enough, but the hand was slick with sweat.

"Ifeanyi will help us, won't you, Iffy?"

Without releasing my hand Iffy turned to Nwosu and said "Of course, of course," quickly, nodding energetically at the same time. Each time he nodded my arm jerked up and then down again, and Iffy looked at it like he didn't know what it was before broadening the smile and letting me go.

"It has been too long, Chi."

Nwosu nodded, but didn't speak.

"Where have you been? We all thought you were dead. Everybody thought you were dead."

"I am alive."

"But the bomb."

"I am alive."

There was a pause, the men looking at one another, their expressions unreadable. Iffy wasn't smiling any more.

"Femi isn't," he said, and Nwosu nodded. Something was passing between them but I was damned if I could figure out what it was.

The moment was over almost as soon as it had started, and Iffy was smiling again, and Nwosu was looking brisk and business-like.

"We need transport, Iffy. We need weapons."

The smile faltered, but only for an instant. Iffy nodded.

"I'll see what I can do. But it's not easy, Chima."

"Sure," said Nwosu, like he'd heard it before.

"I mean it."

"I know you do, Iffy. You always mean it. But you always get me what I need."

"Things are different, Chima. You haven't been here. You don't understand."

"Then tell me, Iffy. Tell me what has changed."

I hadn't noticed it happening, but the men were standing so close together their noses were almost touching. Iffy didn't look comfortable.

"Everything, Chima. Come on. You know what' has happened to this country. You think I control the weapons these days? Everything we had, it's gone. Everything the Government had, too, we can't even steal that."

Nwosu was nodding, like a director hurrying through the padding to the exciting bit. Iffy looked animated, angry, a little scared. I didn't think he was acting.

"And who has it, then?"

"Frentoi."

I'd known it was coming, from what I'd seen Frentoi were the only people in the country with enough guns to make a difference, but knowing it was coming and hearing the word out there, in a place where those men might come running in with those guns at any moment, they were very different things. Absorbed in the conversation in front of me I'd almost forgotten about the fear, but here it was again, an old and unwelcome friend. It was a hot day and we were standing inside a metal building, but I wasn't warm.

Nwosu stepped away, suddenly, turned, walked to the other end of the room, nodding to himself. He stood there, facing away from us, and I found myself looking back at Iffy, who had the air of a man who'd made a heavy bet and was just about to find out if it had paid off. Nwosu walked back, as abruptly as he'd turned away, right up to Iffy.

"Frentoi?" he asked. He didn't sound like he believed it. Iffy just stared at him.

"Listen to me, Iffy. Listen to my words. I don't give a damn about Frentoi and I don't give a damn which bunch of murderers you are selling to these days. But I know you have weapons and I know you have vehicles."

"I don't. I can't. It's impossible."

Nwosu smiled, suddenly, unexpectedly, and said "Nothing is impossible."

Iffy's face fell.

"You remember, Iffy?"

Iffy nodded. Nwosu turned to me.

"You see, Sam, Ifeanyi is an Igbo name. And that is what it means. *Nothing is impossible*. Iffy promised me that, once, when I saved his life. He promised that when I asked for help, he would help, and nothing would be impossible. So now I am asking. And look. It is impossible. Can you believe such a thing, Sam?"

Iffy was muttering to himself, "It isn't fair, it isn't fair," over and over again. Nwosu turned back to him.

"It isn't fair, Iffy? Is it fair that I have been locked up for thirty years? Is it fair that you lived, when all your thieves of friends were killed, and only because I arrived at that moment to stop the killing? Is that fair?"

"No," whispered Iffy.

"No," said Nwosu. "None of this is fair. And I have no weapons. But I can still kill you, easily, right here, if you do not do as I ask. Nothing is fair, Iffy. I thought you knew that."

Iffy said "You wouldn't kill me, Chima," but he didn't look like a man who believed it.

"Perhaps, I wouldn't. But you won't deny me what I ask for, Iffy."

Iffy nodded sharply, once, like he'd made his decision, and gestured for us to follow him. Back out of the shack, into the sunlight. Behind the shack was another, smaller building – not really a building, it was difficult to call anything here a building – a small metal shed. There was a padlock on the door, a tiny thing, it wouldn't have protected a push-bike for five minutes in London. Iffy had it off in five seconds. He pushed the door open and we followed him in.

Everything had gone, that was what Iffy had said. There were no weapons left. And yet here I was looking at what even I could tell were automatic weapons, sniper rifles, smaller handguns, bullets, grenades, row after row of killing machines. Some of the things there I didn't understand at all, they looked lethal enough, in some indecipherable way, but I didn't think Nwosu would be offering a teach-in. I thought, suddenly, of Hans. Hans would have explained. I could have done with Hans out here instead of Nwosu. I could have done with Hans out here instead of me.

There were other shacks around, too, other people living in this village besides Iffy – unless I'd been right earlier and they were all dead – and if they were alive and sentient they couldn't have been stupid enough not to know what was in the shed behind Iffy's place, or dull enough not to care. Something was keeping these weapons safe, and it wasn't the padlock. It wasn't fear of Iffy, either. Even I wasn't scared of him. It was something else, the same thing that had this whole country running scared, and that, more than Nwosu or the weapons or what the hell he was planning on doing with them, had that chill coming down on me again.

"You want to look at it all, take what you need, right, Chima?"

Iffy was crouched in front of us, looking up like a supplicant into Nwosu's expressionless face. Nwosu nodded.

"You can go. Back to your house. We will be back shortly. And also – we need a vehicle, Iffy. Something that can manage these roads."

Iffy nodded, quickly, glanced briefly in my direction and backed out of the shack. Nwosu was staring at the weapons, but he didn't seem to be looking at them, he looked like someone thinking about something else entirely.

Ten seconds went by. Twenty. Thirty. He hadn't moved. I couldn't stand it.

"What's going on? Doesn't he have what you want?"

He turned to me, suddenly, like he'd forgotten I was

there, and held up his hand for silence. I was starting to resent being told to keep quiet, but I didn't feel like arguing about it in a room full of guns I didn't know how to use. There was more going on here than I understood, for sure.

"Show me your phone."

Someone else, somewhere else, I might have said something. Instead I reached into my pocket and put it in his outstretched hand. He looked at the display, nodded, handed it back.

"How do you check for other networks?"

I showed him. There were no networks available.

"Good."

We were in the middle of nowhere with no way of getting a message to anybody in the civilised world, and Nwosu thought this was a good thing. The cold got a notch colder.

He turned away from me and walked out of the shed. It wasn't a big thing, walking out of a shed, but where we were, what we were doing, everything was a big thing, or could be. For all I knew Nwosu walking out of a shed meant the difference between my living or dying here, and I didn't like the fact that he just did it, without a word, like someone getting on a bus or buying a newspaper. I waited a moment and followed him outside.

He was standing by the door, waiting for me as if he'd told me what he was doing half a dozen times and was beginning to lose his patience. He didn't wait any longer, but turned again, walked quietly towards Iffy's shack and pushed open the door, hard, with his shoulder. He walked inside. I didn't know what was about to happen in there, but I followed him anyway. It wasn't like I had anywhere else to go.

It took a moment for my eyes to adjust, but it didn't look like I'd missed anything. Iffy was standing in the corner of the room, staring at Nwosu, an old-fashioned analogue phone in one hand, wired into the wall behind him, and a look on his face like he'd just been caught screwing the boss's wife.

Nwosu was standing in front of me facing Iffy, so I couldn't read his expression, but when he spoke there was a new tone. Cold. Menacing.

"Who are you calling, Iffy?"

Iffy opened his mouth, and closed it, twice, three times, like a fish. Nwosu held up his hands. In the right was a gun, it looked like one of the handguns from the shed but I couldn't be sure. I hadn't seen him take anything, but I hadn't really been looking. I couldn't be sure if it was loaded, either, but if I was Iffy I wouldn't want to be taking any chances.

In Nwosu's left hand was a small length of wire, and for a moment it didn't mean a thing to me, and then I noticed Iffy looking from the wire to the phone, and back again, and I realised why Nwosu had wanted to check for networks and what he'd been doing while I'd been sitting in the car terrifying myself with thoughts of Frentoi.

Iffy was talking, if you could call it that, stammering out something in Igbo, if that's what it was, and English, and what sounded like the odd snatch of Dutch. "Just friends," I heard him say, and "nobody," and, quite redundantly in the circumstances, "it's not working, Chima."

When it happened, it was so fast I wasn't sure I'd seen it, but suddenly Nwosu was standing in front of Iffy, looking a foot taller even though I was sure they'd been around the same height moments before, and the phone was on the floor in three large pieces and dozens of smaller ones.

"They made me promise, Chima."

"Who made you promise?"

Iffy was shaking his head, fast, side to side, like a man having a fit. He was terrified.

"Who was it, Iffy? Listen to me. If you tell me, I won't kill you. That's more than they'll offer, isn't it?"

"I can't, Chima."

Nwosu shrugged.

"We leave now, what will happen to you, Iffy?"

I've got to be honest, I didn't understand this, but Iffy did. If he'd been terrified before, I couldn't put a name to what he was now.

And then he spoke, finally, and I did understand, even if I didn't want to.

"Frentoi," he said, quietly, and Nwosu nodded, and there was the fear again, something almost physical, something behind me, watching me, ticking off the seconds until it came for me.

"What do they want?"

Nwosu had stepped back, a little, and turned to the side, and without noticing it I'd found myself edging towards them, so now I could see them both, in profile. They were standing there with a metal wall behind them discussing their own lives and deaths, and, ridiculously, it suddenly struck me that this was a conversation best had sitting down.

"They want you, Chima. They want to know where you are, and when, and they want you."

"Why?"

Iffy shrugged. The terror had lifted, from him, at least, and I thought I could understand why. Chima Nwosu wanted information, and Iffy had it, or at least Nwosu thought he did. That information might keep Iffy alive a little longer.

"Just you, Iffy?"

"I doubt it, Chima. There aren't many of us left, but you can be sure Frentoi have paid everyone a visit."

Nwosu nodded and stepped back again. He looked down, and then, surprisingly, he turned and looked at me, and the expression on his face was puzzled, questioning, like he expected me to have the answer. I had no idea what Frentoi would want with a man who'd been locked up thousands of miles away since years before they'd even existed, I couldn't imagine how they'd have heard of him, much less of his escape and return. I didn't have Nwosu's answer.

Except, suddenly, I thought maybe I did.

"Iffy," I said, and he started at my voice, even though he knew I was there. "Iffy, when Frentoi arrived, when they first came to this country, how did they arm themselves?"

He shrugged, again, and looked like he had nothing more to say, and for a moment the germ of an idea that was growing inside my head looked like it was going to die before it had even been born. I turned to Nwosu, preparing to shrug myself.

"They just came, Sam." He pronounced my name long and hard on the *m*, like there was something missing, half a silent second syllable. "They just came, they walked into the depots and the compounds, they walked in without firing a shot and they walked out again with all this."

He pointed to the back of the shack, in the direction of his shed. No wonder he'd been so scared. It was bad enough offering your own guns to a man on Frentoi's hit-list. Offering him Frentoi's weapons was close to suicide.

"I don't understand, Iffy."

It had seemed pretty clear to me. I couldn't see what Nwosu hadn't grasped.

"How did they do it?"

Iffy shrugged, again.

"I mean it, Iffy. We fought and died for those weapons and still we could not take them."

"That was then, Chima. That was thirty years ago."

"I don't care. The Government would not have surrendered them, like that."

"It wasn't just them, Chima."

"What do you mean?"

"It was us, too."

"What 'us', Iffy? Who are you talking about? The weapons dealers, like you? The rats, who change sides whenever the money moves?"

Iffy didn't rise to it. He shook his head.

"Not me, Chima. You're right. Getting guns off somebody like me just takes money. But I mean your friends, your old friends, your old comrades."

"What of them?"

"Their weapons, too, Chima. Hidden in the walls of their houses and buried in their gardens, hidden in mines and by trees and near rivers, they dug them all up and they handed them all over and none of them had to be killed to make them do it."

Silence, for a moment. I looked at Nwosu. He looked like a man who'd just been told he had a month left to live. He opened his mouth to say something, to argue, that was obvious from the way his face was set, and then he changed his mind and nodded, slowly. He didn't like it and he didn't understand it, but at least he believed it.

"Why, Iffy?"

Iffy rubbed his second and third fingers against his thumb and said "Why does anything happen round here, Chima?"

Nwosu nodded, again.

"So they paid you, Frentoi? They paid everyone?"

Iffy shook his head.

"Not Frentoi."

"Then who?"

"I don't know."

Nwosu was on the edge. Iffy should have known that, even I could see it from where I was and Iffy was right in front of him. *I don't know* might have been true, but it wasn't the right thing to say. I took a step back, without quite realising why.

"You don't know?"

There was an air of suppressed violence in the question that seemed to reach out and fill the tiny shack. I wanted to get out. Instead, I stepped forward, right up to the two of them, and spoke to Iffy with a calm in my voice that bore no relation to what I was actually feeling.

"How did they pay you, Iffy?"

He started, again – again, like he'd forgotten I was there.

"Wire. To the bank in Ybaddli. And then they send me a paper I have to take to the bank to show the money is mine."

I nodded.

"How do they send you the paper?"

"I have a fax machine. It works well enough. When the telephone line is not cut, anyway."

This was stupid, I thought, complaining about the phone wire, like criticising your firing squad for wearing dirty boots. I carried straight on before Nwosu could take offence.

"Do you have a copy, Iffy?"

He looked at me curiously, then turned and walked away. Unlike Nwosu's shack, there was more than one room here, or at least a bunch of rugs hanging from the ceiling dividing the place up. He disappeared behind them. Nwosu was motionless, his eyes fixed on the spot between the rugs through which Iffy had stepped. If there was another way out behind those rugs I had little doubt Iffy would be half a mile away already, but that was a risk I had to take. Thirty seconds passed, a minute. Silence. If Iffy was still there, surely there would be rustling, breathing, footsteps, the sound of a man looking for something, or at least pretending to look for it. Maybe I'd taken the wrong risk. Another thirty seconds.

The rugs moved, and suddenly Iffy was back, a scrap of paper in one hand.

"Here it is."

Nwosu had his own hand out, ready to take it, but I moved faster.

Iffy hadn't been lying, or at least he hadn't been lying about this. It was an order made out in his name, a certificate entitling Ifeanyi Okore to claim for a particular sum (four thousand Guranesi, which came to about two hundred dollars, which wasn't a huge amount of money for selling out to the most vicious gang of murderers in Africa, but went a fair way round here, and it wasn't like Frentoi weren't going to get what they wanted anyway), on a particular day (six months back) on production of this paper and his identity documents. The funds were to be drawn on the National Bank of Surtalga in its Ybaddli offices, in cash, and the document, on National Bank headed paper, assured whoever would be handing out that cash that the company transmitting the money had already placed the necessary funds with the National Bank.

I looked down to the bottom of the page, to the name of that company, and I read it, but I didn't need to. It had been obvious, from the moment I realised Frentoi were after Chima, these same Frentoi who'd walked into this country less than a year ago, shot and bombed and hunted out of every other place they'd terrorised, and suddenly found themselves the money to buy up all the weapons and power they needed.

Surtalga Resources, Limited.

18: Changing the Game

I took a step back and tried to blank out everything in front of me, so I could concentrate on figuring out what had happened and how the game had changed. I let the facts pile up on top of each other and build a wall between me and whatever was going on between Iffy and Nwosu. Last time I'd seen those words, Surtalga Resources Limited, they'd confirmed what I'd probably already known, what with the dead bodies and the fires breaking out everywhere I went: Ballantine and Poulter didn't give a damn about Africa or peace or anything except the diamonds and what they could get for them. *Surtalga Resources*, a business set up to grab those resources and squeeze them till they bled.

And they'd been prepared to kill for those diamonds. That was obvious. I knew that already.

But this was something new. This wasn't just Freddie, Jayati Mehta, Maurice Harwood, all the other *collateral damage* at Dovesham. This was a war, it was atrocity after atrocity at the hands of some of the nastiest people to have graced the planet since Nuremberg, and Poulter wasn't just happy to work with them, he was the man who'd opened the door and invited them in.

Frentoi were only in Surtalga because Poulter had let them in, and he'd only let them in because he thought, somehow, it would help him get closer to the diamonds. A lot of diamonds, I suddenly realised, if it was worth buying a whole war to get them. I thought about explaining it, setting it all out clearly and concisely for Nwosu, and Iffy. How would he take it? Finding out that the reason for the war in his country, the reason people were being slaughtered and raped and mutilated and kidnapped and forced to kill their own families, that this was all because of his precious diamonds? I looked at him. He was staring at Iffy like he was waiting for something. I didn't think he was in the mood where an apology would do. I decided not to spell it all out, not yet. The shortened version would do.

"Poulter," I said, my finger on the words at the bottom of the paper. *Surtalga Resources, Limited.* "That's Poulter's people. He's paying Frentoi. That must be why they're after you."

And the only reason they're in this country at all, I didn't say. I felt like I was walking on eggshells already. A layer of eggshells sitting on a layer of land mines. I didn't want to step down too hard.

Nwosu glanced at the paper and nodded, and returned his gaze to Iffy.

"Is it true, Iffy?"

"I don't know, Chima. Really. I've never heard of this Potter. But they are after you, Chima."

"You think they're going to let you live, after you give me to them?"

Iffy looked at the floor, and when he looked back up again there were tears in his eyes.

"No, Chima. I think they're going to kill me, if you don't. But I didn't ask for this, Chima. I didn't ask for any of this."

Nwosu nodded. He didn't look like he was going to kill Iffy, but Iffy knew him better than I did.

"You should have stayed dead, Chima," he said, and I gave a small, involuntary nod. The art of staying dead was wasted on people who insisted on being so powerfully alive. Iffy was still talking.

"They know you're here, Chima. In the country. They have people looking for you everywhere."

"They didn't do a good job of finding me, did they, Iffy?"

"They have time. And they don't expect to wait too long."

"Why not?"

"They think you will come to them."

Silence fell. It couldn't have gone on more than five, maybe ten seconds, but it felt longer, long enough for me to go cold, again, for Nwosu's frown to deepen, for Iffy to take a step back so he was standing right against the rugs that looked suddenly and horribly like the hanging carcasses of recently-dead creatures.

"Why would they think that, Iffy?"

Nwosu's tone was normal, almost friendly, the kind of tone you'd use to a child that had made silly mistake, or a friend who'd given you the wrong drink, but his face wasn't friendly at all. Iffy looked like he was about to burst into tears.

"They know, Chima. They know where you're from."

Nwosu stepped towards him, their faces almost touching again.

"How do they know, Iffy?"

And now the tears did come, and the sobs, and I could see why, because it was obvious how they knew, and anyone who knew Nwosu's story, who'd heard what he'd told me the night before, the burning of his village, the killing of his family, anyone who knew about that, and about what Nwosu had then become, and then brought that all back to him, with the added bonus of Frentoi – anyone who did that would surely not be surprised if Nwosu shot them dead right there, and would probably just be grateful if it was all over fast.

"Did you tell them, Iffy?"

Iffy was nodding, the tears falling fast, words bursting out between sobs.

"I – yes – I had no choice – I am sorry."

Nwosu still seemed calm, but I didn't think that really meant anything. I'd given up trying to read the man.

"When did you tell them?"

"It was just yesterday, Chima. Last night. They were here. They said –"

"What did they say, Iffy?"

"They said they would get their men and go in and they –"F

"What did they say, Iffy?"

"They said they would kill every person there, one by one, until you came."

Nwosu nodded, slowly.

"One last thing, Iffy. Did they go there straight away, yesterday?"

Iffy shook his head, almost frantic.

"No. They said twenty-four hours. There were only two men, they had to wait for others to return. They will go this evening."

I'd checked the time shortly before we'd walked in. It hadn't been much before ten in the morning.

Iffy had stopped crying. The silence that fell now was different, subtly, because now everything had come out, and there were no more revelations or horrors to come. Just a judgement, and a sentencing. I was looking at Nwosu and Nwosu was looking at Iffy and Iffy was looking at the ground.

"How long do I have, Iffy?"

Iffy shrugged. "Eight hours. Maybe ten. They did not give me a time, Chima."

"I need your weapons. And I need a car."

Iffy nodded. Nwosu already had a car as far as I could see, but I wasn't about to argue. Nwosu turned to me and told me to go and wait in the car, the one he already had. I thought about standing my ground, because it wasn't like I was just some tourist along for the ride. I had something at stake here, a life to lose and (possibly) a reputation to regain. But there were the eggshells, too. And anyway, there wasn't much doubt who was in charge.

Ten minutes I sat in that car, building up that wall of facts brick by brick, *Surtalga Resources Limited*, Poulter, Ballantine, Freddie, and shivering every time I remembered where I was and who else was here, and watching the bricks fall in a heap of dust and broken stone. The facts were all I had left, the one-liners had dried up long ago in the hot African terror, and it turned out even the facts weren't enough by themselves. So I sat there and looked at my phone, which was useless, and outside, which was pointless, because nothing was happening at all. I could see where the weapons might come from, but as for the car, I had no idea. There were the shacks, and nothing else. When the hard, angry rev of a brand new Land Rover Discovery pierced the silence I sat up so fast I had to close my eyes for a moment to clear my head. I hadn't eaten a thing since the lamb and the whisky, and I'd left most of that in Nwosu's shack. I figured my head would be asking some serious questions about all that soon enough.

For fifteen minutes we drove back in the direction we'd come from that morning, and neither of us said a word, but fifteen minutes was about as long as I could take, because there was a big Iffy-shaped hole in the car. I'd thought he'd be coming with us, if Nwosu hadn't killed him. He wasn't with us. I didn't like where that left him.

"What did you do with Iffy?"

"Why do you care?"

Nwosu's eyes were staring out at the road. He didn't turn, didn't even seem to move as he spoke. If I hadn't seen him losing his temper and torturing himself over the past, I'd have been tempted to think there was something not-quite-human about him. But he was human, all right. He was what happens to a human when you murder his family and lock him up for thirty years.

"Because he didn't have any choice, Chima."

It wasn't the first time I'd called him by his first name, but it was the first time it felt right. There was a feeling I had that I couldn't put my finger on, something I wasn't used to, but even though I didn't have a clue what was going through his head, or what he was planning, even though he was a killer and there was still a chance he was going to kill me, it felt like we were on the same side. More than that. Like we were in something together, more deeply in it than the facts alone accounted for. I'd had the same feeling with Claire, back in London, but I'd put it down to something different and a whole lot more obvious. Now I wasn't so sure.

"We all have a choice, Sam. He chose to sell guns, to the right people, the wrong people, he never cared as long as he got his money. And then he chose to be a coward and live while around him everyone else was dying. I think he had a choice."

"Not much of a choice, though, is it? What did you do with him?"

Silence.

"Is he dead, Chima? Did you kill him?"

More silence. I decided to fill it.

"Do you think he should have just let them kill him, and then they'd never have found out where you were from? Do you really think that would have been it? Christ, Chima, Poulter could have found out easily enough, you can count on it. All they had to do was ask the guy who'd been paying them."

He turned to me, briefly, finally, and looked me in the eye, for no more than half a second, and all I could read in that look was another judgement, only this time it was me that was being judged. I had no idea what it was I was being judged on, or how it panned out. I just felt assessed, quickly and confidently, and that was it.

There might have been more, but the low-rise dead-zones on the fringes of Ybaddli were visible in the distance and that meant the closest thing this country had to civilisation, and, more importantly, a mobile network. My phone rang.

"Sam Williams," I said, without thinking, followed by a silent "*shit*", because the one person I *wasn't* supposed to be was Sam Williams.

Turned out it didn't matter.

"Good to see you're sticking to the cover, Sam."

"Maloney?"

"That's right, pal. Thought you might want to hear the news from this side of the world."

"What's happened to Claire? I tried calling but R —"

"Relax, Sam. She's fine. We've got her."

I took a deep breath, the first one since I'd realised it was Maloney on the line.

"Tell me what happened."

"They figured it out, Sam. Christ knows how. But I've got a couple of boys outside her place all night, and nothing's happening, right – hey, you sure you're in Africa?"

"Yes, why?"

"Because you've got a better signal than I get on the Seven Sisters Road, mate."

I laughed. He carried straight on.

"So nothing's happening, and then I get a call about six saying something's up, there's two cars just shown up and no one's got out, just waiting there, you know what I'm saying."

"Waiting for Claire."

"That's what I figured. So I told them to go in and get her out, and they did, and she's with us now, it's all cool."

I was thinking. *Christ knows how*, he'd said, but if Poulter had discovered Claire was working with me, it was obvious enough where from. Me. I couldn't remember exactly what I'd said when I called her drunk outside that shack the night before, but it would have been enough for anyone listening to put two and two together. Especially if they were already looking around wondering if there was a four in the house. I didn't say anything.

"Sam?"

I smiled, and glanced to the side to see Chima looking at me, registering what happened to my face the moment I heard her voice.

"Are you OK?"

"I'm fine, Sam. What about you? I've been worried."

"It's all go here, Claire. What happened?"

"Maloney's told you, right? It was Poulter's men all right."

"How do you know?"

"Well, I'm not really supposed to know this, but they've got one of them tied to a chair downstairs with a blindfold on."

I didn't like the sound of that. The trouble I was already mixed up in was thick enough. I didn't want it getting any thicker. Before I could say anything I heard Maloney, in the background, saying "Tell the idiot to chill out. Tell him we're not gonna kill the fucker. OK?"

I found myself nodding, realised, and said "OK."

"He doesn't know much," said Claire, and I realised that if Maloney was confident the guy in the chair didn't know much, he must have used some fairly persuasive methods to find out what he *did* know. I didn't want to ask. I hoped Claire hadn't asked, either. Then I remembered the photos she'd shown me. The dead girls. A bloke in a chair getting beaten up didn't seem such a big deal.

"But he admitted he worked for Ballantine. Didn't have a clue who Poulter was. Recognised the name Jenkins. I think he's too dumb to know what's really going on, Sam."

"Fair enough. But tell Maloney not to kill the guy. Please. And Claire."

"Yes?"

"Look, I'm sorry. About the call. I know this is all my fault. I shouldn't –"

"Forget about it, Sam. It was nothing to do with you. Don't worry about it."

Which was kind, but bullshit, and we both knew it. She was protecting me, from being seen as a liability by Maloney and his serious, professional friends and employees who'd put their serious professional skills at my disposal. They wouldn't be happy if they realised how close I'd come to screwing it all up just a few hours after I'd landed.

Claire was still talking.

"Anyway, looks like all this is turning into more than a diversion after all, Sam."

I knew what that meant.

"I'm sorry, Claire. I really am. Did you manage to get your stuff?"

"What, the photos, all that? Relax. I've got everything. And besides, my place hasn't burnt down. Not yet, anyway. Your little diversion might end up being just what I need, Sam."

"How?"

"Well, I can work here just as well as I can at home, or in the office. And your friend Maloney seems keen to help."

He would be. I remembered Hassan. Maloney wasn't fond of people who hurt women. And understandably, he shared Claire's distrust of the police. Which reminded me of something else.

"Did you know Roarkes had shown up at your office?"

There was a silence, a faint buzzing sound, and for a moment I thought I'd lost the connection, but then she spoke.

"It doesn't surprise me."

"Well it surprises the hell out of me, Claire. You've been missing for what, about an hour, and some DI from miles away suddenly shows up and takes an interest?"

"Not suddenly, Sam. He's been trying to get hold of me for a day or so, ever since you left. Leaving messages. He wants to know about you, but he was also asking about Ballantine."

She stopped, and I thought about what she'd just said.

"Ballantine? That's interesting. Think he might be starting to add things up?"

"Not sure. But if he's asking about Ballantine then I reckon he can't know everything. He's probably as much in the dark as we were. Still, he managed to connect you and me well before Poulter did."

I smiled to myself. I had the feeling that once all the suspicion and misunderstanding was out of the way, Roarkes and I might be OK. He was my kind of cop, and if he was smarter than the bad guys, so much the better for me. I pictured him biting into his cress sandwich and smiled again.

"Good. The more people who start to get suspicious, the better. Did you ever hear from that Connolly?"

"No," she said. "And I don't think I will, now. That's the other reason we called."

More news, then. And I doubted it was good news.

"Jim Connolly's dead."

I should have been expecting it, but I wasn't. I was speechless for a moment, and then asked "How?"

"No fire this time. They didn't even try to make it look like an accident. His car was run off the road and from what they're saying, he was shot the moment he got out."

"Sounds like Poulter."

"Right. But of course, this guy ran security at one of the toughest prisons in the country. As far as the police are concerned there's about a hundred suspects and not one of them's our mild-mannered Colonel."

Connolly. I wondered. Had he found something out, let something slip, learned too much? Or had he been in on it the whole time, found himself exposed, and outlived his usefulness, like Major Dawes, or Pedrag Ilic who'd died of a broken ankle? Poulter would have needed people on the inside at Dovesham, it would be difficult to keep the existence of an entire prisoner completely hidden from the authorities. The head of security would have been useful. I thought back to the phone call I'd had with him. He'd been dismissive, one hundred per cent sure of himself, but that was probably just his character and the effect of what he'd been through over the last day and night. It didn't mean anything, and it certainly didn't mean he was bent. But he'd been ready with the answers, and that *was* suspicious. Twenty-three black prisoners and seven black officers, he'd said, like he was giving me his own date of birth. He might be a details man. He might have the kind of memory I had. But on the whole, I thought it was more likely he'd been briefed on what I was going to say, and how he should deal with it. And if I'd had to guess, I'd have said the person doing the briefing was Ballantine.

"Sam?"

I'd been quiet so long she probably thought I'd gone.

"Sorry, Claire. I was just thinking."

"Sam, there's something else."

I braced myself. Whatever it was, I doubted it was a lottery win.

"It's Brooks-Powell."

"What's the bastard done now? Oh, don't tell me," and for the briefest of moments I felt a shiver of pleasure run down my spine, "they haven't gone and killed him too, have they?"

"No such luck. Look, fact is, what with the riot and now Connolly and the fire at your place, and the fact you seem to have disappeared off the face of the earth, well, you're still big news, Sam. And I guess Brooks-Powell's decided he wanted a piece of the action."

"Well, what's he done?"

"He called a press conference."

Even more than Connolly's death, this floored me. The audacity. Brooks-Powell had no more involvement with what had happened in the last week than he had with the Chinese Communist Party. But typical, to try and make a connection, get in on the act.

"Who did he end up talking to? Don't tell me. A couple of his own secretaries and some hack who showed up for the free drink, right?"

"Er, no. No, he had half the national press there, plus radio and TV."

"Well what the hell did he have to tell them? I used to work with Sam Williams and I didn't like him very much?"

"No, no, he was much cleverer than that, Sam. You won't like it.

"Go on then. Tell me."

"He played it all nice. Started off reminding everyone about your 'chequered past', that's what he called it. Went on about Pierre Studeman, how it hadn't been possible for the firm to continue its association with you after that, mentioned Trawden, raised a few doubts, nothing concrete."

"Damn right nothing concrete. There's nothing doing on Trawden. Everything there was legit."

"You don't have to convince me, Sam. I believe you. But anyway, that's not the point. It's what he did next that was the crafty bit. He talked about your comments, Dovesham, the article."

She trailed off for a moment. She meant her article. Not something she wanted to dwell on.

"And then the thing with your flat, and he mentioned Freddie, although no one's worked out that was anything more than an accident, but what he said was something like, and can anyone be surprised, after Dovesham, and getting exposed like that, and then the shock of his old tutor dying so horribly, that Mr Williams has gone completely off the rails?"

I couldn't believe it.

"What?"

"Yes. Exactly. So he starts saying there's nothing suggesting you've done anything really wrong, even with the fire, maybe you've just been unlucky, and with all this, is it really surprising you've gone to ground?"

I didn't like where this was going.

"And he said something about how this stank of the police persecuting a troubled individual who clearly needed help more than he needed to be hunted down like the worst kind of criminal."

The bastard. I could see it now, I could see where it was going, and while half of me was thinking *the bastard*, the other half couldn't help applauding the sheer bloody cheek of it.

"So what he said was that he wanted it to be known that in your absence, and while there was no indication that you'd appointed anyone to act on your behalf, he said that he, that Mauriers would therefore be acting as your solicitors and in your interests. And something about how he hoped that showed their commitment to defending the rights of all people regardless of their past actions or personal issues or something like that."

"The bastard."

"I thought you wouldn't like it."

"Well you were right. I'll bet he figured out the same thing. So he's managed to get himself on the bandwagon, get loads of publicity, come out of it looking like a hero, and piss me off, all at the same time."

"That's about the size of it, Sam."

I whistled, and then found myself laughing.

"You know what, Claire? It doesn't matter. It doesn't bloody matter. We've got more important things to deal with. I'll sort out Brooks-Powell when I've dealt with Poulter, right?"

"Good. So tell me what's going on over there."

I'd been so wrapped up in Connolly and Brooks-Powell I'd forgotten I had news of my own to share. When I told Claire I'd found Nwosu she whooped so loud I nearly dropped the phone. When I told her he was sitting right next to me she whooped again.

"So look, it's complicated. It's seriously complicated, and I'm sure Chima won't mind if I tell you he's a tight-lipped son of a bitch and I don't know a whole lot more than I did when I landed. I've spent more time thinking I was about to die in the last day than I did in the last ten years, and that includes Dovesham. Frentoi are mixed up in the whole thing. We're off to some village and Chima won't tell me what we're doing there, he just expects me to follow him round like a faithful puppy."

I was watching him while I was speaking. He was still staring ahead, but he was smiling.

"I think he's all right, Claire. I don't know what he did thirty years ago and I don't really care. I think he knows we're on the same side this time."

I could hear her breathing down the line, Maloney was right, it was like she was next door, I could almost see her frowning and picking at her lower lip with her finger. It hit me, suddenly, that I wanted to see her. I liked her. I missed her. Which was good, because whatever happened out here, if I got out alive, I'd want something pleasant to come back to. I didn't think I could expect much by way of a career.

"Be careful, Sam."

"It's a bit late for that, isn't it, Claire?"

She laughed. Something that had been bubbling along inside my brain since I'd seen Iffy's bit of paper rose gently to the surface with a pop.

"Claire, can you do me a favour, do you have your notes on Poulter?"

"No, they're all at the flat, but I can get all the info easily enough."

"Good. Can you look into the companies in Serbia and Iraq and get some dates?"

"Dates?"

"Find out when they were set up. But not just that, when they changed their names, when they got serious money in, when they got loans and offices and anything else you can. I want to know when these outfits stopped being shell companies and started acting like real businesses."

"Are you going to tell me what all this is about?"

"I'm not sure myself yet, Claire. As soon as I am, you'll be the first to know."

"Fair enough."

"You be careful too, Claire. Maloney will look out for you. Just do what he says and you'll be OK."

"I'm not used to doing what people say, Sam."

"Everybody's got to learn a new trick sometimes."

She laughed.

"I'll be back soon, Claire."

"Good," she said. I tried to convince myself there was something in that *good*, something more than courtesy. Even down a near-perfect line I was kidding myself if I thought I could get what I wanted out of a single syllable.

"Can I speak to Maloney again, Claire?"

"Sure. Bye."

I was on the line with Maloney for another few minutes. I wanted to make sure there was nothing else going on that I should know about. And I needed another favour.

19: Doing Something

"So this Claire, you like her, right?"

Chima was still looking at the road but there was a hint of a smile. He hadn't said a word since I'd got off the phone, more than an hour ago. We might be in this together, me and him, but I didn't feel ready to chat about Claire. Instead, I decided it was time to go on the offensive.

"That's not important, Chima. What is important is what the hell we're going to do when we get to your village."

He turned to look at me, an expression on his face like he was talking to someone who'd just turned out, surprisingly, to be an idiot.

"We're going to get everyone out, of course."

"Of course," I said, even though it didn't seem quite that straightforward to me. As far as everyone else was concerned, he was just a dead man walking home and telling them all to pack up and leave. He had no proof to back him up. He didn't seem to think that was a problem. I pushed on this, for another minute, but it was like pushing against solid rock. I added it to the list of things I wouldn't think about.

We'd been driving for nearly two hours now and the asphalt had come to an end. What we were on now was still a road, just, but it was the kind of road you had to concentrate on if you didn't want to end up with a broken axle or worse. I remembered suddenly what we'd been talking about earlier, when Maloney had called.

"Look, just tell me, Chima. Did you kill Iffy?"

"Of course not, Sam. I gave him the other car and told

him to get out of the country as fast as he could. What kind of man do you think I am?"

I found myself smiling, because that was what I'd suspected, from the brief flashes of humanity I'd seen in him. *In it together*, I'd thought, and I was starting to understand him. But I hadn't been sure.

"Iffy wasn't too confident, was he, Chima? What kind of man does he think you are?"

"He thinks I am a traitor, and a liar, and in many ways he is right."

I didn't know what I'd been expecting him to say, but it wasn't this. I waited for him to go on, but that was it, he was silent and staring back at the road, and this was a road that needed to be stared at. I couldn't let words like that just hang there, unexplained.

"What do you mean?"

"How long have we been driving, Sam?"

"A couple of hours."

"Can you drive a Land Rover?"

I looked down at the gearbox, and back out at the road. I'd driven on bad roads before, and I'd been off-roading, a couple of times, for fun. This didn't look like it would be fun.

"Yes, but slowly."

"Slow is better than still. I need to rest."

So now I was driving, and it wasn't as bad as I'd thought from the passenger seat. I guess the fact it wasn't my Land Rover – it wasn't Chima's either, really – made me a little more relaxed with the potholes. Not too relaxed, though. We hadn't seen another car or even a building for miles, and apart from some low hills to the left (I couldn't figure out north or south – *left* would have to do) there was just dead and dying grass stretching as far as I could see in every direction. A broken axle out here could kill us.

"So what did you mean, Chima? Why should he think you were a traitor?"

I risked a glance to the side. Chima had his eyes closed but I didn't think he was asleep. I waited.

"You know why I left, Sam?"

"You were captured. You didn't have much choice."

"I was leaving anyway. That's the thing, Sam. I wanted to leave. I had had enough."

"Enough of what?"

His eyes were open now, looking at me, through me, into the past.

"Of everything. Of turning fear into diamonds and diamonds into guns. Of killing people. I didn't want to kill people any more, Sam. Do you understand that?"

I nodded. I did understand. Different worlds or not, we had more in common than I'd have guessed when he was just a guy in the woods pointing a gun at me.

"We were still right, I thought, the People's Army, we were still the good side, but we were fighting the same way the Government fought, and that made me want to get out and stop it all."

"But?"

"But nothing. There was a bomb. You know about the bomb. Many people thought I was dead. This was perfect for me. I took the last shipment and I went to Antwerp, and yes, I was going to keep the money, it was a small shipment but enough to buy papers, get me to America, get me started."

"But Poulter caught you."

"Poulter caught me. Here, most of them think I am dead. Those that know I am alive, they think I am a traitor. They are probably right."

Chima had stopped but I kept my mouth shut. If this was true, he *was* a traitor. I wasn't going to take that off his back. I glanced over again and his eyes were open, glistening, but still set with the same hardness that had been there every time I'd looked at him. His friend had died, his best friend, and he'd got out and run. I couldn't figure out why, but suddenly I wanted to hurt him.

"You know Poulter paid for Frentoi, Chima?"

He nodded.

"You know why?"

He nodded again, and looked at me.

"I am not stupid, Sam. I can read, I can see dates. I can see that without Poulter, Frentoi would not be in my country. And I fear that without me, Poulter would not care. So yes, if you are trying to tell me that it is because of me that these animals are here, if that is what you are trying to say, then yes, and if I had died in that bomb none of this would have happened, I understand all that, Sam. But I can do nothing about it. I could never have done anything about it."

That I couldn't accept.

"You could have told him where the bloody diamonds were, Chima. It's a bunch of bloody stones. He's destroying your country for them. You could have let him have them instead."

He smiled at me, and shook his head, and said "If only it were so simple, Sam. Drive straight. Wake me in an hour."

And that was it.

Five hours, the drive took, from leaving Iffy's shack to reaching the village, with the road so bad that for the last hour I didn't think we'd make it at all. The sun sank so slowly it felt like it was going to be evening for another month, and then suddenly it was just sitting there, half an inch above the horizon, waiting.

Which was what I found myself doing, again, sitting in the car waiting a hundred yards from the nearest hut –

they lived in huts out here, not even shacks – while Chima strolled in and prepared to meet a bunch of people he hadn't seen for three decades. People who thought he was either dead, or a traitor. People he had to convince their lives were in danger. He spoke to me for a moment, before he got out and gave his usual order to wait.

"You could die, Sam."

I nodded. It was a statement of fact, and it was so obviously true it didn't need anything from me. Chima didn't seem to think so, though.

"The people here, if they do not trust me, they will not trust you, either."

"I understand that."

"You can go, if you wish."

"Then why the hell did you bring me here?"

He shrugged.

"I did not know if I trusted you. Now, I know I do."

I shrugged myself.

"I'm here now, Chima. Go and talk to your friends."

He wasn't done.

"And if they do believe me, and escape, then Frentoi will want you as much as they want me."

Frentoi. The fear surged up again – and then subsided, by itself, into a new and unfamiliar emptiness. I'd been about to say something, something glib and pointless, but I stopped and tried to work out why I wasn't afraid. Or why I was, but it didn't matter.

That was it. It didn't matter. I was afraid, but there was nothing I could do about that, in the car, or in the bush, or running all the way back to London. There was something else, too, something more important. Getting the people that had done this, had done everything, to Chima, to Surtalga, to me, Jayati Mehta, Freddie, even Pedrag Ilic. Setting things straight. There was a connection, too, with Bill and Eileen Grimshaw, and

Pierre, Maloney, all the bent cops, but even though I could see it was there, I couldn't figure out what it was. I almost had it, almost, but not quite. Not enough to say it out loud, anyway. I went for glib instead.

"Chima, I'm an Englishman in a village in the middle of Surtalga. If Frentoi stumble across me I'm dead anyway. The fact that I'm with you doesn't make a great deal of difference."

He grinned at me, briefly, and nodded, and got out of the car and told me to wait, and there I was, sitting there, watching the sun doing nothing at all, again, just hanging there a finger's width above the horizon like it was waiting for me to blink first. The heat was extraordinary, far hotter than it had been in Ybaddli, late in the day but still strong enough to feel like something with mass and colour and a dull, impartial hatred for human life. I opened the door. It didn't help. The only sound was water, there must have been a river nearby, but I couldn't see it. I got out of the car to piss, and stumbled, as the hunger and the thirst and the tiredness lined up and hit me with one great big lead-gloved fist. Even outside the car, the only thing I could hear was the water. I could see the nearest huts, but nothing inside them, and nothing moving outside. I pissed, got back in and carried on staring at the sun.

After a few minutes of this I looked at my phone. There was no signal, obviously, and the battery was getting low. But my watch had already died – you get what you pay for – and I needed to know the time. It wasn't like I could do anything about, it wasn't like if it was five I'd get out and if it was six I'd stay put, I just needed to know.

It was six.

By quarter past I'd given up. The sun still hadn't moved but my thirst was getting worse. I gave it another ten minutes. After that, I'd have to see what had happened to Chima.

I didn't have to. He walked back five minutes later with that same casual stroll that was just starting to annoy me. I couldn't read his face. He got in the car, in the driver's seat.

"Well?"

"They've gone."

"They believed you?"

"I showed them this."

He had the totem in his hand, *gris-gris*, he'd called it. I was puzzled, briefly, but then I saw how it would have played out. He'd disappeared, dead, or a traitor, maybe, and now he was back, so why should they believe him?

But then he'd shown them this thing, this relic of his past, something he'd kept with him for thirty years when (if he was telling the truth) he'd kept nothing else, and I still couldn't see why Poulter had let him keep it anyway. It didn't matter. The gris-gris had done the trick. I hadn't noticed before, but there was a leather strap on it, wrapped round his wrist, so that when he wasn't actually holding it in his hand and looking at it it was almost part of his body.

"So now we can go?"

I needed a drink, but I didn't really fancy being around when Frentoi turned up.

"Where will we go?"

He was looking at me as if he actually expected an answer. I didn't have one.

"The road ends here, Sam, and even a Land Rover cannot manage the land beyond. We can drive back the way we came, but that is certainly the way they will come, Frentoi, and if they see us they will kill us just for being on the road."

I could see his point. After everything we'd been through, getting shot on the way back was an experience I'd rather avoid. He went on.

"We can go and hide in the bush with the others from the village. You want to do that? Frentoi might not find us, they probably will not find us, we will live. Of course, that will not stop them hunting all over the country for me, and Colonel Poulter will still be looking for you until you are dead, or he is dead, so I am not sure that will help us much either."

"So what do you have in mind?" I asked, even though it had suddenly hit me. I knew what he had in mind. I'd looked in the back of the Land Rover when I'd given up staring at the sun.

He did it pretty much by himself. I couldn't have been much help if my life had depended on it, it was beyond me, I'd never done anything like this before and never expected to. I lugged boxes out of the back and put them where he told me to, and when there were no more boxes I stood and watched him, for a while, and then I went back and sat in the Land Rover and wondered how the hell my life had come to this.

I'd dropped one of the boxes on my right foot, and it hurt more than I'd have expected it to. I didn't mind that. It was a slow throb of a pain, the kind of pain someone who's clumsy or too often drunk knows like an old lover. I was grateful for something familiar.

It didn't take him long. Twenty minutes, and he was done. The sun had crept about a centimetre lower. He got in beside me and grinned.

"This is good, Sam," he said. I didn't share his excitement.

"Finally, we are doing something."

I'd been *doing something* from the beginning, I thought, and then it hit me again, that odd feeling of emptiness, the fear and the thing which made me not care about the fear. I might have been doing something from the beginning, but I wasn't sure it was for the same reasons I was doing something now.

Not that I'd done much.

"And now?" I asked.

"Now we move the Land Rover, and then we wait."

Which was funny, because waiting was about all I'd done since I'd arrived in the country.

So we moved the Land Rover, just a few yards off the road, but invisible unless you knew it was there. I explained to Chima that if I didn't have something to drink soon I wouldn't be any use to anyone, and he disappeared for thirty seconds and came back with a flask of water. I didn't ask where it came from. By this time I didn't really care. I drank it all in three great gulps and even though my head was still hurting, I knew it was what I'd needed.

And then we waited.

We didn't have to wait long. Another hour, not much before eight, and we heard the engines. A minute later, the lights, which were on even though it still wasn't dark. The lights were useful, because we could see them sweeping over the huts in front and that told us there were six of them, six vehicles, which meant a hell of a lot of psychopaths with guns.

We waited. There was so much waiting. We could hear them getting out, calling to each other, to the villagers, firing shots into the air. Then quiet, as they went from hut to hut, looking inside, and more shouts, as it became clear what had happened, that the village was empty, that they had been cheated of other people's deaths.

Chima looked at me. There was an expression on his face, like he was asking for permission. I shrugged. The shrug was enough.

In Chima's hand was a small black box, and on the box

was a button. He pressed the button. For a fraction of a second, nothing happened.

And then the whole world went red.

20: Where It All Began

I couldn't tell how long I'd been out for. A few seconds, I thought, probably, not more than a minute. My ears were ringing, and when I opened my eyes to see what was going in it felt like someone had cut the top off my head and dropped a chainsaw inside. The sun still hadn't set, it was everywhere, in front of me, above me, beside me. Inside the ringing there were screams and gunshots and a voice, close by, saying the same thing over and over again, *Lukeee, Lukeee, Lukeee*.

Car. I was in a car. Where the windscreen was supposed to be, in front of me, there was a big square of nothing. Beyond the square there was green, which seemed right, but also red, which didn't. It occurred to me that a few moments earlier everything had been red, and now it wasn't, so maybe this was just in my head, something I'd imagined, like the man with the gun at Dovesham.

Oh.

I moved my head to the side, which hurt, but not unbearably. The man with the gun at Dovesham was there. It was his voice I could hear, he was talking to me, repeatedly, and what he was saying wasn't "*Lukeee*" but "Look at me".

I focused on his face. He stopped saying it and smiled.

"You're OK, Sam," he said.

His name was Chima Nwosu. My name was Sam Williams. I was a human rights lawyer from London and I had just helped him blow up a group of terrorists.

I nodded, so gently that I doubted Chima could have seen it at all. It didn't hurt. I nodded again.

"Yes, I think so," I said. My voice sounded different,

still my voice, but as if I was hearing it from somewhere else. Somewhere to my left.

"Your head will be fine."

I couldn't think why I hadn't noticed, but Chima's hand was pressed to the side of my head nearest him. The right side of my head. He took the hand away, and I had a glimpse of green, a scrap of cloth, the canvas that had covered the explosives in the back of the Land Rover. But the green was mostly red.

"I need to drive us away from here, Sam. You take this."

I realised I was having to concentrate to hear the words. The ringing had faded, mostly, but there was still a persistent high-pitched tone in my right ear. I knew what that meant, what that might mean. I shook my head, to get rid of the thought and, if I was lucky, the ringing. When I stopped shaking both the thought and the ringing were still there.

But at least I was alive.

Chima pushed the rag into my hand and pressed my hand against my head. I remembered that just before he'd pressed the button I'd looked across and noticed he was wearing his seatbelt and wondered why. The roof. The force of the explosion had lifted me up and smashed my head into the roof of the Land Rover. At least the pain was starting to fade. He was right. Whatever might have happened to my right ear, my head would be fine. Still. He could have told me about the seatbelt.

We were moving. Reversing, then bumping back onto the road, then spinning round to face the other direction, where it wasn't red, just the darkening yellow of dead land in the evening sun. My head was clearing, and in my good ear I could hear everything now, except everything was just the sound of the engine. No more explosions, no more screams, no more gunshots.

Everyone was dead.

I looked down. Chima had strapped me in while I was unconscious. What with that and the rag pressed to my head it must have been more than a minute. I wanted to ask him how long and what had happened but the effort was too much. I closed my eyes and willed myself to sleep.

Sleep wouldn't come. The car was jerking around a bit, but that shouldn't have stopped me. The moment I closed my eyes there was Chima pointing a gun at me and Iffy looking like he was on his way to the firing squad and Freddie with a broken neck and Claire being tortured by Ballantine, which I knew hadn't happened, but that didn't stop it showing up in my head among the whole horrible series of images that had planted themselves there in the last few days. And the Grimshaws, of course, no more out of place here than anywhere else. I was, I reminded myself, a human rights lawyer. I should have had plenty of images stored away there, massacres in refugee camps, water-boarding of terror suspects, bombings and assassinations. Instead I had drug busts and minor car accidents. I unsuccessfully fought back a laugh.

"What is it?" asked Chima. I opened my eyes. He'd slowed the car down and was looking at me with concern, like the explosion had turned me into a lunatic who laughed in his sleep.

"Nothing, Chima," I said. My voice sounded closer this time. My throat was hurting, but that was hardly surprising. Flight, air conditioning, dry heat, more air conditioning, bad meat, bad whisky, vomit, fear, lack of sleep, lack of food, lack of water, concussion. The fact that I'd got away with a sore throat and a ringing in one ear was a bona fide miracle.

Of course the pain didn't matter, and so far I hadn't got away with a thing. We'd saved Chima's village, temporarily, we'd killed a few terrorists, out of hundreds, and Ballantine and Poulter were still out there looking for us. Whatever we might have done, it wasn't over.

"Where are the diamonds, Chima?"

He looked over at me and shook his head and I closed my eyes and this time, I slept.

We weren't moving. I opened my eyes again. It couldn't have been much later, because the sun was still there, fat over the horizon, hanging around like a West End taxi driver who wouldn't take no for answer. I yawned. My throat still hurt.

I looked to the side. There was nobody there. Suddenly I didn't feel like yawning any more.

A tap-tap-tap, close to my head. I looked up. Chima was there, outside, flicking a finger against the window. He looked at me briefly, and then away. I opened the door, tried to get out, forgot the seatbelt and found myself dragged back down. Second time round I managed it.

By the time I made it out of the car Chima had already moved off. I glanced around. A tired-looking bush and a few dying trees to my left. Might not sound like much, but that made this a unique spot, a landmark. I didn't remember many trees on the road. Still no birds. I remembered what Chima had said. *Even the birds had left our country by then.* From what I'd seen of the place, I couldn't blame them.

Chima was round the other side of the car, looking over at the trees. I coughed, and he looked round.

"Toilet break," he said.

While he was gone I felt in my pocket for my phone. It was still there, and there was a notification. A text message, which meant we must have gone through somewhere that had a signal, which was another surprise.

The message was from Claire, and it was short and to the point.

"Bor Platinum 1990. Iraq Oil 2001. Also Mali GoldCo 1989 Suriname Bauxite 1985 Khartoum Copper 1970."

I sat down on the ground and tried to figure it out. Frentoi and Surtalga, 2011. Serbia, 1990. Iraq, 2001. I had a degree in modern history and a photographic memory, so Mali, Surinam and Sudan rang some pretty loud bells. The dates that went with those bells were a little out, but that was what I'd expected. That was the whole point.

I found myself smiling. The strange and unidentifiable emptiness was suddenly clear and obvious, and it was nothing to do with hunger or thirst or lack of sleep. What was it I'd said to Claire? *It's not my war.* She'd told me that was bullshit, and she'd been right. I might get killed out here, I might make it as far as Ybaddli, I might get all the way home and find myself with a broken neck and a burning body, but at least I was on the right side. I could see how zealots were made. For as long as I could remember things had been complicated, voices in every direction, what I should do, what I had to do, what I wanted to do, there had been doubts and confusions and a million different shades of grey. Suddenly that was all gone, swept away by one simple fact. I was on the right side.

Did it make a difference?

I thought it did.

Still, all things being equal, I didn't want to die.

Chima was taking a while. I thought maybe I'd take a look around, but it didn't take more than fifteen seconds to see there wasn't anything to look at. A bush. A few trees. The same dead yellow everywhere else. The sun still hadn't set, but the heat was easing. I looked back at the phone. Still not yet nine, I couldn't have been asleep more than a few minutes. I walked back to the car but didn't get in. I'd spent enough time sitting in that thing already.

A sound behind me. Chima was coming back, walking slowly. There was something in his right hand.

I didn't think he'd had anything with him when he'd gone down there. In fact, I was sure of it.

He walked over and stood in front of me and put the thing down. It was a briefcase. Worn, and caked in dried mud and the detritus of decades of flood and drought. Somehow out of place, in the scrub and the dirt. But still, and clearly, a briefcase.

"Is that what I think it is?" I asked.

He stared at me.

"The diamonds?"

He looked past me, back the way we'd come. There was a faint chill in the air now, it seemed a little darker than it had been just a minute earlier. I followed his gaze. I could still see the smoke from the explosives we'd detonated. He'd detonated. We couldn't be far from the village.

"You know where we are, Sam?" he asked, and suddenly, I did.

"It was here, wasn't it?"

He nodded. I walked right up to him, without thinking what I was doing, and put a hand on his shoulder. It didn't feel like the kind of thing Sam Williams would do, but I didn't feel like that Sam Williams any more, and I wasn't sure that was such a bad thing. He started at the touch, briefly, then nodded again.

"It was here. It was here we cowered while our families burned, it was here we heard their screams, it was here we saw their bodies float away in the smoke. There was nothing we could do that day, except hide like cowards and wait for the murderers to drive by, but this was the place where we became soldiers."

And then an unexpected sound, from behind me. From behind the car.

Applause.

One man, clapping.

And a voice.

"A charming story, Chima. A soldier, was it? Of course a few years later you decided to run off with all the regimental silver, but we can't let a little detail like that ruin the story, can we?"

I'd heard that voice before. *"Milk? Cream? Sugar?"*

I turned, slowly.

There were two of them, standing behind the car. Christ alone knew how long they'd been waiting there or how they'd even got there without us seeing them. I couldn't see another car, but they couldn't have walked all the way from Ybaddli, which meant they must have something parked close by.

The silent one, the one standing tall and straight and pointing a gun at the narrow space between Chima's head and my own, the last time I'd seen that elegant sweep of hair we'd been in his "rooms", the last time I'd heard his voice he'd been telling someone he'd have his own people out there – out here – shortly. We'd just blown up a bunch of those people, I realised. And here he was, in person.

But he wasn't the man running the show. The man running the show was a quiet white-haired fellow with creases round his eyes, and he was still smiling, but the smile wasn't so nervous this time. Jenkins, last time we'd met. But the time for pretence was long gone.

I was looking at Colonel Poulter.

21: A Briefcase

The next few moments seemed to take place as a series of unrelated incidents, things shifted outside the normal world of cause and effect, and then back in again. It began with Poulter raising one arm to reveal that he, too, was holding a gun. He nodded towards the briefcase. Words were unnecessary.

Chima bent down, towards the case. I tried to remember if he'd taken a gun with him when he'd stepped out of the car, but I couldn't picture it. I'd been asleep. I visualised the car, the front, the boot, whether there had been any guns lying around, but my mind was suddenly blank, all I could remember were the explosives under the green canvas cover, and anyway, it wasn't like I expected to be able to do much even with a gun in my hand.

Then I was looking at Poulter, and Poulter's gun was pointing at my head. I heard a scuffing sound and sensed dust rising, and realised that Chima had kicked the case towards me. Without thinking, I bent down to pick it up. While I was down like this, the car was between me and Poulter's gun, and even though I couldn't see Ballantine I felt suddenly safe, like I was wearing Kevlar or just looking at the whole thing through a bullet-proof window. I glanced at Chima. In the empty space between us the dust he'd kicked up was circling slowly back to the ground, the setting sun picking out individual specks and painting them red or gold for an instant, snatching them out of reality, and then releasing them back into dull brown obscurity. I forced my gaze away.

Chima was holding a gun. He turned, just in time, because Poulter and Ballantine had moved round to our side of the car and for the briefest of moments, Ballantine had his own gun pointed at Chima's head.

Poulter's weapon was pointed at me.

Three men holding guns and one holding a briefcase. Chima had made up his mind instantly, and aimed at Poulter. Two guns against one. I couldn't see what good the briefcase would be against a bullet, but still, it was a standoff. Poulter didn't want his head blown off, and Ballantine wouldn't want his boss shot dead in front of him, even if he could take out the killer a second later.

"How did you find me?" asked Chima, and Ballantine laughed. Poulter just smiled.

"We know what's important to you, Chima," said Ballantine, and laughed again. "I know you so well I can probably tell you what's going through your head right now."

"I doubt it," said Chima.

Ballantine shrugged.

"You're trying to work out how to kill us both and get out, and you're picturing our bodies rotting in your shithole of a county, Chima. Am I right?"

Now Chima laughed, which surprised me.

"Even this shithole of a country is too good to be a graveyard for people like you, Mr Ballantine. But how did you find me?"

"I told you. We figured out what mattered to you. After that, it was easy."

I glanced to my side, to Chima. I had that luxury. The others had to stare where the guns told them to. Chima looked puzzled.

"You did not follow me to the village. I was watching the road."

"That's right, Chima."

"So what do you mean?"

Poulter had stayed silent, and he still didn't speak, just inclined his head gently towards Chima's hand, the one that wasn't holding the gun. The hand was empty, and I didn't understand what the gesture meant. Chima did, though. The expression on his face turned from puzzled to furious in an instant.

"You would not."

Ballantine was laughing again, and now Poulter with him.

"Oh, we would, Chima," said the older man.

"You know what this is?"

I didn't have the faintest idea what they were talking about.

"Yes, Chima. It's a lump of metal."

The gris-gris. It was still strapped to his wrist.

"You didn't like to talk about it, Chima, but we knew what it was."

Ballantine had taken over the conversation again.

"Of course, you didn't like to talk much about anything, but I always liked the way you *particularly* avoided discussing the one thing that was so obviously important to you."

"You opened this."

It wasn't a question, but Ballantine nodded. I'd been trying to work out why we were having this conversation, like a collection of villains and victims in a Bond movie, why there hadn't just been two or three gunshots and a survivor. And why they were taunting a man with a gun pointed at them. I tried to put myself where they were, two guns, us, one gun and a briefcase, and I saw it straight away. This wasn't idle chat. They were waiting for a slip, a tiny gap in the window they could get their fingers into and push.

"You knew it contained the spirits of my ancestors, and you opened it anyway?"

Poulter laughed again, and broke in.

"Oh come now, Chima, you don't believe that any more than we do."

He was right about that. Chima's obsession with the thing had nothing to do with magical or spiritual power. It was his way of remembering his family.

With a flick, Chima had the disk in his hand. Keeping his eyes on Poulter and Ballantine, he reached out and passed it to me.

"Open this," he said. He couldn't do it himself, not without dropping the gun, or at least letting his concentration lapse, which was just what Poulter was hoping for.

It was heavier than I'd expected, but it wasn't solid. There was a clasp on the side. It looked like it hadn't been opened in decades. I picked at the clasp with my nails and prised it open easily.

At first glance the thing looked empty. It wasn't. A tiny bit of metal and plastic was half-embedded in its inner wall like a midget staple. I picked it out and held it up. Chima glanced towards it and nodded. Poulter and Ballantine were still smiling.

"For someone so determined not to let us in, Chima, your attachment to that thing was touchingly stupid."

Poulter was brave, I had to give him that. If someone was pointing a gun at my head, the last thing I'd have wanted to do was annoy them. I reminded myself why he was doing it. And, of course, someone was pointing a gun at my head, and all I had to stop the bullet was a briefcase. I was stood there with my mouth open holding the damned thing like I didn't know what it was, like I'd never seen a briefcase before, like an actor who'd forgotten his lines and was stuck out there on stage with the wrong prop waiting for a cue. There was no cue. There was nothing I could do.

Except, of course, there was something I could do. There were four of us here, three holding guns, and Chima wasn't the only one who had to keep his concentration.

I coughed. I was about to say something that might, if I was lucky, save my life. I didn't want it to come out as a croak.

"Chima," I said, and I saw him twitch in surprise. He hadn't expected me to be doing the talking any more than I had. He didn't take his eyes off the others.

"Chima, we've lost. I'm sorry."

He nodded. I hadn't expected a nod. I knew I was playing a game. I wasn't sure he did.

"I just want to go home and forget about all this. Let me give him the diamonds, Chima. It's over."

My right ear was still ringing, a little, but I could hear laughter again from Ballantine. I kept my eyes on Chima. He nodded, and spoke.

"Why do you think they will not kill you anyway?"

Which was true, and remarkably similar to what Claire had said half a world away in London. I tried to think of something plausible in response.

"Maybe they will. I can swear to keep my mouth shut, they've got enough dirt on me, and I'm sure they can make up more if they need to. That might be enough to keep me quiet, at least. And the fact is, if we don't give up the diamonds, they'll kill us and take them anyway. If we do, there's a chance we might live."

"I still have a gun, you know, Sam."

There was the ringing, and underneath that the quiet laughter from Ballantine, but there was something else. A scuffing noise. Chima was still glancing between Poulter and Ballantine but his brow was somehow lower, his face pointing down, and drawing my gaze down with it. Towards the sound of the scuffing. I looked at his shoes, pushing forward and back, forward and back, tracing tiny ephemeral patterns in the dust.

I wasn't the only one playing a game. In between the shoes, visible to me but hidden by them from Poulter and Ballantine, lay another gun.

The gun was on the ground, so I couldn't get to it, not without being shot. And even if I did get to it, it would be two armed men against two armed men, one of whom didn't have a clue what to do with a gun. Not for the first time, I wondered why it couldn't have been Hans instead of me, Hans on the step of the helicopter staring into Chima's gun. Chima could have done with someone like Hans, and here he was, here we were, stuck with me instead.

But the gun was something new, it was something we knew about and they didn't, it was an edge, a twist, a tiny nudge back in the direction of not getting killed after all.

All of which is to say that once I saw the gun, even though it didn't change things all that much, I felt better and more confident. It was a screwed up card game, in the middle of nowhere, with guns. My partner had spotted my bluff, which was good, but now I knew we had something that might actually win us the hand. Ballantine was still laughing and if I was going to die I didn't want Ballantine laughing to be the last thing I heard.

"What the hell are you laughing at?" I asked.

He stopped laughing, abruptly, and turned to Poulter, who replied on his behalf.

"Diamonds," he said, simply. "You still think this is about diamonds."

I looked back at Ballantine. He looked serious, again. I turned to Chima, still keeping his eyes on the other guns, but he was difficult to read at the best of times. No one else was saying anything, and even with the gun on the ground I had the feeling delay was my best chance of staying alive. And I was curious, anyway.

"Isn't it?" I asked.

Poulter shook his head.

I glanced at Chima. Nothing. I thought that was probably best. I didn't want him distracted. Poulter went on.

"The fact is, Sam, Surtalga – Mirandano, it was, then – this place never really had anything. You've got oil to the north and diamonds to the south but this little oasis of shit has neither. Oh sure, a few diamonds, enough to keep a bunch of guerrillas together a few years, but even that was running out, wasn't it?"

His eye wandered back towards Chima. I followed it, and thought I saw an almost imperceptible nod.

"Which is ironic, really, because if it hadn't been for the promise of diamonds the war probably wouldn't have happened in the first place. And if the war hadn't happened, well, none of this would have been necessary at all."

No diamonds. I didn't understand. If there were no diamonds, or not enough diamonds to make much of a difference, what the hell was I here for? Why had Chima kept his mouth shut for thirty years, why had he escaped and come home, why had Poulter let loose the rabid dogs of war on the place, why had he followed us here himself? None of it made sense.

I started to put the case down, and then remembered what they were trying to do, Poulter and Ballantine. I stopped my arm before it had moved more than a couple of inches, but my face must have given away what I'd been feeling, because Poulter piped up again.

"Sam doesn't understand, Chima. If he's going to die, don't you think it's only fair that he understands why?"

I glanced over. Chima nodded, again, more clearly this

time, and then, to my astonishment, he started to talk.

"It's true I was a traitor, Sam."

"You've explained all that. You wanted to get away. Doesn't make you a traitor."

"But I haven't explained it. Not at all. Colonel Poulter," – he pronounced *Colonel* in three long, sarcastic syllables – "he is right about one thing. You need to know the truth."

I waited. I was worried, now, because apart from the small matter of the gun on the ground the one thing that was keeping me going, and keeping the terror to one side, was that nice, simple moral framework, Claire's text, the sense I was with the right team. Burrowing its way up through that moral framework I could sense something else, the growing and horrible possibility that I was going to die for worse than nothing at all.

Chima had stopped talking. It looked like he was trying to work out where to begin. Ballantine decided to give him a hand.

"Tell him about Femi."

Chima nodded, again, and started up.

"Femi died, you know. In the bomb."

"Yes," I said. Everyone knew that. Even Freddie had known that. Remembering Freddie, I was reminded that whatever Chima was about to tell me, I was still with the right team.

"I did it."

I nearly dropped the briefcase.

"You killed Femi?"

Chima nodded.

"Your best friend?"

He nodded again, and I waited. I couldn't quite believe it. He could have killed Iffy, he'd had reasons enough, but he hadn't done. Or maybe, I suddenly thought, he had. Maybe he'd just told me what I wanted to hear.

"You must understand. I had to do it."

"Go on." I hadn't meant to sound cynical, but the moment the words had left my mouth I realised that was exactly how they'd come out.

"If you had seen what he was doing, Sam."

I'd probably been doing my Grammar School entrance exams in Reading. Whatever Femi and Chima were up to in Mirandano was so far away it might as well have been the moon.

Chima had stopped, and now there was something else to worry about, because although he was still looking where he was supposed to be looking, there was an unfocused quality to his gaze. The moral picture might be getting cloudy, but there was still one simple, life-and-death fact underneath it: whatever Chima had to tell me, he had to concentrate on Ballantine and Poulter at the same time.

"Tell him, Chima," said Ballantine, and to my relief the words seemed to snap his face back to reality and the present. He nodded, and went on with the story.

"I did not set the bomb myself. I wish I had done. It would have been more honest. But I could not. Instead I told *them*."

"Told who? Told them what?"

"I knew of people. Channels to the enemy. To the Government. While we were busy killing each other we were talking to each other, too, or some of us were, the men on both sides who could see the war ending and us all having to live together one day."

"And these were the people you spoke to?"

He nodded. I felt I was owed a little more than a nod.

"What did you tell them?"

"I told them where Femi's building was located and how they could get to it. Even as I said it I knew he would die. I wished so many times I had set the bomb myself, and waited for it to explode, to die alongside my friend and stay dead, and so much would have been spared. But I was a coward. And I suffered a coward's punishment."

Ballantine laughed, again, and interjected.

"It's true, you know. Thirty years we had him, and between you and me, we tried things even the Americans don't know about. But we couldn't get to him. The only thing that could do that was own conscience."

"Why?" I asked. I couldn't understand it. He was still a traitor, and that was a fact, but something didn't add up. The facts didn't fit the man I was starting to feel I knew.

"You have to understand, Sam, I was going to leave anyway. I told you I did not want to kill any more. That is true. And for every one of us who wanted peace, there were others who wanted victory even if it meant there would be nobody left to celebrate that victory."

"You mean Femi?"

"I mean many people. But yes, I mean Femi. Femi told me once he saw his father's body every night, the moment he closed his eyes."

And there I was thinking I'd got a bad deal with Bill and Eileen Grimshaw.

"He told me the only way he could rid himself of that picture was by killing the men who had put it in his head. He built bombs and guns that killed those men by the hundred, by the thousand, but even that was not enough. And then he found something that was."

That faraway look was returning to Chima's face. I coughed and clicked a finger and he was back among us.

"Have you ever seen a man die, Sam?"

It was a strange question and for a moment I genuinely couldn't remember the answer. In Dovesham I'd seen the recently, violently dead. I'd been with my grandmother minutes before she had died in hospital, painfully and inevitably, with everyone knowing what was coming. I'd seen accidents and not waited to find out what had happened. But no, I'd never seen a man die.

I shook my head.

"In England, it's funny, you have cancer and stroke and heart attack, in America, too, I see all this on television and certainly it is terrible, when it happens to you, or your wife or your children, but it is nothing out of nature. In this country we have something different. It does not come often but when it comes it is worse than you can imagine, I have seen it and I know that it is worse than I can remember, because my mind would not allow me to recall the worst of it. Do you know what I am talking about?"

I tried to think, again. War? Famine? No. Chima was talking about something different. I turned my mind to news reports. *Mirandano* wasn't a word you heard these days, but *Surtalga* was, and not just recently, with Frentoi. The borders, the rivers, the inaccessibility and ignorance and lack of clean water or hygiene or trust in medical science. Of course.

"Ebola," I said, and saw him nod.

"When this disease comes, so many die", he said, "and those deaths are not good deaths. The sickness gets into everything, into the head, the heart, the eyes, under the skin, and those that are dying die alone, or if they do not die alone then those who are with them will die too, a week later, two weeks, a month, it does not matter, it will come for them. It came to our village once, before I left for the university. It killed eight people and spared the rest of us, because the elders did what they had to do."

"What?" I asked, and Chima shook his head. Whatever it was, it was too painful for him to talk about, and given what else he was happy to discuss, I guessed it wasn't going to be a happy ending. Ballantine decided to fill in the gaps.

"What they do, round here, Sam, they're not as stupid as some. They know how the disease travels. They fear the dying. So it's quite simple, Sam. They burn them."

"They burn the bodies?" It didn't sound so extraordinary. It sounded perfectly sensible to me.

"No, Sam. They burn the living."

I shook my head and turned to Chima, but he was nodding. Still looking at Ballantine and Poulter, nodding, with tears in his eyes.

"It is true, Sam. The elders told the families to leave the village and not to come back for twenty days. And then the sick, seven of them, dying in their huts – they burned those huts and we heard the dying scream."

"You said eight, Chima." I couldn't help it. I've never been able to help it. He nodded.

"I told you the families went away. When they came back, one had died. She had become sick. Her nephew hit her with a rock and pushed her in the river. It was better that way."

I was beginning to feel sick. I'd heard the stories about Ebola, how it killed, how it raced through towns and villages and turned flesh to blood and the agony it brought with it. But this was somehow worse.

"I hated Ebola more than I hated the Government, more than I hated the army, more than I hated the men who had slaughtered my family. But for Femi, Ebola was something different. Femi was a scientist. Femi was very clever, he could do things no one else could do even if they had thought of them."

I waited. By now I knew what was coming, but I had to hear Chima say it.

"Femi turned Ebola into a weapon."

22: The Reason Why

The sun was almost down, finally, but that wasn't the reason I was shivering.

It was in my hands.

The most evil thing in the world, that was the way Chima saw it, and he'd seen some evil. I'd been an idiot. There were no diamonds, there never had been. There was a briefcase full of weaponised Ebola and I had no idea how it had ended up in this particular spot, but that didn't matter. It was in my hands.

"He had been telling me for months he was close, but I did not believe him. He was clever, certainly, but if you could really just make Ebola, like that, make it airborne and even more virulent than nature had already made it, if you could do all that then surely cleverer people would already have done it, and New York, London, Moscow, Tel Aviv, Seoul, these places would have been flooded with the dead. My friend could not do what nobody else in the world could do, I thought."

He paused again. For a quiet man, he was doing a lot of talking. I'd found the same thing last night. Push the right buttons, give the quiet man a chance, and he won't shut up.

"I was wrong. A week before, he told me he had finished. I did not believe him, and then he showed me what he had done to a prisoner, a Government spy who had made the mistake of allowing himself to be taken alive. It was a brutal war, but this was something different. I remembered what I had seen and heard, in my village. Now I believed him."

Ballantine was laughing again. I was starting to wonder if there was anything the bastard wouldn't laugh at.

"You see, Sam? These freedom fighters of yours? Lovely people."

I ignored him. So did Chima.

"I told him he had to stop. I told him this was not right, even in war. And he said something which I thought was very stupid, for a clever man. He said *it is fine, Chima. We will never actually use it.* But had he not already used it, had he not already shown me he could use it? And now he was saying it was enough for it to be known, it would win us the war, it would deter our enemies and make them put down their weapons and we could have the peace we had always wanted."

He sighed.

"I think that he really believed this, Sam. Even though there were people on our side, powerful people, who would not hesitate to use any weapon, he believed he could keep it from them. I told him this. I told him they would kill him if he stood in their way. He said they would not dare. One more week, he said, to complete the tests, and then he would give them their weapon. One vial. But, he said, there would be another. His own. His insurance. It was hidden, he said. I asked him how this would help if he was dead, and he would not answer. *Insurance*, he said, again. And if he did not survive, I would avenge him."

He stopped, again. His voice seemed distant, but as I stared at his face I knew his mind was right there with me. A gentle scuffing, below. He was reminding me about the gun.

"Six days I tried to persuade him not to do this thing, and then I went to these channels and told them – I did not tell them about the Ebola, of course, I was not a fool. I told them where the building was, and I told them that if they destroyed it, if they incinerated it, if they wiped every trace of it from the earth, then peace might come to our country sooner. I went back again, that day, even though I could not be sure when the Government would strike. I pleaded with him one final time. It was no use. I left, and minutes later I heard the explosion and I knew that I had killed my best friend."

He had killed Femi because he had no choice. Iffy was probably still alive.

"I had reported my presence when I entered the building. I made sure not to report out when I left. I was listed among the casualties. I thought I would take the diamonds I had, my final shipment, take them to Antwerp and start my life again. I remembered the insurance Femi had spoken of, but what could I do? I did not even know where it was. It was not until I was in Antwerp that I realised I probably did. Because if I was supposed to avenge him, then I had to know where he had hidden it. And that could only be one place."

He flicked his head towards me, towards the briefcase.

"I thought I would sell the diamonds, return and destroy the last vial, and leave forever. But these men had other ideas. I had been in Antwerp for one hour when they found me. I thought maybe they were just street thieves when they took the diamonds from me."

"Not all of them, Chima," said Poulter, who had remained silent during the confession. No doubt he thought he'd done enough, he'd wound Chima up so far there was no way he'd be able to stay focused. Poulter didn't know about the gun. Chima ignored him.

"And that was it. For thirty years. I do not know how they knew about the Ebola, perhaps they did not and I said something I should not have said, early on. It does not matter. For thirty years these men have been trying to obtain this briefcase, and for thirty years I have known of the death they will release if they have it."

Poulter was nodding.

"He's spot on, Sam."

I could see it. I could see it clearer than Chima, because he could only see what might be to come. I knew what these men had already done.

And now, suddenly, Poulter was the one with things on his mind.

"Thirty years I've been waiting. I figured we'd break the bastard, and then I realised we wouldn't, and I came up with this idea, let him go, follow him back, that was twenty-five years ago, and I wake up and the damn war's over."

"So?" I said.

"Peace was fine with me, I couldn't give a shit about this place. But with peace came the UN, and for all the money I threw about, for all the disappearances I arranged, I couldn't get myself or my people or this bastard in here quietly with thousands of blue berets walking around getting in the way."

I was surprised. The way Poulter operated, I wouldn't have thought the UN could stop him. He looked at me, and paused. Working out whether to go on, or leave me dangling. Playing the percentages. He went on.

"There were people here who knew about me, Sam. I'd been involved since the beginning. I had to arrange for them to be removed before I could do anything. And the blue berets were keeping those bastards safe, too."

"Hence Frentoi."

Poulter looked surprised.

"Clever, Sam. I didn't expect you to figure that out."

"Surtalga Resources. 2011. And Serbia before the civil war. Iraq before the invasion. Mali and Sudan before the coups. Suriname before the guerrillas. At first I wondered how you did it, Poulter, how the hell you knew what was going to happen so long before it did. I mean, I know you had friends in high places, but this was something different, wasn't it? And then I saw what you'd done here, and it all made sense. You saw something you wanted, and you brought those murdering bastards in to help you get it. I thought it was for the diamonds, but it could have been anything, right?"

Poulter was nodding again.

"You're right. Diamonds would have been enough, you know, even a handful, even that little case you're holding. Because you know what it cost to bring Frentoi in, to arm them, to bring this shithole of a country to its knees?"

I shook my head.

"Half a million dollars. That's it. Half a million dollars for a country. A briefcase full of diamonds would have been just fine. But this, Sam? This is something different. Imagine a weapon so powerful the whole world fears it. Imagine owning that weapon. Imagine if you could divide it as many times as you wanted, use it, sell it and still have enough left over to do it all again."

"You'd be the most powerful man in the world."

He shrugged.

"I'm not greedy, Sam. I think you might be exaggerating a little. But yes, it's true to say I'd be able to do whatever the hell I wanted. Of course what I want to do is sell it, piece by piece, whenever it suits me. But first, I had to get it."

"So you created a war."

"Yes. That's precisely what we did. That's what we do. Other people make computers, or food, or money. We make wars."

"For your own benefit."

Poulter shrugged. I'd wavered, briefly, when they'd told me about Femi, and the diamonds, but since then I'd been steady enough. Chima had been too, I thought. Unless Poulter had something new, I didn't think keeping everyone talking was going to work out for him. He hadn't given up on it yet, though. On he went, expansive, almost persuasive, and it struck me that Poulter was a chameleon. Soldier, salesman, killer, businessman, politician. And always, I reminded myself, liar. Above all, liar.

"Sometimes," he was saying. "Sometimes we identify something we want, and yes, we make sure we can get it. If that means a rebellion or a coup or a secession, well, these things are always on the verge of happening anyway, aren't they? All we have to do is give them a gentle nudge. On occasion we act for paying clients, people with interests in countries that need to be pushed in a certain direction. In the sixties the CIA used to do it, but they were amateurs. It's always happened, Sam, all over the world. It comes in waves, in patterns, in the jungles and the mountains and the dust. Someone has to draw the patterns. We're just the ones holding the pencil."

"The Scourge," I said, and heard an intake of breath beside me. Chima's mouth had fallen open and for a moment I was afraid this was it, the moment he slipped, and I was the idiot who'd driven him there. I coughed. He nodded, and spoke.

"Since the beginning, you said?"

He was addressing Poulter, who nodded in reply.

"You were the Scourge?"

Another nod.

"Was this – was Mirandano, was it another of your wars, the ones you created?"

Poulter was smiling now.

"It's taken you long enough to figure it out, Chima. But well done. Yes, it was one of ours. And what a waste that was. No diamonds to speak of. We'd torch a village and say it was the Government, and everybody would be furious, and then we'd lob a few bombs and call ourselves rebels, and the Government would get cross, and pretty soon the Government and the People's Army were doing all the work for us. But no diamonds to show for it."

"You torched villages?" asked Chima. I could see his mind turning it over, working out dates and times and possibilities.

"Yes. Several. Many. One of them might even have been yours."

Chima collapsed to the ground. It was sudden and unexpected and that's probably what kept us both alive, because until that point, whatever he'd been saying, Chima had kept his head and Poulter couldn't have imagined he'd lose it so suddenly. I was on top of him half a second later, straightening his arm, pulling him up, and neither Poulter nor Ballantine had yet reacted. Chima was back on his feet, gun pointed in roughly the right direction, and I was back on my spot, a couple of feet away, the briefcase in my left hand in front of my stomach.

Stomach, or head. Now I knew what was in the case, I was guessing they wouldn't want to shoot it. My stomach was safe, this way. My head wasn't. You can't have everything.

"Give it up, Chima," said Ballantine, which seemed somewhat optimistic. Chima had resisted for thirty years. He'd been tortured and imprisoned and he couldn't have expected to get away, alive, safe. He wasn't going to hand over the case just because someone asked him to. Nothing had changed. That's what I thought.

I suppose, like the CIA, I was an amateur.

"Your village," said Poulter, softly, as if nothing had happened since he'd last spoken. "Not far from here, is it?"

Chima shrugged. No point in denying it.

"The thing is, Chima, you're not going to make it out of here alive, are you?"

Another shrug.

"But there's dying, and then there's dying, isn't there?"

For a moment I didn't understand what he was saying, and then I saw him nod towards the case in my hand and I realised. Chima must have realised too, I thought. Now we knew how Poulter operated, it didn't take a genius to figure out his next play.

"I am not afraid, Colonel. Like you say, you will kill me anyway. I will be dead. I have lived with pain. Why should I not die in pain?"

I'd been wrong. Chima hadn't realised, yet, hadn't read the play, couldn't see where Poulter's thoughts were leading. Poulter shook his head slowly, and smiled.

"You remember the spy, Chima? The man who Femi chose, as an experiment, to infect?"

Chima swallowed, and nodded. I started to worry, something sharp and tangible inside the bubble of fear around me. We had the gun, our secret, our *something new*. But Poulter had his own something new, too, and if Chima didn't see it coming it might be the window the bastard was looking for. He was still talking.

"We need our own little experiment, Chima. If we're going to sell this thing, we need a demonstration. Not you, Chima. One man isn't enough, not if I'm going to show the world what I've got. I was thinking of infecting a prison. No one would care that much. No one would go in and try to save them, a prison, in Ybaddli or some other shithole, a bunch of murderers and thieves and rapists, no one would risk themselves for that. They'd probably just burn the place down and blame a mob. But now, Chima, I'm thinking of something else. I'm thinking your village would do nicely."

"No, Poulter."

Chima looked scared. I hadn't seen him look scared. I hadn't believed he could. Nothing had changed, I'd thought.

I really was an amateur.

"No," Chima said, again. Nothing happened. Nobody spoke.

Poulter stood there, with a quizzical, almost gentle look on his face. I was reminded of Jenkins, of Poulter-as-Jenkins, wearing a shy, nervous smile as he asked whether I'd like milk, or cream, or sugar. The choice he was offering Chima was very different, but the look was the same. The fear was fading from Chima's face, but I couldn't forget I'd seen it. On the plus side, at least he'd stayed on his feet this time. As for me, well, the case was in my left hand, still, in front of my stomach. My left arm was slightly bent, and even though the case was light enough, it was awkward and uncomfortable and I hoped to hell this didn't go on too long because I didn't know how long I could go on holding it that way.

I had to hold onto it that way because that was the only way I could hold it in front of my right hand without drawing too much attention to myself. And I had to hold it in front of my right hand because in my right hand, cold and surprisingly light, was the gun Chima had slipped to me in the split second I was pretending to pull him up.

23: Any Dog Can Turn

A gun in my hand.

I suppose that makes it sound like it just happened. It didn't. There was a moment, down there in the dust, when there was a decision to be made. Take it, or don't, and hope for the best. *Any gun's better than no gun*, you'd think, and usually you'd be right, but it depends who's holding that gun, and I'm no Chima Nwosu, or Ballantine, or Ilic, I'm Sam Williams, fumbler of kebabs, repeated smasher of my own head, dropper of high explosives. A gun might be better than no gun, but no gun would be better than a stumble, a hand passing through empty space, and the gun still lying there in the dust. There was no time at all, really, hardly half a second, but still. It didn't just happen. I didn't just do it. I weighed it up and made my decision and for once, it had turned out right.

For now.

The pause stretched into a silence. There was nothing left to say. I guessed Ballantine and Poulter were thinking they'd done all they could and there weren't going to be any more open windows. It was over to Chima. He had a decision to make, about how he died, about how his friends died, and even if he didn't care about himself any more, even if he didn't care about me, he'd just driven halfway across this hellhole of a country to save his village from Frentoi, so from where I was standing the card Poulter had played looked a good one.

Chima was waiting. Maybe he was still hoping one of them would slip up, would tire of the heat or just of standing there, doing nothing, for so long. I didn't think it was likely. Of the four of us here the one most likely to slip up was me.

The pain in my arm was becoming intense. I kept trying to think about something else. Something nice. Claire. I thought about Claire, her face, her smile, her body. That bought me a few seconds, and then my brain was off, Claire, Maloney, Ballantine, Poulter, Chima, Ebola, the briefcase and the agony in my arm.

Something nice hadn't worked. I backtracked. Ebola. Long, lingering death. Organs liquefied, they said. Weeping blood. But even though I'd read about it, heard about it, even though I was holding the damned thing, it was still too abstract. Ebola gave me the briefcase and the briefcase gave me the pain.

I don't know why, because it wasn't exactly useful, but briefly I got a glimpse of the four of us as we might look from somewhere else, from someone else. Three men with guns, one with a briefcase so nasty it made Pandora's Box look like a Christmas cracker, and the same guy holding another gun, hidden, one he didn't really know how to use. All those ingredients, plus the gathering cold, the tiredness, the things we knew and the things we didn't, all balancing out in a perfectly-poised equilibrium. A tableau, one of those extraordinary gigantic full-colour Renaissance paintings strewn with figures frozen in battle or in the moment of martyrdom, in the chase or the sacrifice or the long, painful walk. Equilibrium. A stupid, pointless thing to think, but it took my mind off my arm for a few more seconds, and it was right, too, because without something else happening we'd stay like this until one of us collapsed for real.

And then something else did happen.

It started so faintly I thought it was just the ringing returning to my right ear. But subtly different, and as it got louder I realised it wasn't getting louder, it was approaching, and it wasn't a ringing, it was the sound of an engine. The way we were standing, we could all look at the road without turning around, but I was the only one who could do it without taking much of a risk, because as far as Poulter and Ballantine were concerned my gun wasn't part of the balance.

I glanced to my left. Lights. It was getting dark now, so even though they were a long way off it was clear there were two lights, one vehicle, heading towards us. I thought about what was back that way. *The road ends here*, that's what Chima had said. This vehicle had come from the village, and there might have been a car or a truck hidden there, but I doubted it.

Six had come. We hadn't stuck around to see what had happened to them. I'd just assumed everyone was dead, or on the slow painful way there. Now I wasn't so sure.

The others had noticed the sound now, and one by one taken the fraction of a second they needed to see what it was and where it was coming from.

"Frentoi," said Chima.

Poulter smiled, and shrugged.

"Then they can finish the job I paid them for, can't they?"

Chima smiled back.

"You think they'll want to do that now?"

I glanced back at the road. The vehicle was getting closer. I couldn't tell for sure, from this distance and in the dark, but from the outline it looked like a Jeep. I'd noticed Poulter's smile briefly waver, but by the time I looked back at him it was there again. Poulter was a liar, and his face was half the lie. I didn't believe that smile for a second.

"I've been giving them food and weapons for a couple of years now, Chima. I think they'll be happy to finish off a couple of nobodies. I think they'd do it for fun, anyway. You know what they're like."

Chima nodded.

"I do. They are dogs, and like dogs they remember wrongs that have been done to them. I know six vehicles came in and only one is coming out. Do you think they will remember who sent them there?"

Poulter's smile faltered again, briefly, returned, then disappeared. And that was all it took. With the mask gone, without the smile, his face was so changed that I'd have been hard-pushed to recognise him. The creases round the eyes were still there, but now they looked more like lines etched out by wind, sand and pain than by laughter. Jenkins was gone. This was the Colonel.

"Move," he said, and gestured with his gun. He wanted us to turn and back away. And even though the balance hadn't changed at all, or shouldn't have, somehow it seemed natural that he was the one giving the orders.

Chima nodded and took a step back. So did I. The Jeep was getting closer. It was all very well moving away from the road, I could get that, if there was a chance of not being spotted that was probably best for all four of us. But surely they'd see the Land Rover, even in the dark. And chances were that would be enough to stop them.

I could hear the whine as the Jeep over-revved. Frentoi weren't what you'd call careful owners. Poulter was talking, saying "It's OK, they work for me," and for all he was addressing the words to Ballantine, he sounded like a man trying to convince himself. He waved the gun. I took another step back. So did Chima, although he had turned, a little, so that his angle of backward motion was around sixty degrees from the road rather than directly away. It was dark enough now that I couldn't see his face clearly, but Poulter didn't seem to react, which meant either he hadn't noticed or he didn't care, so I followed suit. I didn't know why Chima had done it, but doing what Chima did was probably my best chance of surviving.

"The stomach," he said. I stared at him. He was

speaking quietly, and in the noise of the approaching Jeep I didn't think Poulter or Ballantine could hear.

"The stomach. Head is best, but there is a lot of stomach."

He spoke a little louder, and this time I was sure Ballantine had heard, because five things happened at the same time, or almost at the same time, since logically one had to follow the other, but so close together it was difficult to tell where one thing ended and the next begun.

The first thing was Ballantine saying "What the hell", but I never got to find out if that was the whole question or just the beginning of a longer one, because the second thing happened immediately.

The second thing was the whine of the engine reaching a crescendo and then cutting out entirely, abruptly, to be replaced by the sound of raised voices close by.

The third thing was Chima disappearing. One moment he was by my side, the next moment he was gone, and even in the flurry of all these things happening as close to simultaneously as it's possible for consecutive things to happen, I had time to think "What the hell?" myself.

The fourth thing was light, sudden bright light, side-on but still strong enough to make me blink and then squint and only then think to myself *the Jeep, dammit, now they can see us.*

The fifth thing was several things, but most of them were thoughts running through my head and that really is as close to simultaneous as makes no difference.

They can see us, I realised. *I can see Poulter.* The darkness had fallen so fast he'd been little more than a vague outline moments before. Now he was shining like a bonfire. Poulter was the obvious choice because his gun was still pointing at my head. Ballantine's was pointing at the bit of empty air Chima had been in before he disappeared.

The stomach, I thought.

Where the hell is Chima? I thought, but that didn't seem to matter.

I adjusted my right hand so that it was pointing the right way. I moved my left hand up and to the side, so there was no longer anything between the gun and what it was pointing at. *I hope this thing's loaded,* I thought, and squeezed the trigger, and as I did it I felt a pain in my arm that I assumed was the recoil, even though it seemed to have started before I'd finished squeezing.

Five things.

The gun was loaded.

The noise wasn't as loud as I'd thought it was going to be, but it was loud enough. Poulter looked at me and smiled, and then suddenly stopped smiling and fell slowly to the ground. He was clutching his thigh – I couldn't figure out which one – and even as he fell I could see the blood spreading out and up and around. I'd missed. But the leg would do. The voices stopped, briefly, and then began again, louder and closer already. I turned to point the gun at Ballantine but he was gone, a shadow in the distance, fading.

Five things. Or more. It's up to you. But to me it felt like five, plus the after-effects, all over in a second or two which felt like no time at all, like the time it takes a finger to click. And then time started again.

The voices were getting closer. Chima had disappeared and Ballantine had already fled and I thought about doing the same thing, alone at night hundreds of miles from anywhere at all, and then from nowhere I felt a hand on my ankle pulling me down. There was an instant in which I couldn't help picturing myself sliced up like a horror movie victim, and then I landed on my side and there was a hand over my mouth stopping me from screaming. A dark shadow rose in front of me and turned suddenly into Chima's face.

"Quiet!" he whispered, and this time I didn't even think about arguing.

The men out there had fallen silent. Listening, I guessed. They'd seen the Land Rover, that must have been why they'd stopped. And then they were out and on the hunt, lights in our faces, maybe they'd seen us, maybe they hadn't. They might not have done. It was dark now, they might have given up and gone off to kill someone else. But then I'd shot at Poulter – I'd *hit* Poulter, I realised, with a sudden inappropriate burst of pleasure – and they must have known for sure someone was here.

A moan, close by. Poulter. He wasn't stupid, he'd survived this long working with the kind of people Genghis Khan would have considered unfit for society, so he knew what Frentoi were like. I suppose when you've been shot in the thigh it's difficult to keep your mouth shut.

Which reminded me of the pain in my arm. My right arm, up high. It was still hurting, a long slow burn of a pain which felt like it was taking its time, circling me, waiting and wearing me down before it went in for the kill. I needed that pain at a distance, though. I didn't want to be attracting the kind of attention Poulter was about to get.

They'd heard him. The moan gave way to a short burst of loud whispers, then lights above – and thanks to those lights I could see we were in a ditch, a bend in a tiny ancient dried-up river. That was why Chima had turned. A ditch, that was all it was, a little knowledge local of the land, and it had saved our lives. So far.

We were feet away from Poulter, and the noises above told me Frentoi weren't much further. I could hear footsteps now, and my own heart beating, and more moans, and whispers again, and then, finally, a word, an English word, but driven from somewhere so deep in the throat that at first it sounded more animal than human.

"You."

They'd found him.

"Yes. It's me. I've been shot."

He sounded like a man speaking through gritted teeth.

"Yes."

It was a neutral kind of *yes*, an observation. It was difficult to tell from the voice alone whether the speaker was pleased or unhappy that Poulter had been shot.

"You let Nwosu get away. And the other one."

I could have found that insulting, but I chose not to. And I couldn't help admiring him a little. Straight on the offensive.

"We are three."

I didn't see how that was relevant. There was a brief silence, Poulter no doubt trying to work out the appropriate response, but in the end it was broken not by words but by another sound altogether. An engine. Not the Jeep, or our Land Rover, something-higher pitched, four stroke, smaller than a car. A ride-on lawnmower. A quad bike.

Of course. Ballantine. That was how they'd got here, him and Poulter. A quad bike. Fast enough, able to cope with the ground, and small enough to hide, too. They'd have parked it somewhere with a decent view of the road and just waited for us to show up. It wouldn't have the fuel to get all the way back to Ybaddli, but they probably had a car waiting somewhere within range.

Not *they* any more. Just Ballantine.

"Your friend has gone," said the man I assumed was the Frentoi leader. I couldn't place the accent, but that was hardly a surprise. There wasn't a country or a tribe this side of Lagos that Frentoi hadn't been through in their short but bloody life.

"Yes. Yes, I rather think he has," replied Poulter. He sounded disappointed. "I must remind him of the importance of loyalty."

"We are three," again. This time the silence was brief. "We were eighteen."

Three to a vehicle. Fifteen dead. Christ.

"You knew the location. You gave them too much time. And you have men enough to spare."

"We were eighteen," said the leader, again. He didn't sound like he was getting past the arithmetic.

"You have plenty of money. In a project like this, people die."

I wasn't up there with Poulter. I couldn't see his face, the face of the man talking to him, the faces of the others, two of them, standing either side, I imagined, holding the injured man up while he spoke. But even from down here, I thought Poulter was taking a risk with a line like that.

"That is true, Mr Poulter. We have your money, now. We have all the money we need. And you sent us there."

"It's Colonel Poulter. You had time to get there before Nwosu. You could have killed them both and lost nobody. Don't blame me for your mistakes."

There was a short silence, and then the wet, angry noise of someone spitting. It didn't sound like Poulter's line was going down well.

"You are right, Mr Poulter. People die."

Poulter didn't bother correcting him this time. It was obvious what was going to happen. I wondered, briefly, whether Poulter knew, whether he hoped something would save him, and then he spoke, and his voice was the voice of a man who knew it was over.

"Yes. Yes, they do," he said, and a moment later there was a single shot followed by the sound of flesh hitting dirt.

It took everything I had to stop from shouting out, I don't know why, it wasn't like the man hadn't deserved to die, I'd shot at him, I'd have killed him myself if I'd had the chance and I am, in normal times, a pretty peaceful kind of guy. But hidden in that bland, impartial sound of metal hitting man and man hitting the ground was a coldness that wasn't bland at all. It was brutal and its impartiality wasn't the impartiality of justice or fairness, it was the impartiality of blind, unthinking death, of killing without question or thought. It was vicious and it was evil, a plague, a scourge on humanity, and it had been unleashed on this particular part of the world by Colonel Poulter.

And now, finally, it had turned on him.

24: Flesh Wound

I managed to control myself. Chima's hand round my mouth helped, but if I'd been determined to get the pair of us killed, I reckon I could have managed it.

The pain in my arm was getting worse.

There was shouting again, and I couldn't understand the words. Not English. Three voices, moving further away. I tried to put myself in their position. One of us was dead. At least one had got away. How many of us had they seen in the first place? Ballantine had run and Chima had vanished into the earth. Poulter had been slumped on the ground with blood running out of his leg, but had they got a glimpse of me before Chima pulled me out of sight? Maybe it didn't matter, now they'd shed a little blood themselves. Frentoi liked killing, but it was dark and if there were any of us left, we might be armed, and we'd already killed fifteen of their men. In their position, I wouldn't have thought it was worth going after us. But of course, I wasn't a murderous psychopath.

And it was always possible they hadn't seen me. One man shot, another escaped on a quad bike. Who was to say there was anyone else there at all? Poulter might have said something, but he'd had other things on his mind.

I allowed myself to think I was going to survive, and instead of joy a tremendous tiredness welled up inside me, alongside the pain. I forced myself back to the present. It was dark, we were miles from anywhere in the dirty dead scrub of a dying country, and the psychopaths up top hadn't gone anywhere just yet.

Thud. The sound of something landing. I didn't want to hope, but it sounded like something being thrown into a Jeep. A gun. Or a man, jumping in. The voices were distant now, audible, but hardly clear, even if I'd understood the language.

The engine. I forced my fingernails into my left hand and that helped me focus on something else. The engine was starting. My arm was hurting. The engine was starting and Christ, wasn't that the sound of wheels spinning? *Please let them not be stuck. Let them not be stuck.* The engine noise grew louder and higher and then stopped and all the fear flooded back, which at least kept me quiet.

Someone was getting out of the Jeep. Someone was walking. The voices were raised, shouting. One word, over and over, *Okuta! Okuta!* Someone else got out and I started to pray that *Okuta* didn't mean *there they are!* or *let's go hunting!*

It took me a few seconds to realise the gentler sound nearby was Chima, whispering to me.

"A rock. Okuta is a rock."

Please let it be a rock.

More footsteps, the sound of exertion, and then *thank Christ* back in the Jeep and the engine, once more, only this time it didn't get so loud and it didn't get so high and the wheels didn't spin and that was it, they were off.

They slowed down, briefly, and I heard something metallic, and then they were gone, and five seconds later there was an explosion, another explosion, a whole series of explosions. I'd had enough of explosions by now, but this time I was down in a ditch and it was far enough away not to hurt.

We stayed in the ditch another five minutes. Chima assured me it was five minutes, still whispering, even though it felt more like an hour, and I was so desperate to get out and stretch my body and do something, anything about the pain in my arm that I'd have taken the small chance Frentoi had left someone behind, just in case, if Chima hadn't stopped me.

By the time we emerged the fire was almost out and what had been our Land Rover – Iffy's Land Rover, I reminded myself – was just a few lumps of metal. I didn't see how a car could go up so fast, but the shreds of green canvas picked up by the last flickering tongues of flame reminded me. There were still explosives in the car when the grenade had hit it. I was surprised there was any of it left at all.

What with the fear and the pain in my arm, I'd not been thinking about the other thing that was here, besides me and Chima and the burning car. I followed Chima back towards the ditch, towards the darkness, and found myself gasping in surprise when a sudden glint of light picked out the body on the ground.

"One shot. Head. See?" said Chima. I didn't need him to point it out. It wasn't a nice clean hole in the forehead, it was half a face and half a Halloween pumpkin, the insides exposed, the openings bigger and cruder than they should have been, the whole thing bathed in a constantly-moving orange light. I tried to feel something, pity, anger, revulsion, but there was nothing there. I was looking at a corpse. That was all. I shrugged, because something was called for, a word or a gesture, and immediately winced, because the shrug brought the pain slamming back like a hungry and forgotten foe.

"Let me see," said Chima, and steered me back to the brighter area around what remained of the car. He pulled me down to the ground and tore the right sleeve off my shirt. It was red, but I didn't remember my head wound bleeding that much – the pain *there* was gone now, and the ringing.

"A flesh wound. Nothing serious."

My expression must have asked the question I couldn't

get into words, because he went on.

"He saw you coming, Sam. A good thing you were fast, because he did not have time for a proper shot."

So Poulter had shot me, had he? I was missing him even less than I had done. And this was a flesh wound. I had a vision of Che, screaming into the semi-darkness. I couldn't see my arm but at least I could move it. And Christ did it hurt. No wonder the poor bloody mammoth had screamed.

"Up" he said, and pulled me to my feet. "We have a long walk."

I don't remember much about that walk. It was dark, and we stumbled a lot, that much I could have guessed before we'd even started. Ten miles, I remembered Chima saying, the first time he'd talked about this place. It was ten miles to the village, on a road not fit for human legs, in the dark, and it was cold – I couldn't believe that now, finally, the damned heat had gone and it was *too cold* – and the pain in my arm wouldn't let me go for more than a few seconds at a time.

So we walked, and talked, or at least Chima did, because I really wasn't in the mood for talking and it took every ounce of concentration I had to keep one foot in front of the other and not just fall over and die right there on the road. He talked about what he was going to do now, now that Poulter was dead, how he could return to his country and tell everyone the truth about Frentoi, rid his country of them, make it great again, and he laughed when he said *great* because one thing Surtalga, or Mirandano, or whatever you wanted to call it, one thing it had never been was *great*. He had one arm round my waist, so it wasn't just my willpower keeping me going, and I knew he was talking for the sake of it, and I knew it was important, too, for both of us, so I wouldn't have bothered interrupting or arguing even if I'd felt capable of it, which wasn't like me at all.

It was pure fantasy, of course, and he knew it. Just because Poulter was dead didn't mean all our problems were over, with a single shot to the head, just like that. Frentoi, Ballantine, Henderson, Roarkes, the list of people who wanted one or both of us locked up or six feet down was still longer than I felt comfortable with. But I nodded along and smiled at his vision, taking over some rag-tag little army and driving the animals out for good, and we both pretended that when all this was over he'd be staying in Surtalga, where every other person seemed to want him dead. We were talking for the sake of talking, and we both knew it, making up an impossible future to get us through the present. I didn't know where the safest place for Chima might be, but sure as hell it wasn't here. I figured Chima knew it, too.

The sky was already beginning to lighten when we finally got to the village. Not that there was much of a village left. What the explosions hadn't smashed to bits, the fire that followed had taken care of, and long before we could see anything at all we could hear the sound of people hammering, heaving, moving what had survived around to make some kind of shelter while they set about the task of rebuilding the rest of it.

I'd like to say they were pleased to see us, but I guess I should have been grateful they weren't on the list of people who wanted me dead. They gave us water, and a little bread, and once Chima had washed my wound, which had me screaming loud enough to bring half a dozen of them running, they found some rags to tie around it which were slightly cleaner than the blood-and-dust-stained shirt that had been there in the first place.

Chima confirmed his earlier diagnosis. A flesh wound. A minor one. Nothing that would keep me out of the ring, he smiled, and when I looked puzzled he threw a couple of punches. I smiled back at him. He really didn't know me at all.

Later that morning we argued. We were waiting – there was a man coming from Ybaddli, apparently, with a truck, bringing supplies, he came once or twice a week and was expected later that day, and everyone seemed confident he'd be willing to take us back with him. I certainly hoped so, and after what had happened last time Chima had shown up, I had the feeling the villagers did too.

We were arguing about the briefcase. Chima wanted to burn it, right there, just get rid of the thing. He'd have blown it up if he could, but we were all out of explosives, finally, and anyway, he thought setting fire to it would be good enough.

I wasn't so sure. Neither of us were scientists, after all. We didn't know what the virus could survive. It had been weaponised, after all, whatever that meant. If I'd been Femi, I'd have worked on making it tough, fire-resistant, as close to invincible as I could, the Incredible Hulk of viruses. For all we knew, fire would just spread the thing around. And after everything they'd been through, did Chima really want to expose the people here to that risk?

That shut him up. He nodded.

"OK," he said. "What is your idea?"

I think he was guessing I didn't have one. He was wrong. I did. It had a lot of moving parts, but if it worked it would take care of more than one of our problems.

"We need to go back to London," I said, and he shook his head, as I'd known he would.

"We cannot. It is not safe. Poulter may be dead, but –"

He didn't need to finish the sentence, but I was glad he'd recognised it, in spite of the nonsense we'd thrown at each other while we walked. Even with the head cut off, a flailing limb could do some damage. And it wasn't like blowing the stuff up in London would be any safer.

"We'll turn it over to the authorities. Someone will know what to do with it."

"You trust them to do that?"

I grinned. He went on.

"And you know, Poulter's friend, Ballantine, he will have friends there, in these authorities of yours. As soon as we contact them he will find out. He will be waiting for us, Sam."

I grinned again. I knew.

"That's OK, Chima. We just need to be one step ahead of him. Get me to Ybaddli, let me make some calls. I think I can do this."

The truck came early in the afternoon. I don't know what I'd been expecting, the word *truck* had conjured visions of ten-wheelers streaming up and down the M6 by night. This was basically a tractor pulling a trailer filled with bags of rice and live chickens. Now I understood why the villagers had been rebuilding the chicken shelter before they'd started work on their own homes.

There was no room for us up front, so we lay in the trailer with a few empty rice sacks to shield us from the road. If you have to take a long trip on a bad road in a wood-and-metal trailer with a bullet wound – sorry, a *flesh wound* – in your arm, have something better than rough canvas sacks to lie on. They didn't do the job, and even though I'd been awake longer than I cared to remember, I couldn't sleep. Chima had given me some leaves to chew, "For the pain," he said, and I don't know what they were but they seemed to do the trick, because that pain had settled into an occasional grinding ordeal. The driver seemed to be in a hurry, so the trip was over quicker than I'd expected, even if we did seem to go via every pothole in West Africa. It was still light when we hit Ybaddli. I had a vision of walking into the Majestic Hotel, stinking and bloody, marching straight back to my room, bath, sleep, food, sleep. As for Chima, yeah, I'd pay for him, too. I just didn't care.

It was a stupid idea. We needed to stay off the radar, still. Chima's shack, the one he'd taken me to – Christ, it was only the night before last, it felt like weeks ago – it would have to do. No one knew about it. I shrugged. Anything was better than the trailer.

We had to walk the last couple of miles, but this time I knew where we were heading, it was light, the ground was flat and the pain in my arm had dwindled to a dull forgettable throb. The place looked the same as it had when we'd left it, which after the last twenty-four hours was as close to luxury as I needed. I went to sit in the chair, but Chima shoved me out of it and onto the sofa and by this point I was too tired to argue. When I closed my eyes sleep came so fast I didn't even have time to be grateful.

25: Getting Out

I made my calls. At the shack there was a mobile signal and there was electricity, which came as a welcome surprise. "Not my electricity," said Chima, and winked towards the outside, the other shacks. I didn't care where it came from as long as it charged my phone.

Chima made some calls, too, in a language I didn't understand. I asked him who he was talking to. He shook his head and I didn't take it any further.

Things were in place. It was a risk, but everything I'd done since Dovesham had been more or less of a risk, and at least this time there was a plan. That's what I kept telling myself, there was a plan, so far everyone had done what they were supposed to do, and there was no reason any of the moving parts should stop moving in the right direction.

I knew that was no more likely than Chima settling down to herd goats in the scrub outside Ybaddli. I knew the one sure thing about every plan anyone had ever made was that at least one bit of it would screw up, and you had to hope that it wasn't an important bit or if it was an important bit that you had enough time to fix it. I knew we didn't have any time and all the bits were important, so if anything went wrong at all we'd be in the worst kind of shit. I just kept on telling myself it would be OK, everyone would do what they were supposed to do, everything would fall neatly into place.

The first sign that the plan wasn't going to work like I'd hoped came right at the beginning, at the airport, before we'd even got on the plane. We'd been stewing in the shack for the best part of a week and I was itching to get home, to a real bed and food and beer, but there was nothing I could do. A direct flight, and the right papers, that was what we needed, and that was something we had to wait for. Maloney had done his bit, so we had new documents and tickets and everything else we might need waiting for us in a stinking dive in downtown Ybaddli where even waiting outside while Chima went in to retrieve them felt uncomfortably like waiting in that ditch for Frentoi to find us and blow our heads off. I'd known Maloney had fingers in a lot of pies, but to get this kind of thing done, that quickly, out here, with him getting ready to hang the "closed" sign on the door back home – that was impressive. It made me think maybe everything else would be just as smooth.

I'd forgotten. I was an amateur.

Having travelled out on false documents I was pretty relaxed about travelling back on them. Of course the fact I was carrying a weapon of mass destruction with me this time made me a little more nervous, but the seals and certificates Maloney had procured for us looked good enough to convince a UN weapons inspection team. They'd fool the bored customs officers at Ybaddli International, I thought. No problem.

And there was no problem with the papers or us or the briefcase, as it happened. The people who were supposed to be keeping an eye on things had those eyes set behind dark glasses and my guess was they were closed. We were through and onto the runway (Ybaddli International is one of those airports where you stroll from the terminal direct to the plane and hope no one's trying to land at the same time). Nothing could go wrong.

And then, suddenly, the first sign of trouble: shouts from behind. I turned. There were four men in uniform running towards us, guns out, no sunglasses, barking out words I couldn't understand. Chima dropped to the ground and put his hands behind his head and I thought I'd better do the same thing. I scratched my knee on the ground as I went down and swore and hoped to Christ that a scratch on the knee was as bad as it was going to get. I twisted my neck to look back up and knew straight away it wasn't.

The four men had slowed to a casual walk, guns swinging by their sides. Behind them was someone I really hadn't thought I'd see again. Wishful thinking.

Ballantine.

He was wearing a suit and smiling, and I couldn't blame him, because it looked like everything was going to turn out just perfectly as far as he was concerned. The boss might be dead, but Ballantine would be walking out of here with the briefcase and me and Chima out of the way, permanently.

I couldn't think of anything to say. I turned my head, my neck was aching like hell, and looked at Chima.

Chima was smiling.

He could see what I could see, but he was still smiling. I didn't get it.

He got to his feet.

"Get back down," said Ballantine, calmly.

Chima shook his head. The men with the guns looked at him, at one another, at Ballantine. Chima grinned. Ballantine frowned, but didn't say anything. He might have said "shoot him," or even "shoot them." But he didn't. The men started to look confused. I liked that. I thought I'd add to it.

I got to my feet.

"Get back on the ground," said Ballantine, "or I will have you shot."

He spoke slowly, precisely, no inflection or intonation at all. If it hadn't been for the remnants of the frown on his face, he'd have passed for a man in complete control.

More people were walking towards us now, from the far end of the terminal. Ballantine couldn't see them, he was facing the wrong way, but a couple of his men could, and the confusion on their faces turned suddenly to fear.

The newcomers were striding calmly in our direction, eight of them, in uniforms but with sunglasses, and another guy in a plain shirt and shorts bringing up the rear. Something about him looked familiar.

They seemed utterly relaxed, more like a bunch of guys strolling into a bar after work than a bunch of guys walking into the gunfight at the OK Corral. And they were quiet. Ballantine must have noticed something on someone's face, because he turned, now, and saw them, and the frown deepened.

"It's OK," he said. The approaching men stopped, about ten yards away, with the guy in shirt and shorts further back. Their uniforms weren't the same as the ones Ballantine's men were wearing, the uniforms of all the military-looking people at the airport. These were darker, less tidy, less ceremonial. Their guns were hanging casually by their sides, but that didn't make them look any less dangerous. It made them look like people who knew what they were doing.

"I've got the situation under control," said Ballantine.

"You are under arrest," said one of the men, the man nearest us.

I recognised that voice. *People die,* it had said, last time I'd heard it. Suddenly I knew what was coming next.

"I don't think so," replied Ballantine. He still sounded like he thought he was in control. His men didn't seem so sure.

"You will come with me."

The man in shorts who was standing back from the action turned, slightly, and suddenly I could see his face. Iffy. He looked scared, but I'd only ever seen him looking scared. Maybe he always looked like that. He was smiling, though. Looking beyond me, and smiling. I turned. He was smiling at Chima, and Chima was smiling back. I wasn't certain, but I thought I saw him wink.

Ballantine's men seemed to have made up their minds. They knew who the newcomers were. So did I. Ballantine didn't seem to, or he wouldn't have been quite so calm. His men were outnumbered and afraid. Their guns, which had been pointing alternately at us and the newcomers, were lowered.

"What will we do with these, sir?" asked one, jerking his elbow towards us.

The man who'd spoken before, the leader, the one whose face I'd never seen before but whose voice was burnt into my memory, walked right up to us. He stared at me, into my face, an inch or two away. His breath smelled of whisky, which didn't exactly fit in with Frentoi's religious line, but I didn't think this was the time for a theological debate. He moved over to Chima and did the same. He turned around and walked back to his men, then past them, to Iffy.

Iffy wasn't smiling any more. I suddenly realised I wasn't breathing.

"They may go."

I breathed. Iffy turned, started to walk away.

"Wait," called the leader. Iffy stopped.

"I did not say you would be allowed to go as well."

An expression formed on Iffy's face that mixed desperation and injustice. He was trying to speak, but couldn't. If he had, the word would have been "But…"

The leader nodded.

"Yes. You may go. We no longer hold you responsible."

Last time round Ballantine had run before he'd had a chance to hear the voice, so he couldn't yet know who these men were, but surely that was a clue. I turned back to look at him. His own men had retreated, walking slowly back to the terminal building with the air of people who knew they were being watched and were trying to look like they didn't care. Iffy was a few paces ahead of them and trying the same act, with considerably less success. Two of the newcomers stood either side of Ballantine. He didn't seem to have got it yet, despite the clue, he was talking about his friends in the Surtalga Government and how these men would be hearing from their superiors and they were making a terrible mistake. They were ignoring him, steering him gently towards a car I hadn't noticed until now, parked on the runway beside the terminal. I couldn't figure out why they hadn't just shot him on the spot, and then I remembered who they were. They were going to have their fun with him first. I had a sudden flashback, me, on a bus, picturing Ballantine dying slowly and horribly by fire. I had a feeling he'd be begging for fire before it was all over.

Chima and I were alone. We walked towards the plane. The steps were down, a stewardess at the top, smiling at us, beckoning us on board. I was holding the briefcase. I climbed the steps behind Chima, showed her my pass, followed her directions, found my seat.

Against all expectations, it looked like I was getting out of Surtalga alive.

We had ten hours on the plane. Ten hours for Chima to explain what the hell had just happened. Ten hours for everything else to start working, because while we could plan all we liked, the plan couldn't turn into action until we were in the air. That had been the idea. Set things up any other way and Ballantine and his friends might track us down.

Turned out I needn't have worried about Ballantine.

It was simple, really. We had just about the most dangerous thing in the world in a briefcase. We couldn't destroy it because we weren't clever enough. We had to get it to the right people, the people who were both clever enough and not planning on selling it to the highest bidder, and we had to make sure the wrong people didn't beat them to it.

I tried to figure out what had gone wrong, where the plan had slipped. I decided it hadn't. Ballantine had been waiting at the airport, that was all. He knew we'd have to show up eventually. He didn't know what we were planning. He couldn't. The plan was still going to work.

The theory was simple. While no one knew where we were, we were safe. But the moment anyone heard about us and what we were carrying and where we were taking it, we were exposed. The right people would get the news, sure. But we couldn't be sure that the wrong people wouldn't as well.

Only, that might not matter. As long as there were enough of the right people there too.

Ten hours. Ten hours to get enough of the right people to the right place so that no one, not even Ballantine (if he'd been free) or Poulter (if he'd been alive) or anyone else who worked for them or with them, not even the devil himself would risk taking us on.

Chima had a look on his face I hadn't seen before. He was happy. That wasn't so bad. But it wasn't just that. He was pleased with himself. The guy was *smug*. Whatever it was that had just happened, he was luxuriating in it. So he was human. He kept turning to me, and smiling, and then turning away, which was annoying enough. I knew what he wanted: he wanted me to ask the question. I thought I'd make him wait.

Five minutes was enough. There was a screen in front of me and a complicated menu promising all kinds of treats. It didn't work, any of it, and there was no way I could face ten hours of smug Chima grinning at me. I caved.

"So what did you do?"

He was suddenly serious.

"You know, I thought, if I was Ballantine I'd be waiting at that airport. I would wait there for years if I had to, because there was not a chance that a soft white guy like Sam Williams would risk the land borders. I knew Ballantine would be there, so I called Iffy and reminded him that he owed us."

"So Iffy didn't leave the country?"

"Iffy? He wouldn't risk the land borders either. And he is afraid of flying. I spoke to him, and I told him what had happened, at my village, what had happened to Poulter. And then I asked him who it was that had sent Frentoi to my village, who had given them this location."

I pictured Iffy in his shack, on the other end of that phone call, hearing the news, digesting the implications.

"I'm surprised he didn't have a heart attack."

Chima smiled.

"He seemed afraid, yes. He said to me that no, they would not blame him, he had only given them information they had asked for. I said to him that was true, and that any reasonable person would be satisfied. He understood what I was saying."

So did I. Frentoi weren't exactly known for being reasonable.

"He begged me for help, and I suggested that perhaps, if he was able to provide them with Poulter's colleague, they would not kill him. He was pleased with this opportunity."

So that was it. At the end of it, I'd been on their side, the worst people the world had yet produced, I thought, and all it took for us to work together was a common enemy. I felt slightly sick, slightly dirty, but only slightly. I was too tired for much more, and my head was hurting, and my arm, too, which had stopped bothering me for whole hours at a time over the last few days, but decided to remind me of its injury the moment we hit the first bit of turbulence. And I'd spent years feeling slightly dirty. Pumping a self-congratulatory fist. Paying cops. Working for dealers. I was used to being on the wrong side.

It felt different this time. Not because Frentoi made Pierre and Maloney look like saints, but because I hadn't been on the wrong side. Not really. This one, I could wash clean. No problem. And I had other things on my mind, anyway. So much done, so much yet to do. I turned away from Chima, to the window, just in time to see the edge of Africa receding, yellow, to brown, to a faint dark line in the distance, to nothing.

Just the sea, cornflower blue, glittering at me. And whatever was waiting the other side of it.

EPILOGUE

Exposure

I'd been wrong about the Butchers. It was still my kind of pub after all. That night I'd come here with Claire – the day it all began – must have been an unfortunate one-off. The posers and the fighters were all cruising Upper Street tonight, anyway, and the Butchers was down to the bare bones. Two couples, a few harassed-looking middle-aged men, alone, in for a quick half on the way home and *"oh look is that really the time heavens how much have I drunk?"*, and us, the whole crew, everyone bar Maloney (whose temporary truce with Roarkes wasn't enough to drag him out of Tottenham) and Freddie (for obvious reasons).

I'd been back a week, and it was safe to say things had changed since I'd left. No apartment (again, for obvious reasons), and a whole new set of clothes (same), and no office, either, which was something different but only a few days away from being put right.

I'd seen a couple of places that afternoon, as it happened, and one of them was a real possibility. Still Islington, still walking distance from the apartment, if the apartment had still been there, but bigger, cleaner, nicer: two rooms, one for me to put all my stuff in and another to sit the clients down and offer them crisps and fags and legal advice. And a window in each, which was something my old place had been lacking. Yes, I thought. That one would make the list. There were still a few more to look at, but I needed to make up my mind by the weekend.

Claire was sitting next to me smiling and sharing a joke with Paul like they'd been friends for years. She could turn it on when she wanted to. If he hadn't been a happily married man with the kind of moral fibre they make comic book superheroes out of, I'd have been worried. She'd asked if she could see the office before I made my final decision, which I thought was none of her damned business but probably a good sign overall, so I'd said *sure*, and she'd smiled and suddenly it seemed like maybe it was her business after all. Still, if I was getting anyone's advice on the place, I'd get Pierre's, because he'd seen the inside of more cells and brief's offices than anyone else I knew. I leaned across the table and tapped him on the shoulder.

I'd known Pierre would show up tonight. I'd told him there would be police, started to explain how Roarkes was one of the good guys, and he had nothing to worry about, but Pierre had interrupted me before I'd got to the DI's name and reminded me it wasn't an issue.

"You forgetting I'm straight now, Sam?" he'd said. "I got no problem with the police. They got no problem with me. They like me. I'm doin' their job, man!"

And to my amazement, because "good guy" or not, I didn't have Roarkes down as someone who'd be entirely comfortable in a social environment with someone like Pierre, the DI and the ex-dealer seemed to be getting on like a house on fire. I winced at the image. Hardly appropriate, given recent events. Good job I hadn't said it out loud.

Pierre looked up at me but Roarkes was still talking. No need to interrupt. Pierre was still under the impression he owed me, even though I'd finally got round to telling him he didn't. I'd been living off his gratitude too long, and that was another bit of dirt washed away. No need to ask now, anyway. He'd come and check the place out with me if I wanted.

Of all the things that had happened since the moment we'd landed, dealing with Henderson had been the most unpredictable. I had a plan, of course, but I'd already seen how wrong plans could go. Ask Poulter. Ask Ballantine. In the event, this one had gone pretty well.

I'd been nervous when I'd walked in, which, I thought, was pretty reasonable of me. I owed the guy money. He'd sent his man round to get it, and his man had ended up dead. There were a lot of ways this conversation could go, and most didn't end with a smile on my face. I had Pierre waiting outside, of course, in case things got nasty, but if Henderson wanted things to get nasty he could probably get them there quicker than Pierre could get in and help me. I was going to have to rely on luck and charm. I'd have to find some first, I thought, and smiled.

Henderson was sitting behind a desk made of some kind of expensive-looking dark wood. He had a look on his face like he knew he wasn't running the show but had to pretend he was. That was good. It meant he was nervous, too, and my unaccountable smile couldn't have helped. I'd given him an hour's notice that I was coming, no more, and he hadn't seemed too keen to see me but I hadn't given him much choice. Better that way, I thought.

"What can I do for you, Mr Williams?" he'd asked, his fingers drumming gently on the desk. He kept glancing at my face, and then away, as if he didn't want to be caught making eye contact. Again, good. The fear was flowing one way in this room. I was starting to feel like everything would turn out fine.

"This," I said, and handed him the envelope. He should be pleased, I thought. It was obvious what he was afraid of: for all the press conferences and police statements and absolute, unequivocal confirmation that I was an innocent man, as far as Henderson was concerned I'd been mixed up with some thoroughly nasty people, some people who were a lot more serious about being nasty than he was, and I'd come out alive. If I didn't know better, I'd be scared of me. It was no surprise he was. And here I was handing him some money and clearing out of his face for good.

I was right. A Henderson with nothing to fear would have taken one look at the cheque and asked for twice as much, in cash. This Henderson looked at the cheque and started making noises about how there was no need, certainly there was no urgency. He tailed off, and picked up the letter, which stated that I was quitting the offices with immediate effect and bringing to an end our contractual relations. He read it once, quickly, then again more slowly, and put it back down on the table. He looked relieved. "A shame, Mr Williams," he said, "but I wish you luck in whatever it is you're doing."

Like he didn't know.

And that was it. Off I went, picking up Pierre on the way. He'd got talking to a couple of kids on the pavement and was trying to convince them to go back to school. They couldn't have been more than twelve years old and anyone else, my guess is they'd have spat in his face, or stabbed him, and walked away. But they were taking in every word and gazing up at the guy like he was Martin Luther King, or maybe someone off the X Factor, and that was when I realised Pierre was wasted in security. Marketing my business, that would be a far more appropriate use for his talents.

I was thinking a little bigger these days. Hence the new offices. Samuel Williams & Co. was going places.

The fact that all this was down to Maloney, and the "favour" I'd asked him for, and the way he'd taken it upon himself to develop that favour into something quite different when I disappeared off the radar for a mere thirty-six or so hours, well, that was just another one of those surprises I was learning to take in my stride. I wasn't sure if all my new clients saw it that way. I wasn't sure how long they'd stick with me, either, or what Maloney had said to convince them (because whatever it was, they weren't hanging around out of respect for my legal skills). They were lawyers themselves, for Christ's sake. The leading role played by a well-known North London gangster in the whole affair can't have filled them with confidence.

The favour I'd asked Maloney for, at the same time I was asking Claire to figure out the dates of Poulter's operations, was quite simple: I wanted David Brooks-Powell destroyed.

I might have laughed about it with Claire, but the truth was I was almost as angry with David Brooks-Powell as I was with Poulter and Ballantine and Frentoi and Henderson and his stupid curly-haired broken-necked *associate*. I'd had enough of them, of all of them. *Find me something*, I'd said. Something on David Brooks-Powell. There was no way the bastard was as clean as he pretended. Find me something, and I'll wrap it round him so damned tight he'll spend the rest of his life trying to pick it off.

Maloney figured he still owed me, so he'd gone out there and found something. At first, when he'd told me, I was a little disappointed. There was nothing obviously criminal there, for a start. And no solid proof, either. But Maloney was a big-shot businessman (of a sort) for a reason, and I wasn't. I hadn't seen the big picture.

Brooks-Powell's sordid little secret wasn't precisely sordid, or even much of a secret. He was a bully, that was all. *I could have told you that*, I'd said to Maloney, which was a little ungrateful, but I was out of my comfort zone at the time.

Brooks-Powell was a bully, and a sexist, and probably a racist, too, although that one was going to be harder to prove because Mauriers hadn't got round to hiring any minorities he could hound out of the firm when the fancy took him. But that was precisely what he had done to a surprisingly high number of smart, well-qualified lawyers. Mostly women, but not all. The sole criterion for incurring the implacable hatred of David Brooks-Powell seemed to be intelligence, which made me feel briefly rather good about myself before I remembered where David Brooks-Powell's hatred had landed me. Anyone who did a good job, who looked like they might be getting somewhere, who worked hard and broke a case and in general behaved in a manner you'd expect to be congratulated for, found themselves out within months. Step one in Brooks-Powell's workplace bullying playbook was to take credit for the successes. Step two, just in case there was any chance the glow of victory still adhered, even slightly, to the unfortunate victim, was to get the poor sod working day and night on cases that were no-hopers, that were already closed, or might as well be, that no one would ever hear about, that the firm probably wouldn't even be paid for. This would take the process up to step three, where he'd accuse them of wasting their time and the firm's resources and question their involvement in anything that had ever gone right. His model for these campaigns was, it appears, one Sam Williams. The Studeman debacle had taken the shine so thoroughly off the Trawden win (with a little help from Brooks-Powell himself, of course), he realised the same methods could be applied time after time. So he'd just create his own little Studemans to screw up his employees' Trawdens, failures to taint their victories, complain persistently and vocally to the rest of the partnership about them, and have them out the door before they knew what was happening to them.

Maloney had tracked down a dozen of these unfortunates before he had his genius idea, and another seven by the time he'd managed to get hold of me, by which time he'd managed to get sixteen of the nineteen into a room together (the other three came on board the next day) and put his idea to them.

It really was a good idea.

David Brooks-Powell was a cunning bastard, and he'd played the game so well and so carefully that each of his victims thought they were the only one. Oh sure, others had left, with clouds over their heads and tears in their eyes, but they were the incompetents. They were the failures. All the fiascos Brooks-Powell had concocted had worked so well they'd blinded everyone who saw them, even people who were going through or had gone through or were about to go through precisely the same thing.

Until, that is, Maloney got sixteen of them into a room together and asked them to tell their stories. The way he told it, so many scales fell from so many eyes you'd have thought there had been a mass breakout at the reptile house.

But Maloney wasn't just after screwing Brooks-Powell. He knew that was what I wanted, sure, but it wasn't what I needed. What I needed, as I'd mentioned when I was hiding out with him, was clients.

And what these poor, bullied, abused, constructively-or-wrongfully-dismissed victims needed, was a lawyer.

Like I said, I didn't know how long they were going to stick with me, but while they did I was going to make sure I got so deep under their skins and did such a good job they had no damned reason to go anywhere else. I'd been a half-decent lawyer, once upon a time. The spark might not be dead after all. I was cleaner than I'd been for years. Maybe I could be a better lawyer, too.

Of all the crazy things that had happened at the unscheduled press conference in the middle of the Heathrow Airport Terminal 5 arrivals lounge, the bit about David Brooks-Powell had been the most satisfying.

"Ladies and gentlemen," I'd announced to the assembled hacks. Rachel had done a great job on that, there were more than twenty newspapers there, plus TV and radio, plus (most important) the disease control people with their military escort who'd taken the briefcase and left as soon as I could be sure they were who they said they were. I made certain Claire got the pick of the questions, her and Olivia. Olivia's campaign to find the missing Serbs had petered out when no one had risen to the bait. Claire had been stuck with Maloney and unable to get a word in print the whole time I'd been away. They deserved a break.

"Ladies and gentlemen," I'd said, "you've heard everything I have to say on the subject of Dovesham and Surtalga and the extraordinary events of the last couple of weeks." They had done, too, in five spellbinding (even if I say it myself) minutes. Chima had managed to sleep on the plane. I hadn't, but that was OK. I'd needed the time to work on my speech.

"If you're in any way sceptical – and I wouldn't blame you if you were," (scattered polite laughter) "feel free to check the facts with Detective Inspector Roarkes over there."

I'd gestured to Roarkes and he'd rewarded me with a less-than-friendly gesture that could be seen later that night on the one TV news outlet whose producers hadn't spotted it and had it cut in time. I couldn't really blame him for it. He couldn't have enjoyed having to go through Maloney to get to Claire and the rest of the facts. I owed him. I'd buy him a drink, I thought, as I smiled cheerfully back at him.

"In the meantime, there is one other matter to bring to your attention."

Five minutes, the murderers and warlords had got. David Brooks-Powell got twenty, and as much detail as I could throw in without a defamation action. Nothing the press like more than a spat. The legal feud got nearly as many column inches next day as the murderers and the warlords. I'd signed off by thanking him, through the assembled press, for offering to represent me in my hour of need, but given I was now suing him on behalf of nineteen former employees, I thought it best our professional relationship came to an end.

There was one other person missing, of course. I thought I was safe enough now. I'd told everything there was to tell, I was going to square things with Henderson, I wasn't a threat to anyone any more. But Chima was. Even with Poulter and Ballantine out of the picture, Frentoi were still out there, plus all the people he'd fought against and alongside all those years ago. He knew too much, in England, in Surtalga, he knew where the bodies were buried and he knew who'd buried them. We'd parted before Arrivals, before immigration, Chima's path illuminated by giant purple "Flight Connections" signs. He wouldn't say where he was going, he'd sorted all that out with Maloney and I hadn't pushed. I thought I knew, anyway. Poulter had said, "*not all of them, Chima*", and at the time, what with all the guns and the briefcase, it had seemed utterly insignificant, but I could see a glimmer of significance now. I'd turned to him and offered him my hand, and he'd looked at it, and nodded.

"Thank you," he said, and grabbed my shoulders and squeezed so tight I thought if he carried on much longer I'd be able to fit in the briefcase myself. And then he nodded, and turned, and walked away.

Ten minutes at immigration – "Richard Collins" was a UK citizen, which made life a little easier, but I was so wound up every time someone glanced in my direction I half-expected shouts and guns and more dark glasses. I had no luggage to collect, which sped things up. And then arrivals, and the flash-bulbs, and the shouts, and I thought, for a moment, it was a shame he'd missed this, he deserved to be here.

And then I saw, at the front of them all, the blonde hair and the eyes and *that* smile, and my heart gave a tiny little lurch.

Now that was something new.

She had a car waiting for us at the airport, a local minicab, and I didn't say anything when she gave the driver her address. Before we'd hit the M4 and got beyond a few awkward '*How are you?*'s, her phone had rung and she'd passed it to me without answering.

"Hello?" I'd said.

"So now you're *really* famous," said Maloney, and I'd laughed and congratulated him and then, suddenly, thought this was the moment, even with Claire sitting next to me, this was the moment I had to find out if I could ever really be clean again. So I'd asked the question.

Maloney had laughed.

"Hassan?" he'd said, and laughed again. "Dead? Of course he's not fucking dead. I didn't even have to break his legs. I gave him a choice, and he made the right choice, and I've kept an eye on him ever since. He hasn't put a foot wrong. He knows what'll happen if he does."

I'd slumped back into the cheap fake leather seat and unwound a little more. There was a lot more unwinding to do, but there'd be time for all that. Claire was looking at me with a quizzical little half-smile, but I shook my head and she shrugged and that was it. No need to bring all that up. And no need to worry about dead bodies in fields any more, either.

Paul had gone to the bar to get a round and now Claire

was chatting across the table with Olivia Miles and Rachel. Pierre and Roarkes were engrossed in some kind of political debate on the reasons for street crime. They weren't agreeing, but they still seemed to be getting on well enough. I sat back and sipped on a whisky – a real scotch, no ice, a different species from the stuff I'd forced down my throat in that shack on the edge of Ybaddli.

Technically, I should have been looking for a place to live even more urgently than a new office. But this time round, I had alternatives. Paul had offered me his spare room. Pierre had offered me some space in his "pad". Maloney had plenty of places I could stay, if I didn't mind turning a blind eye to whatever else was going on in them. Even Rachel had grudgingly mumbled something about a little room, if I needed it.

I didn't. I was perfectly happy where I was, for now.

I was staying at Claire's. I'd been staying there since I'd got back, since Roarkes had confirmed it was safe for her to go home (and Maloney had confirmed it again, which had a little more weight). I'd been through her notes on my African trip, and made sure every detail was in the right place. And then I'd gone through her notes on her case – her project – the real story she'd been working on and still was. I thought I might be able to help. Maloney had offered to help her, after all. She'd even discussed it with Roarkes, despite her insistence that the police were about as reliable as Chima's friend Iffy. I had a few ideas of my own, how to find out more, how to get deeper, even though getting deep into anything at all was a whole new thing for me. I told her my thoughts. We discussed them. It turned out most of them were stupid, or impractical, or so obvious she'd been through them right at the start. But not all of them. Not all.

So in the meantime, I was staying in her flat – I was looking for my own place, it was temporary, we both knew that – except I hadn't started looking for my own place at all, yet, and although Claire was entirely aware of that, neither of us seemed to think it was worth discussing. It was starting to dawn on me that maybe I wouldn't be looking for my own place at all. I certainly didn't feel any great need. Except for that fact that Claire's place was a mess, and a bit dingy, and probably too small for the two of us to live in.

So maybe we'd end up looking for a place together. A bigger place. I allowed myself to picture it, a nice top floor flat with a roof terrace or a ground floor with a patch of garden. Still Islington, of course. I wouldn't dream of anywhere else. It was just an idea. Nothing more. I hadn't discussed it with anyone. Not even Claire. And anyway, it would cost. I'd need all my new clients to stick with me, and win, and pay me, and then I'd need some more clients to replace them. There were a lot of variables in there.

But still.

There was a man standing in front of me, coughing. Wearing leather. I hadn't thought it was that kind of pub.

"You Sam Williams?" he asked. I nodded.

"Got this for you."

He held out a small package and passed me a clipboard. Now the leather made sense. I signed beside my name and watched him walk out.

"This one of you lot?" I asked, waving the package at the table, and watched half a dozen heads shaking back at me. No one else knew where I was, not that it would have been that hard to work out, if someone wanted to. Who would want to?

Black plastic wrapping. I tore it off. A small wooden box inside, and a postcard. Nothing written on the back. On the front, some buildings, gothic ones, modern ones, a crazy red one that looked like it was built out of Lego.

I shook the box and thought I heard something rattle inside. A momentary terror gripped me as I considered the possibilities, micro-explosives, poison, polonium. Ebola.

None of them seemed very likely.

I looked back at the postcard. On the front, apart from the buildings, no words, nothing. On the reverse, in tiny blue script down the middle of the card, were the usual references to the photographs and the rights and the location.

"Antwerp," it said.

Very slowly, and with infinite care, I lifted the lid off the box, looked inside, and smiled.

She was on at me in the pub for the rest of the evening, and on the short walk back to her flat, and in the end, she won. She'd taken off all her clothes in the thirty seconds it took me to pour us both a drink, and by the time I'd turned around and seen her she was disappearing into the bathroom in a blur of hair and soft skin with a swagger and a finality I knew was entirely dependent on whether she got her way.

"OK," I said. "Just take it."

Out she came, modesty itself in a cream bath-towel, and took the box from me, and when she opened it and saw what was inside she didn't swoon or scream or do any of the things I'd worried she might. I should have known, really.

"We have to give it to the police," she said, and I nearly screamed myself. It wasn't like it was stolen, or if it was, it had been stolen so far away and so long ago nobody would really care any more. It was Chima's diamond, and he'd given it to me. It was my diamond. *Our* diamond, I caught myself saying, too late to stop.

"Is it a blood diamond?" she asked, and that made me pause. I didn't think so. But I wasn't sure.

"We'll see what we can find out in the morning," I said, and that was enough to move onto the drinks and the love-making, and the diamond was back in its box somewhere among the papers and forgotten food cartons on the floor. I watched her as she fell asleep, the gentle rise and fall, and knew that in a minute or two, I'd be right there with her.

I didn't know if it was her, or everything else I'd been through, or just the fact I was so damned tired there wasn't time to dream any more, but since I'd set foot back in England, I hadn't seen the Grimshaws once.

Acknowledgements

A heartfelt thank you to my wonderful family and friends, north and south, home and abroad, real, virtual, and entirely imaginary, who have tolerated, encouraged and conspired in my whimsical fantasy of being a novelist. Thank you for reading, advising, reviewing, commenting and offering your thoughts on what I should do, how I should do it, and how pleasant it is to hear me going on about it every time we meet.

So many people have helped that simple printing economics prohibit my mentioning them all by name, but special thanks go to my parents, sister and brother-in-law, old friends from school, university and work, newer friends from Lancashire, the contributors to THE Book Club, and my long-suffering wife, Sarah.

Printed in Great Britain
by Amazon

43526125R00179